Party of One

PARTY OF ONE

ENDORSEMENTS

"Clarice James is that smart, hilarious, authentic, sometimes ironic friend you always want to be around, and her writing is all that and more. *Party of One* had me at hello, and I immediately felt I was part of the dinner crowd at Cranberry Fare. It's the kind of book you hate to start because you know, at some point, it will end. Funny. Poignant. Real. And smart—did I mention smart? You'll want to form a book club just to discuss this book. Invite me when you do. We'll have dinner!"

—LORI STANLEY ROELEVELD, author of *Jesus and the Beanstalk: Overcoming Your Giants and Living a Fruitful Life, Red Pen Redemption,* and *Running from a Crazy Man (and Other Adventures Traveling with Jesus)*

"*Party of One* is a celebration. Of life and love. Humor and heart. Faith, family, and friends. Clarice James serves up authentic, captivating characters I want as friends. I smiled, chuckled, and laughed out loud. And even cheered. RSVP Yes! to this party. You won't regret it."

—LINDA BROOKS DAVIS, author of *The Calling of Ella McFarland* and *A Christmas to Remember*

"As I turned the pages of *Party of One*, I imagined stepping into the story, pulling up a chair, and sitting at the table with Annie and the rest of the gang. Their stories captivated me with every joy and sorry, heartbreak and celebration, and I kept wondering if I could start a Party of One in my own town. *Party of One* entertained me, but more importantly, Clarice James inspired me to walk off the pages of her novel into a local restaurant to write a new chapter in my life. James proves that reading changes our perspective and opens new doors our imagination hadn't seen yet."

—LISA BELCASTRO, author of
Winds of Change and *Possible Dreams* Series

"*Party of One* is a heartwarming story about finding love again in the most unexpected places. Endearing, eccentric characters spring off the page making it bittersweet to finally bid them goodbye. Add to that the candor and comedy I've come to expect from Clarice G. James, and you won't want to put this book down."

—CHRISTY BRUNKE, author of *Snow Out of Season*

"In Clarice James' *Party of One*, you'll find several reasons for reading a good book: a heartwarming story that whisks you away on the first page; characters you'd swear you know in real life—or wish you did; a witty delivery that makes you smile on every page; and a lilt to the prose that plays background music in your head as you read. If you're looking for a serious light-hearted read to help you "get away from it all," then curl up with *Party of One*. Clarice James won't let you down."

—JIM HAMLETT, author of *Moe*

"Once again, Clarice James brings together wit, wisdom, and a winning tale in *Party of One,* a heartwarming story of grief reaching beyond self to bring comfort and joy to a group of lonely and sometimes unlikeable strangers. You'll be tempted to start your own "party of one" after reading this rewarding novel!"

—**STEPHANIE PRICHARD,**
co-author of *Stranded* and *Forgotten*

"*Party of One* is a humorous and uplifting tale of moving beyond grief and loneliness to healing and serving others in a very creative way. Colorful and lovable characters will have you laughing out loud while discovering the source of all comfort."

—**JANET GRUNST,** author of *A Heart Set Free*

"If you're looking for a heartwarming read with the literary power to make you laugh out loud on one page and grow teary-eyed on another, you'll enjoy *Party of One* by Clarice G. James. The author's sense of humor often kept me in stitches. Yet, she blends those skills with her ability to bring to life the experiences of widowhood, adjusting to spousal loss and the single life again, and the challenges of moving outside one's usual social circles to begin a second chapter in life. The author's descriptions of the many varied characters who people this modern-day novel, paint word pictures that bring the characters and the story to life. I highly recommend this cozy, hopeful, and inspirational tale."

—**MELINDA V. INMAN,** author of *Fallen* and *Refuge*

"Clarice James' novel, *Party of One,* is a poignant look into what it feels like to be a "single" in a world of couples. The author's humor and talent shine in this story as widow Annie McGee finds her independence, a second chance at love, and a relationship with her Savior."

—**SHARON SROCK,** author of
The Women of Valley View Series and *The Mercies* Series

Party of One

Clarice G. James

Elk Lake
PUBLISHING, INC.

Plymouth, Massachusetts

Cover Design: Jeff Gifford
Interior Design: Melinda Martin
Editors: René Holt, Deb Haggerty
PUBLISHED BY: Elk Lake Publishing, Inc., 35 Dogwood Dr., Plymouth, MA 02360

Library Cataloging Data
Names: James, Clarice G. (Clarice G. James)
Party of One, Clarice G. James
334 p. 23cm × 15cm (9in × 6 in.)
Description: Elk Lake Publishing, Inc. digital eBook edition | Elk Lake Publishing, Inc. POD paperback edition | Elk Lake Publishing, Inc. 2017.
Identifiers: ISBN-13: 978-1-946638-12-0 (ebk)| 978-1-946638-13-7 (POD)
Key Words: baby boomer fiction, Cape Cod, Christian widows, uplifting fiction, finding Jesus, women's beach reads, funny Christian fiction.

508746173405152017 NF

DEDICATION

To my husband, David,
who every day *shows* me he loves me,
makes me laugh, and keeps me
out of trouble as best he can.

ACKNOWLEDGMENTS

Shortly after I was widowed in 1998, I returned to the local diner my husband and I had frequented for decades. I chose a small table in the corner. A waitress approached and asked me to move to the counter, saying, "Sorry, but our tables are reserved for two or more." I'm grateful that in the midst of one person's insensitivity, the seed for this story was planted.

Originally, *Party of One* began as a non-fiction book about the struggles and surprises of the middle-aged single life. When I remarried in 2006, my husband, David, suggested I turn my manuscript into a novel. I took his advice. Later, while agonizing over what theme to employ in naming chapters, he calmly responded, "How about Chapter 1, Chapter 2, Chapter 3?" Those common-sense suggestions and much more won him a forever role as my sounding board and first reviewer. David, thanks for being mine ... all mine!

The mother-daughter relationship in *Party of One* was inspired by my relationship with my own daughter, Erin Hennessey. To have a daughter who gets you is a blessing. Thanks, Erin, for being my inspiration—not only for my character, Casey but in life.

During my eight years of widowhood on Cape Cod, I had three special friends who supported and protected me: Kellie Parham, Susan Loud, and Brenda Loud. Like the characters Maddie, Susannah, and Robin in my story, they "hovered closer than blood." Their roles in the book may be minor, but the roles they played in my real life were huge. Thank you for your love, prayers, and encouragement. (Special thanks to

Kellie for being extra bossy. She saved me from myself more than once.)

Thank you to those who helped me—perhaps unintentionally—create some of my more colorful characters: Stephanie Blaisdell for being my inspiration for Lavender, Mary Choharis for Sarge, Ralph David James for Webster, and Shannon Loud Jovan for Gracie. Without your uniqueness, my characters wouldn't be nearly as fun or interesting.

Kudos to my critique group members who pick and poke at all my manuscripts until they fix them for good: Michael Anderson, Ellen Davison, Ralph David James, Cricket Lomicka, Steve Moore, Jeremiah Peters, and Teresa Santoski.

I will be forever grateful to Editor Michael Ehret for connecting me with my fellow 2011 Jerry Jenkins Operation First Novel Contest finalists: Kimberley Gardner Graham, Jim Hamlett, Peter R. Leavell (the winner!), and Terrie Todd. We've been aiding and abetting each other ever since.

Heartfelt appreciation for the suggestions and support from my friends and family, aka beta readers: Debra Bock, Elsie Bush, Dawn Ditty, Andrea Hamilton, Erin Hennessey, Darleen Hildebrandt, Ralph P. James, Sheryl Kall, Brenda Loud, Susan Loud, Diana MacEacheron, Kellie Parham, Jillian Patrick, and Cathy Tully.

I owe Deb Ogle Haggerty of Elk Lake Publishing, Inc. big time for believing in *Party of One* with its mid-life protagonist, and for connecting me with talented and thoughtful editor, René Holt.

Above all, praise and thanks to my Lord!

Great is Thy faithfulness!
Great is Thy faithfulness!
Morning by morning new mercies I see.
All I have needed Thy hand hath provided,
Great is Thy faithfulness, Lord, unto me!

Lyrics by Thomas Chisholm.
Music by William M. Runyan:
Hope Publishing Company, 1923

CHAPTER 1

My husband was dead—I wasn't—and I hated eating alone.

Yet there I stood, a party of one, on the steps of the Ebb Tide Diner. With Exxon pumps out front and the motto "Eat Here and Get Gas," you didn't expect fancy. The home-style cooking is what kept this place packed.

Ned and I had discovered this local favorite after our move from the Boston area to the Upper Cape Cod town of Sandwich. Ebb Tide transitioned into our Friday date-night eatery after the kids were grown and gone. I hadn't been back since he died.

Now, two years to the day, I needed to deal with some things. Coming back here *alone* was one. The start of the New Year was as good a time as any.

I'd had my hair done for the occasion, covering a few grays which threatened to dull my natural nutmeg. I even wore the peacock-blue sweater set and dangly silver earrings Ned had given me. Why? I guess for the same reason I spent time staring out over the ocean rather than the cemetery: Ned would've been pleased.

The place was crazy busy as usual. The smell of Yankee pot roast and fried clams awakened tasty memories. A fast-walking waitress, plates running up her arms, slowed down long enough to tip her head in the direction of the last vacant table—the one Ned and I had called *ours.*

I took a seat, *my* seat. With my hands clasped under my chin, I leaned on my elbows and stared across the table at the empty chair. I let my mind drift back in time until the word *pathetic* chided my resolve. I recovered, then scolded myself.

Keep moving, McGee. Self-pity is not on tonight's menu.

Summoning images of us in times past brought a smile instead of tears, consolation in place of sadness. I could feel grief turning.

I can do this.

A waitress startled me out of my reverie, but her familiar face put me at ease. She extended a pair of menus. "Will someone be joining you?"

A bit bruised she hadn't recognized me, I pretended not to notice. "No, just me tonight," I said, my voice an octave too high. What I wanted to say was, "Don't you remember? I'm *Annie* of Annie and Ned, your old regulars?"

"Oh." She pulled the menus back before I could accept one. "Then would you mind moving to the counter? We like to save our tables for two or more."

I managed a phony "no problem" before my face turned red, then got up and sat where she pointed.

I loathed sitting at that low counter. The hem of my coat dragged on the floor, and the stools always rocked. Even tonight, despite my repeated efforts to control the stubby bugger beneath me, the seat wobbled and swiveled at will. No matter what expression my face tried out, looking composed on a stool the same height as a toilet was impossible.

I straightened and re-straightened my flatware and map-of-Cape-Cod placemat while waiting for someone, anyone, to take my order. The more time passed, the more invisible and conspicuous I felt. The internal berating began: *You're either invisible or conspicuous. Make up your mind; choose one or the other. You can't be both.*

I wanted to bolt but didn't because I couldn't breathe. When the tears came, I had to leave. With my best interpretation of the term *lady-like*, I gathered my puddle of coattails from the grubby tile floor, stood tall, and tucked my purse under my arm. Wending my way through the crowd waiting both inside and out, I smiled and nodded as if I'd just dined at the White House.

Somewhere between the door and my car, a cause was born. The natal cry: Power to the party of one!

Or, at the very least, respect.

With my mission infused with a passion rivaling Patrick Henry's, I started my car, put it in gear and pulled out—right into the side of an SUV. A gray-and-blue Ford to be exact, with the words "Massachusetts State Police" emblazoned on the door.

My immediate reaction was to wish the accident away. I closed my eyes, banged my head on the steering wheel, and chanted, "This did not happen, this did not happen, this did not happen."

I stopped when my forehead hit the horn.

Ned would be so proud. He'd been on the State Police force for over thirty years with a record of zero accidents.

The crowd outside the restaurant grew as those waiting inside joined them to watch the show. This almost topped my being spurned as a single diner.

Bloodthirsty rubbernecks! I bet they're hoping the Statie pulls out his gun and shoots me. Part of me hoped he would.

I knew I had to exit my car at some point, but I froze. The SUV door opened. A middle-aged uniformed officer got out. His mirrored sunglasses hid his frame of mind—but not his good looks. I put my window down and stuck my head out. "I am so sorry. I didn't mean to hit the horn."

"Are you saying you meant to hit my vehicle?"

"No, I mean, uh, after I hit your car, uh, I was …"

He walked toward me. I stiffened. He bent over and peered in my window. I leaned back hard against the seat. Why? Did I think he wouldn't see me?

"Annie, is that you?"

I knew the face but spaced on the name. "Yes, um ..."

He removed his glasses. "Gabe Reilly. I worked with Ned, remember?"

I let out my breath. "Yes, Gabe, of course. You came by the house. Sorry, I'm having difficulty remembering my own name right now."

"You're not hurt, are you? Hard to believe you could reach a dangerous speed traveling three feet out of a parking space." He grinned and more importantly, he didn't shoot me.

I sighed. "Today's been one of those days. And this ending fits like the last piece of a used jigsaw puzzle."

"Don't worry. These things happen all the time. I should know, right?"

I got out of my car and glanced back at the crowd on the steps. I'm sure they were hoping for a gory story to tell, and an SUV sustaining a few dents in its left rear panel didn't cut it. They mumbled and dispersed while Gabe and I exchanged insurance info and license numbers.

He walked me back to my car. With a hand on my arm, he stopped me before I got in. "Annie, the promise I made to you after Ned died still stands. If you ever need anything, and I mean anything, feel free to contact me directly."

"Thanks." I raised an eyebrow. "I'll do my best to be less literal next time."

He shook his head and laughed, then waved goodbye.

Deciding to forgo the whole fine dining experience, I drove home and fixed myself a bowl of cereal. I plopped on the couch and watched *Jeopardy*. On the plus side, I got four answers correct. On the minus side, the show was a rerun I'd seen the day before.

I spoke to the game show host: "I'll take PATHETIC for 600, Alex."

So, Gabe Reilly, huh? I wonder what his story is.

4

Running into Gabe had brought me back to the weeks before Ned died.

Not a day passed without one of his fellow officers stopping by. Gabe, nicknamed "The Deacon," was the last one to visit. I left them alone and stepped into the next room. I heard their voices but couldn't make out the words. After a while, I went in to see if Ned needed anything. When I entered, I heard them praying. I tiptoed backward into the hall.

On his way out, Gabe turned back to Ned and said, "The Lord will show you the way home now, brother."

Ned struggled to speak, "I owe you, Deacon, big time."

After Gabe had left, I saw a small religious booklet on the nightstand. When Ned died, I put the booklet in my keepsake box along with our love letters and his watch, pocket knife, and wedding band.

I wasn't sure what had transpired, but Ned's countenance seemed unclouded for the first time in months. I recalled the last words he spoke to me: "Find God, Annie, find peace." I thought the medication was talking.

After losing Ned, my whole perception of life was askew. When one of my coworkers whined about her job, I outwardly sympathized. But what I thought was, *Do you really believe a bad day at work compares with my husband being dead?* When my friend raved about the latest blockbuster film, I nodded and said, "Wow!" Inside, I recoiled. *Movies? Have you forgotten my husband is dead?* When I ordered a salad at a restaurant, and the waitress asked what kind of dressing I wanted, I said,

5

"bleu cheese." But what I screamed inside was *Oh God, oh God, my husband is dead!*

For years on my way to work—long before Ned got sick—I passed this little old man, walking to the corner store for his morning paper. He was hunched over and needed a cane, yet he strutted with determination. His morning constitutionals inspired me. I searched for him daily and worried when I didn't see him.

On my first day returning to work as a widow, I passed the same little old man. Resentment flared at the sight of him. I felt if he'd only died when he was supposed to, Ned would still be alive. My feelings were senseless, but that didn't change them—and I didn't want to change them.

Weeks later, when I passed the old man and caught myself smiling, I knew my perception was shifting—if not by leaps and bounds, then by tiny steps.

CHAPTER 2

A few days had passed before I ventured out to dine alone again. Driving past Ebb Tide, I stuck my tongue out, grown-up that I am, and stopped a half mile up Old King's Highway at Cranberry Fare. There, the staff greeted me as if they'd been awaiting my arrival all evening. I turned to see if someone important had walked in behind me. *Nope.* They seemed pleased to accept me as I was—a party of one.

The hostess, Gracie, maybe all of twenty-one, wore her reddish blonde hair in shoulder-length waves suggestive of another era. She was dressed in a cap-sleeved, pale-pink chiffon dress with a fitted bodice and satin waistband. Her petticoat rustled when she strolled in her pink open-toed heels. Her ensemble might have been designed in the 1950s.

She led me to the center section of the dining room not far from a big stone fireplace, which crackled with the sound of seasoned oak. The wide-planked pine floors, hand-planed tables, and rustic Windsor-style chairs were in sharp contrast to the patched blue vinyl and cruddy chrome of the Ebb Tide stools. When we got to the table, Gracie pulled out my chair. I thanked her for seating me near the fire.

"You're welcome. Besides, don't you know?" she asked as if everyone did.

"Know what?"

She changed her stance and tone. "At Cranberry Fare, nobody puts Baby in the corner."

I took a few seconds to recognize her reference to the hokey line from an old movie. "'Baby,' as in Jennifer Grey?"

"Yes. That was Patrick Swayze's line as Johnny Castle in *Dirty Dancing*. I wonder how many takes it took before he could say those words with a straight face."

Without waiting for me to comment, Gracie circled the dining room like she was walking the red carpet, posing and smiling at customers along the way. She stopped to converse with an elderly gentleman a few tables over.

"You look mighty pretty tonight, Gracie," the man said.

She raised her chin and said in a sultry, mid-western drawl, "Pretty? Is that all I am?"

He laughed. "You're dressed like Kim Novak as Madge … what was her last name? … in *Picnic*."

"Right! Madge Owens. Made in 1955. William Holden played Hal Carter. Don't you think Miss Novak should've received the Oscar that year?"

He nodded. "I believe you may be right."

This might be interesting, fun even.

A young waiter approached me with a smile. His wavy hair was the color of onyx, a nice complement to his cobalt-blue eyes.

"Good evening, ma'am. My name is Ian. I'll be your server tonight." He won me with his lilting Irish brogue. "May I get you something to drink?"

"Yes, Ian. I'll have a club soda with a splash of cranberry juice and a wedge of lime."

"Right away, ma'am."

"I'm ready to order too. The sweet chili grilled salmon special sounds delicious."

"Excellent choice."

When Ian came back with my club soda, he placed a magazine and a newspaper on the corner of my table. "I thought you might enjoy something to read while you wait, ma'am."

With the Ebb Tide experience still fresh in my memory, I wondered at the difference one simple gesture could make. I wanted to hug him but decided on a good tip and a report to the maître d' instead. "If you don't mind my asking, have you been in the States long?"

"Going on three years, ma'am."

I motioned to the reading material. "I commend you on a job well done."

"For that, you may thank my mum and dad. All of us siblings worked in their pub from the age of six. We were taught to treat our guests like family."

While waiting for my entrée, I studied the other patrons. Over the past few years, I'd been so preoccupied with myself I hadn't noticed others eating alone. Tonight, I found some in the dining room and more at the bar.

In addition to the elderly gentleman, there were two people dressed in suits, sitting at separate tables. One ate while using his laptop. The other had a phone to her ear and a legal pad to the right of her plate. A guy at the bar, dressed in dusty jeans and encrusted boots, jabbed his straw up and down through the ice in his drink, while another man, sporting business casual and polished shoes, stared at the muted flat screen.

I wondered about their stories. Single, divorced, widowed? Bored, sad, or had a fight with their spouse? Maybe they enjoyed traveling; maybe they didn't. Did any of them ever feel self-conscious eating by themselves? Or did they prefer dining alone?

What would they think if I asked them to join me?

While eating, my mind fiddled with that idea like a Rubik's Cube. Before leaving, I introduced myself to the restaurant manager. After complimenting Ian's service, I asked about reserving a table each week for single diners. When I suggested Friday, he hesitated, telling me Fridays were his second busiest night. After I had pointed out the singles eating at separate locations on that very Friday, he agreed to allow the reservation on a probationary basis.

I promised to print some handouts and write an announcement for the local papers and online sites. He agreed to post flyers in the restaurant and talk up the idea with his regular singles. We shook hands, mutually satisfied with the deal we'd made.

I left the restaurant and got in my car. Before I could put the key in the ignition, the cold realization of the plan I'd concocted made me shiver.

Good grief, McGee, your brain needs a warning label. You'll be sitting alone at a table for eight, looking more pathetic than before. While your mind was busy fiddling with that so-called Rubik's Cube, did you recall ever having solved that puzzle?

Doubt taunted my confidence over the next two weeks. But occasional spurts of mania gave me the wherewithal to make flyers and write copy for the internet and newspapers. I named the group Party of One. Since my profession is marketing, I classified my efforts as a marketing exercise. Therefore, if or when Party of One failed, I could declare it a business loss rather than personal.

I didn't get one response. Even so, I still had to show.

CHAPTER 3

At the appointed day and time, I braced myself for a singles' supper fiasco. I walked into Cranberry Fare at exactly five forty-five. A host led the way to the table. In an effort to gain the high ground, I wanted to be the first one there.

I wasn't.

Seated at the table was a man dressed in plaid—shirt, slacks, and jacket. I guessed him to be in his late seventies, early eighties. I didn't know what to make of him. I guess I'd expected nobody or a few middle-aged women.

With a half-shrug and a grin, he stood to greet me. "Good evening. Will Anderson. Hope you're not disappointed to find an old guy like me sitting here."

Even through the thick lenses of his circa 1990 glasses, I could see a spark in his eyes, which made me smile. He looked familiar, but I didn't know why. I reached across the table and shook his hand. "On the contrary, I'm pleased to meet you. My name's Annie … Annie McGee."

I *was* glad to meet him, and I didn't mind being glad. In truth, he moved me from grumpy to hopeful with a single handshake. Will and I chatted. He told me the manager had mentioned Party of One. I admitted I was the usually-sensible person who'd come up with the idea.

"A supper club is a fine idea, Annie. Don't you worry …" Will stopped mid-sentence and gestured toward the entrance. "Well, I'll be … looks like our hostess Gracie has gone *Gone with the Wind* tonight."

I followed his line of vision across the dining room to Gracie. She wore a floor-length, green and white flowered dress with a full skirt and ruffled off-the-shoulder bodice. A dark green sash emphasized her small waist. Her hair had gone from Kim Novak's reddish blonde to Vivien Leigh's dark brown—parted in the middle with the sides held back by matching green bows.

"Oh, my." I realized Will was the one I'd overheard bandying movie quotes with Gracie my first night visiting Cranberry Fare. "Does she always dress in character?"

"You'll get your money's worth. Gracie Camden is our resident actress."

I laughed. "She certainly has more courage than I do."

"More than most of us! Beyond the show, Annie, this night is a godsend. Since I lost my wife to Alzheimer's seven years ago, mealtimes haven't been the same. I can cook a little, but suppertime is more about the company than the food—although my Ruth did make one fine pot roast."

"I know what you mean. My husband died two years ago after a five-year battle with cancer. Not much joy in cooking for one."

Will told me he kept himself busy volunteering. "You can usually find me at the SCORE office or at the Sandwich Senior Center, getting my next assignment. They keep a running handyman's list to help the seniors."

"SCORE? Service Corps of Retired Executives? Did you own a business before you retired?"

"Yes. Manufactured a variety of rubber products for over forty-five years. Sold the company in '98."

I teased, "And as if that wasn't long enough to work, you've taken on odd jobs for seniors?"

"It's more puttering than working. I do some painting and a little carpentry—handicap ramps and the like. We've got a few young men who help us with the big jobs."

"Sounds like you're in demand."

"Seems so." He lowered his voice. "There is one thing you should know about me. My Ruth always accused me of being a flirt."

I laughed. "I'm quite sure she was right."

Like a child let out for recess on an April day, a woman bounded through the swinging kitchen doors and headed toward our table. Her shiny brown-black hair was pulled up in a neat twist, and her dark eyes danced. Her smile was wide and sincere. "Hi! I'm Martina Vargas." She pulled out a chair, then hesitated. "This *is* the Party of One table, right?"

"Yes, it is. It's a pleasure to meet you, Martina. This is Annie McGee, and my name is Will Anderson. So, you'll be joining us?"

"I will!" Martina sat. "I usually work nights as a prep cook here, but I was able to switch shifts. Finally, I'll have something fun to do at the end of the week!"

Note to self: Don't complain about your life anymore.

Martina was an empty-nester whose eyes clicked to high beams when she mentioned her son, a structural engineer in Houston, and her daughter, a nursing student in Boston. "Though their dad and I are divorced, I can never be sorry we married because we wouldn't have our children."

I believed she meant what she said for there was no trace of anger or bitterness when she spoke of her ex-husband. I found her attitude refreshing. Most exes I knew weren't that kind.

"Any children, Annie?" she asked.

"Yes, one of each. Both married. Fortunately, they don't live too far from me."

"I must be older than I feel," Will said. "Neither of you ladies looks old enough to have grown children."

"How about your family, Will?" Martina asked.

"Ruth gave me three wonderful daughters. Now I have grandchildren and great-grandchildren scattered throughout New England."

A few minutes into our conversation, Gracie steered a tall, fiftyish man to the table.

"Here you go. Have a seat; they won't bite, I promise. This is … what's your name?"

"Uh, Webster Townsend, but, uh, I, um …"

"Fiddle-dee-dee," Gracie sang. She swished her full skirt around and pouted. "Now don't fuss and take a seat."

Will shook Webster's hand. "Good to have you with us. What do you think of our own Scarlett O'Hara? Something else, isn't she?"

Gracie curtseyed. "Miss Scarlett thanks you, Mr. Anderson."

Webster Townsend didn't look too sure of himself *or* any of us. He glanced from Will to Martina to me. "There may be some mistake. This young woman caught me by surprise. I hope I'm not taking someone's seat."

Will assumed the role of patriarch. "No, no, this table's reserved for those who don't want to dine alone. If you fit the bill, you're welcome to join us."

I'm not sure if Webster was intimidated or confused when he pulled out a chair and sat.

I thought I should explain. "This Party of One dinner was my idea. This is our first night. If you three hadn't shown up, I'd feel pretty silly sitting at this big table alone."

I didn't get a verbal response from Webster but detected a slight nod.

Martina practically bounced in her chair. "It'll be fun! You'll see."

Will directed a question at Webster. "Is this your first time at Cranberry Fare?"

"No, but tonight qualifies as a contradistinctive visit for sure."

14

I wasn't certain if a "contradistinctive visit" was good or bad, and I didn't dare ask. After a few silent seconds, we perused our menus.

Since I had a soft spot for the Irish waiter Ian Quinn, I'd requested him for Party of One. I suspected his patience would be needed to deal with a mix-n-match group of strangers.

Ian approached the four of us at the table for eight. "May I get you something to drink while you wait for the rest of your party?"

"Well, we're not sure there'll be a 'rest of the party,' but yes, I'll have a decaf coffee, black." The others fell in line and ordered beverages too. Once Ian delivered our drinks, we placed our dinner order.

Thankfully, we had an ally in Gracie, who wasn't about to let anyone single get past her. That's how we got twenty-something Kate Kerrigan that night.

"I came in for a salad and found a support group," Kate said. "With a new apartment in a new town and a new job, I'll take all the support I can get!"

"So, you haven't been on the Cape long?" I asked.

"Long? Since this morning! I was in the middle of unpacking when I realized I hadn't eaten all day." She smiled like she'd just won a door prize. "This was the first place I saw."

"Well, aren't we the lucky ones!" Will said. "If you don't mind my asking, what's the job that brought you to Sandwich?"

"I'm a pharmaceutical rep. My territory includes the Cape and Islands—Nantucket and Martha's Vineyard—all the way to Boston. I chose Sandwich because of its central location, and I wanted to be near the beach."

I broke the bad news. "I'm afraid the beaches are pretty rocky on this side of the Cape. You'll need flip-flops and a thick blanket."

Martina shrugged. "On the plus side, you'll have us every Friday."

Webster pointed to his bowl. "And the soup's good too."

Oh, yeah, good soup's always a big draw for young women.

Kate smiled, making eye contact with each of us. "It's a date."

Will toasted her with his water. "We'll be here!"

His use of the corporate *we* tickled me. But did his *we* include everyone?

That was the count for the first Friday night. Five—not a bad start, I conceded. Painless in a pleasant sort of way. I liked Will from the start, and Martina was friendly and open. While Webster was tentative, I couldn't fault Gracie since he was in our target market. Kate, a fresh mix of college degree, old-money-poise, and the wide-eyed wonder of a child, reminded me of my daughter a few years back—without the old money. I found it remarkable someone so young had agreed to join us. I wouldn't have at her age.

The archetypal naysayers would have been quick to say a communal table would never fly in stiff-necked New England. Since we beat the average three percent return on our investment (of time and materials), I embraced my moderate-to-high expectations for the following week.

Still, me being me and a New Englander, I wasn't exactly ready to franchise the idea.

CHAPTER 4

I spent the first part of the week finishing my marketing plan for a new client in Nashua, New Hampshire. Since their company was large, my boss and I needed three solid days with the various department heads. The account was a challenge, but that's how I liked my clients.

I majored in marketing at UMass and was fascinated by the subject. Still am. I remember thinking once I'd mastered the basic principles I would be set for the duration of my career. Wrong. Technology, social standards, business needs, and consumer savvy have all played a role in this ever-changing field.

Years back, when I first told my employer Ned and I were moving to Cape Cod, I thought our relocation would mean the end of a job I loved. At the time, none of us knew the company would open a satellite office on the Cape a few years later. Our move turned into a bonus we hadn't expected.

After our daughter, Casey, and son, Griffin, were born, I took about five years off. I missed the work and toyed with running my own consulting business from home. In the end, I preferred to keep my home a sanctuary—especially when our kids were young.

When I was ready to go back to work, my old boss accommodated my need for "mother's hours." The twenty-minute drive, on roads public enough to get plowed in the winter but not choked with tourists in the summer, was just long enough to gear up for work, then wind down for family.

All told, I've been working for the same company for nineteen years. I couldn't have survived Ned's sickness and death without their understanding. I don't take their support for granted.

The trip to Nashua included a successful presentation to a new client and two nights in a decent hotel. But by Friday, I was anxious to leave. During the final contract meeting, two of the mid-level managers niggled their way through every jot and tittle, dueling with redundant questions. Their blatant attempts to climb the corporate ladder were embarrassing— and tedious.

As the morning yawned into early afternoon, I checked my watch. If I wanted time to get home to freshen up before our second Party of One, I needed to be on the road soon.

Thankfully, I cleared the city limits minutes ahead of rush hour. I put my mind on cruise control and wandered back to the previous weekend at my parents' home. Seventeen of us had celebrated a month of special occasions, including my fifty-second birthday. Since Ned's death, I noticed our family *fandangos*, as my dad likes to call them, always encompass my special days. I'm sure their timing is deliberate. My family is like that.

Whenever I wondered if my parents, now in their late seventies, were tired of the whole gang descending on them, they'd orchestrate another event. This one began at noon and lasted till evening. The whole time there, I made a concerted effort not to drop a word about Party of One. My family would never understand why I needed anyone but them.

Especially my daughter Casey. She idolized her father in life, even more so after his death. Any hint I was in a social setting, which could lead to a romantic opportunity, was tantamount to infidelity. I figured she'd come around one day. In the meantime, I wimped out and put her attitude in the I'll-cross-that-bridge-when-I-come-to-it category.

For the first three months after Ned died, those who loved me didn't leave me alone for more than a few hours at a time. When they did, I was too exhausted to grieve. My friends Maddie, Susannah, and Robin hovered closer than blood. Maddie's role was to keep me centered, while Susannah and Robin acted as buffers.

Trying to navigate the straits of life's choices without Ned wasn't easy: Should I sell my house? Should I refinance? Should I trade in my car? When I would run my plans or problems by my trio of confidantes, I could always count on Robin's answers to caress: "I understand." Susannah's practical responses would hold me by my shoulders: "Is this what you want, Annie?" Maddie's words were more like blunt force trauma: "No way, absolutely not, don't even think about it."

After a while, my protective entourage had to return to the normalcy of their lives, and I had to go back to work. The first time I came home to my empty house at the end of the day, the loneliness punched me in the gut like a heavyweight boxer. I stared at the phone, no longer ringing on the half hour. The quiet overwhelmed me.

In years past, like most wives and mothers, I savored solitude. Interruptions from Casey, Griffin, or Ned were never far away. Now, with the kids grown and my husband gone, I don't have anyone to tell "Turn the music down so I can think" or "Shut the game off, it's time to eat." There's no one to ask, "Can't you leave me alone for five whole minutes?" I'll never again wish Ned would stop flipping through channels or talking about work.

This solitude felt permanent.

I soon found excuses to go places after work. I accepted any and all invitations to dinner until I felt like a leech. At the end of the night, I still had to go home. I didn't tell anyone how I felt. My friends and family had staved off my grief for as long as they could. I needed to hike that trail on my own now.

I had trouble sleeping for quite a while too. I'd lie in bed, shut my eyes, and slide my hand across to where Ned had slept for thirty years, hoping to feel his warmth. Other times, I would keep my arms tight to my body to avoid Ned's side, so his being gone wouldn't seem so real. There's nothing so cold as the empty side of a widow's bed.

Trying to escape the pain, I spent nights pacing the floor until I thought I'd go nuts. Eventually, after eighteen months, I joined a few online single's sites. (I waited months to tell my friends—but I still haven't told my kids.) Initially, I contacted widowers in far away states, wanting someone to talk to, someone who could relate. Then I got braver and narrowed my search criteria. When I was finally emotionally ready to meet someone, I realized the odds were against my age and gender.

Missing the one-on-one closeness of a loving relationship, I exchanged pacing the floors with pacing the websites. I waited for responses that didn't come or perfect profiles that didn't appear. When I found a match, he was more often a *mismatch*. Most contacts never got past the introductory email. Some ended after one phone call, never making the date stage. And the few first dates I had didn't move on to a second.

There was the man in his seventies who I contacted by mistake. (I punched in the wrong profile code from a personal ad my mother had cut out of the paper for me.) He'd planned a trip to Nova Scotia in his motor home and sought a woman to join him. "I could take my sister, but it wouldn't be the same if you know what I mean."

I didn't make reservations.

Then there was the guy who'd been married four times. He and his latest ex-wife took turns doing time for domestic assault. She'd threatened to kill him if she ever caught him with another woman.

I saw no need to become her motive.

The fifty-three-year-old guy who still lived with his mother and mowed lawns for a living was oh-so-tempting. His older brother had a paper route and lived with them too. While cutting grass, he might want to think about cutting the cord.

Being lonely did strange things to my discernment, and that scared me. Although I didn't admit my concerns to Maddie, Susannah, and Robin, some days I felt safer knowing I had friends like them monitoring my activities.

Loneliness is bad, but foolishness is worse.

CHAPTER 5

I arrived at Cranberry Fare a little before six. I was pleased to see Will and Martina. Her laugh caromed across the room as Will entertained her with one of his stories, his charisma full-blown.

Although Martina had spent eight hours working in a steamy, maybe greasy kitchen, she appeared more refreshed than I did after spending all day in a temperature-controlled environment. I was quick to dismiss her freshness as having anything to do with her attitude. Instead, I thought it might have something to do with ethnicity.

Hispanic people are naturally upbeat. I'm part French, part Irish. We're more reserved.

How did I come up with that theory?

I figured we might see Kate Kerrigan again but doubted Webster Townsend would show up. After Gracie had coerced him with her movie performance the week before, he was quiet through most of the meal. Still, I was hopeful others would find us.

I didn't have to wait long. Taking half-steps like a child on her first trip to the edge of a diving board, a woman approached us. I recognized her as the Sandwich librarian, who'd helped me with the Party of One flyers.

"Hello, my name is Olene Hanssen. Perhaps you remember me? I am the librarian with whom you spoke a few weeks back."

"Yes, of course, Olene, you showed me where to post the flyers. My name is Annie McGee. Nice to see you again."

Olene twisted and untwisted the strap on her shoulder bag. "I did not mention my singleness to you then, perhaps because I am not accustomed to having free time. My brother recently passed. As his main caretaker, my outings beyond work were limited."

Will rose and pulled a chair out for her. "We're pleased you decided to join us, Olene. Meet Martina Vargas. I'm Will Anderson."

We didn't prod or pry. I couldn't tell how old Olene was, but I knew she looked the worse for wear in her washed-out maroon corduroy jumper and faded rosebud-print turtleneck. There wasn't much of a color contrast between the gray-streaked, light brown hair and the pallid complexion of this librarian-caretaker.

"How long have you been a librarian, Olene?" I asked.

"Almost twenty-two years, since graduating college."

I wanted to add, "The job must be interesting" but thought I'd sound insincere. Despite the books, the job seemed dull and boring to me.

"Being a librarian must be so interesting!" Martina sounded like she meant what she said.

Olene nodded. "We have our exciting moments."

Exciting? I couldn't imagine what they might be. Cataloging? Shushing? Assessing late fees? Good thing Martina thought so because Olene seemed to perk up.

After studying the menu, I decided on the chicken pot pie with the puff pastry top. When I lifted my head, I was startled to find Webster seated across the table. "You do fly under the radar, don't you?"

"I'm more stealth drone than fighter, so no need to worry."

"Did Gracie have to drag you over this week?" Martina asked.

"Nope. Dragged myself."

I caught a hint of a grin.

"Good to have you back, Webster," Will said. "I thought I'd have to fly solo with these three lovely ladies. Let me introduce our latest—Miss Olene Hanssen."

He smiled and greeted her.

I would have bet my paycheck we wouldn't have seen him again. Not that I'm fluent in body language, but he seemed less tense this week.

When Olene mentioned she planned to attend her first major librarian conference in October, Webster teased, "You can't be too careful at those conferences, Olene. After one glass of Chablis, my old school librarian got a tattoo of the Dewey decimal number for *The Librarian's Handbook.*"

Olene's eyes widened, and her mouth fell open ... until Webster winked at her.

He made her smile. Nice.

We had already placed our orders by the time Kate arrived. "So sorry I'm late. The traffic was unbearable." When Ian dropped off the rolls and butter, she ordered. "I'll make it easy. I'll have the house salad, no onions, with low-fat Italian dressing on the side. Oh, and no croutons. I'm trying to stay away from carbs." She whispered a confession to us, "I've only been to the gym twice this week."

I teased, "My, my, what shall your penance be?" Kate was as thin as bone china. "I've only been to the gym twice this month, and I might have seconds."

Kate laughed. "By the way, my parents are pleased I've met some friendly people already."

"Do they live far away?" Will asked.

"Not that far. Newport, Rhode Island. Between their work schedules and mine, we hardly saw each other when I lived at home. Now that I'm living alone an hour and a half away, they'll worry."

"You might not want to tell them *how* you met us," Webster said. "They might worry more."

Wow, he's on a roll tonight. What a difference a week can make.

Ian served our meals. Unable to resist the aroma of my pot pie's savory velouté sauce, I took a forkful to muffle my growling stomach. As my taste buds sang their satisfaction, I noticed Martina with her head bowed and her hands folded. *Was she praying?* Out of respect, I guess, I slowed my chewing.

Will caught my eye, nodded once, then bowed his head. The others fumbled to follow his lead.

Martina didn't draw attention to herself. I don't think she noticed we had, well, sort of joined her. After her prayer, she segued seamlessly into a rave about the chef's specials and her recommendations for our next meal. Will nicknamed her our "Watergate mole." When we had to explain the term to Kate, I sighed at the years between us.

Part of me was a bit embarrassed at my less-than-holy table manners. In my defense, we never said anything about praying. Another thing occurred to me. This was my second meal with Martina. Did I chew through her prayer last week too?

To be honest, Martina didn't seem to care at all about what we thought. I sort of admired that quality. Nevertheless, I decided to keep an eye on her. I hoped she didn't turn out to be one of those religious fanatics because I already liked her.

The third week, two newcomers joined Will, Martina, Webster, Kate, Olene, and me.

Vito Falconara showed up first, all big and loud and friendly. He shook our hands while restating his mantra to each of us, "Hi, my name is Vito, and I'm an alcoholic."

Not sure how to respond to this proclamation, we listened as he told his story—his whole story. How different people are. After three weeks, I don't think any of us knew if Kate had a boyfriend or what Webster did for a living, but in ten minutes' time, we knew all about Vito.

He grew up in Providence, where he and his wife, Renata, met when they were kids. He lost his business, his house, and Renata because of his drinking. He'd been sober for two years without a slip. He once did a masonry job for Ted Kennedy in Hyannis Port. He suspected his sister's husband was in the mob. And he attended Mass every Sunday to pray for his wife to come back.

Not much anonymous about this alcoholic.

Just as we were getting used to Vito, a purple, crushed-velvet cape appeared alongside the table. The occupant pushed the hood off. "Is this the table for people who can't eat alone? I saw a flyer at the herb shop in town. I'm a vegan. My name's Lavender."

Lavender? Great. First a fanatic, then an alcoholic, now a fruit loop.

This must be the young woman who'd left me the long, ethereal message over the weekend. I'd tried to reach her but got her voice mail, which had an even longer outgoing message for which I had no time.

"I'm Annie. I believe you called me last weekend."

"Oh, did I? Yes, I think so. Did we speak?"

"No, but I got your message. There's room to squeeze a chair in on this side."

She paused to assess her surroundings. "Uh, could someone switch seats with me? I have to have my back to the wall so my chi can flow."

I dropped my head before I rolled my eyes. How did people on-the-road-less-traveled always find their way to my street? I wanted to ask her what we were supposed to do with our clogged-up chi while hers flowed. Somehow, I managed to keep my sarcasm in check and my mouth shut. Olene gave up her chair and moved to the opposite side of the table.

Lavender wore no makeup, but some would argue her large blue eyes were all the color she needed. Much of her shiny, honey-colored mane hung loosely to her shoulders. The rest was pulled up by a large dragonfly clip, clinging precariously to a lopsided clump of hair. When she took off the satin-lined cape, I was surprised at the contradiction: worn Nikes, faded Levis, and a blue plaid flannel shirt that looked like it'd finished drying at the bottom of a full laundry basket. Sort of like Fantasy Faerie meets the Salvation Army. If I had to guess, I would say she was in her early thirties … and had spent the night in a tent.

When Ian came over to take our order, Lavender turned to us. "Anyone wanna split a pitcher of beer?"

Oh, terrific, the vegan drinks beer and lots of it.

I worried about Vito sitting next to her and wondered if I should intervene.

Vito took care of my concern. "Hey, Lavender, I'm a recovering alchy. I can't drink booze the same way you can't eat animals."

To my surprise, Lavender switched from beer on tap to 7Up on ice.

When we ordered our entrées, Vito said, "I tell you what, Ian, why don't you hold the sausage on my rigatoni this time."

Following a semi-awkward break in our chatter, Lavender spoke. "I'm a research assistant at a marine biology lab in Woods Hole. What do you guys do for work?"

Vito answered first. "Construction Superintendent."

"Way cool!" she said with a level of interest I didn't expect.

28

I took my turn. "I work for a marketing agency."

"A marketing agency? Wow!"

"I'm one of the prep cooks here," Martina said.

"You are? Neat!" Will, Webster, and Olene never had a chance to answer because Lavender had more in-depth questions for Martina. "Do you get to eat for free? Can you have anything on the menu? Do they have tofu?"

Somehow I got the feeling her "Cool! Wow! Neat!" response would have been equally enthusiastic if someone had told her they were a windsock repairman in East Podunk. I found Lavender's genuine fascination with us disarming, and a tad charming—right up to the point when the dinner checks arrived, and she said, "Does anyone have a five I can borrow till next week?"

CHAPTER 6

The staff at Cranberry Fare played an important role in our Party of One evenings.

Was Gracie Camden truly the best hostess in the world? She acted as if she was, which was good enough for us. Even when she asked, "How's everything this evening?" we knew she was honing her craft. The benefit was a dinner *and* a show. We might not have been so cooperative if she'd had no talent—but she did.

Knowing servers made more money than hosts, I asked, "Gracie, any reason you chose hosting over waitressing?"

She answered like she'd been asked before. "Yes. I might earn more as a server, but my decision came down to the whole uniform thing. I couldn't see myself dressing in the same outfit five nights a week."

Neither could we. Her uniforms ran the gamut from Cinderella to Princess Leia to Annie Oakley.

When Kate commented on her attractiveness, Gracie answered without guile. "My future is in *front* of a camera not behind one, so my looks are part and parcel of my calling. I'm obligated to maintain my appearance as any other professional would keep up in their field."

As such, she primped in front of any object in which she could find her reflection—mirrors, windows, flatware, or our eyes. She didn't apologize for her vanity either. Not even for the time she stopped alongside a server carrying a full tray of meals to fluff her hair in the reflective stainless steel plate covers.

Per our request, Gracie assigned Ian Quinn to our table. Not all servers wanted to wait on us. We didn't arrive together, we seldom ordered at once, and we stayed longer than the time we took to eat. And what little leverage we had as regulars didn't negate the truth that turnover is the key to making money. That much I remembered from my teenage summers of waitressing.

Vito remarked one night, "Hey, Quinn, you're a natural. You should think about opening your own pub."

"As it happens, sir, my goal is to have my own electronics business someday. I will have to work a good bit of time in the States before I have a proper amount saved."

The following week, Will came in with a packet for Ian. "While I was rummaging through a closet, I came across my first business plan. I thought our young Ian might get a kick out of it."

When Will presented the aspiring entrepreneur with the handwritten plan, Ian acted like he'd been handed the original Magna Carta. He held the paper close to his chest. "Mr. Anderson, you have no idea what this means to me. I would spend a full university semester to learn this much."

Serious about his dream, every week he waited on us, Ian came with questions for Will. That week was, "Mr. Anderson, what do you think about seeking funds from capital venture companies?"

"Not much. I kept my business simple. The only people I wanted to answer to were my customers."

We learned a lot about business through these mini-mentoring sessions—but more about Ian and Will.

Ian's relief server the following week was Althea Pappas, a sixty-eight-year-old veteran who still hustled through her job. Althea's nickname was "Sarge"—which pretty much summed her up.

She approached our table, pad in hand. "Listen up, people. I'm only sayin' the specials once."

"Bossy, huh?" Vito smiled. "I like it."

"Bossy? Nah. I'm Greek and from Queens. Now, d'ya wanna hear 'em or not?"

"Please," said Olene, fidgeting with her eyeglasses.

"You bet," Vito challenged her. "Now make my mouth water."

The rest of us snapped to attention.

Sarge ran through the specials, then paused a few seconds. "Okay, folks, decide already. I don't have all night."

I was caught off guard by her frankness, even a bit intimidated. Barking out orders seemed as natural for her as belting out ballads was for Streisand. I envied her ability to say what was on her mind, without sounding mean or seeming not to care what we thought.

At the end of the night, Sarge dropped off our checks and gave us a verbal push. "Come on people, let's settle up. The train is leavin' the station, and I plan to be on it!"

Before we left that night, we invited her to join us the following week as an honorary member of Party of One.

"Maybe," she said. "But only if my poker game is canceled."

CHAPTER 7

"Where have you been? I've called you at least three Friday nights in a row. Are you not answering your phone or just ignoring *my* calls?" It was Maddie, full of fear and fret for my well-being.

How had I managed this long without telling her about Party of One? I took a deep breath. "I've been having dinner with some people at Cranberry Fare on Fridays."

"What people?"

"At, um, a dinner club for single people."

"How did you find out about this club? This better not be an internet thing. You never know what kind of whackos you'll meet—"

"Maddie, seriously, it's okay. The dinner club was *my* idea."

"Your idea? Who comes to these dinners? Do you do background checks? Why didn't you tell me?"

I wanted to say, "Gee, let me see, maybe because of how you're reacting right now." Instead, I said, "It's harmless and certainly not dangerous. I share a meal in a public place with an engaging octogenarian, a prom queen turned sales rep, a proper librarian, a vegan new-ager, a woman who prays every week, and a geeky introvert. Oh, yes, and a man who spends the whole evening pining over his ex-wife. Not one serial killer in the bunch."

Seconds passed before she spoke. "And you do this ... why?"

"I don't know, maybe because we need each other."

Saying those words made me think they might even be true.

Martina and I arrived ahead of everyone one week. After seeing yet another look of happiness on her face, I asked why she always smiled. I tried to give credit to a man.

She shook her head, then reached into her handbag, pulled out a tattered piece of paper and read: "I've cried my eyes out; I feel hollow inside. My life leaks away, groan by groan; my years fade out in sighs." She folded the paper and put it back in her wallet. "It's from the Bible. When I read those verses six months after my husband left me for another woman, they scared me because they were a perfect description of my life. I decided I had a choice—wallow in self-pity and fear or choose joy. I chose joy and never looked back."

"It can't be *that* easy." I hoped she'd elaborate, but the others arrived before she could respond.

Will took his seat at the head of the table. "Ask me about my week. No, never mind, I'll tell you. I installed two handicap ramps, and I was in a bathtub with a woman."

"Cast iron or fiberglass?" Webster asked, poker-faced.

Martina closed her eyes and shook her head. "Too much information, Will."

Unable to keep up the ruse, Will explained, "Before I attached a couple of grab bars for one of the senior ladies, I made her hop in the tub, clothes and all, to see if the height was right."

Olene cautioned him. "I sincerely hope the dear lady does not overhear you telling that story."

Will said, "She's the one who started the telling!"

Everyone laughed.

When Vito arrived, he shouted, "Soft drinks all around! I got a raise this week!"

"Atta boy, Vito!" Webster slapped him on the back. "I'll take a Pepsi."

"Congratulations!" Kate said. "Make mine a diet."

Lavender scrutinized the menu. "If I don't get a soft drink, can I get potato skins instead?"

The interaction that night between Party of One-ers left me feeling ... what was the word I was looking for? *Verklempt.* My emotions bubbled up when I saw these people enjoying each other. This simple concept seemed to have far-reaching and positive effects. But would they continue?

You're such a buzz-killer, McGee.

I dove into my psyche and discovered the answer. Ever since I'd lost Ned, I doubted good things could last. After having gone through significant growth spurts in our marriage, we'd finally arrived at a peaceful plateau. We were enjoying that feeling, believing we'd earned it. He died, and the peace ended.

Will I always feel this way?

At home later that night, Martina's quote lingered in my thoughts long enough to bother me. "I've cried my eyes out; I feel hollow inside. My life leaks away, groan by groan ..." The verse ended with something about years fading away. The sentiment hit close to home, tempting me to embark on an unscheduled soul-searching journey.

I usually do my best to avoid that trip. I don't know why. I think I'm afraid—of what, I'm not sure. Maybe finding big things like Wisdom, Success, or Wealth, then not knowing what to do with them. I didn't have to go far to find smart people who still had questions, successful people who were miserable, and rich people for whom more was never enough. I concluded with all their education, efforts, and wealth, they had arrived at the same place I had. In my case, I'd done it with a lower IQ, less time, and much less money.

Worse, what if I found nothing new? Though my cynicism wore thin, I thought it best to shun the soul-searching trip.

Besides, finding peace might be as simple as losing some weight and keeping it off.

CHAPTER 8

On Monday, my phone rang as I arrived home from work. I checked the caller ID. Private number. Feeling generous, I picked up. "Hello-oo."

"Annie? Gabe Reilly here."

Over a month had gone by since I'd hit his SUV, so I was surprised to hear his voice. "Gee, Gabe, I hope this call isn't because there was a problem with my insurance."

"No, no, nothing like that. I thought I'd check in on you."

"I'm fine. Thanks for asking. How about you?"

"Good, good, I'm good."

Okay, awkward.

"Another reason I called is because a bunch of Ned's old barracks buddies and their spouses are getting together next week. We were wondering if you'd like to join us?"

My brain stalled. Thus far I had avoided activities connected to Ned's job because at first, it had been too painful, then too weird.

"Annie? You still there?"

After a cerebral jumpstart, I decided time had moved beyond painful and weird. "Sounds nice, Gabe. Where and when?"

"The wives are the ones doing the planning. You probably know most of them. I'll have Karen call you with the particulars, okay?"

Karen? So he did have a wife.

A few days later, I got a call from her. She told me how to get to their house and a little about the other guests. Most were from work, others from their church.

How bad could this one evening be?

I had four days to decide what to wear to this casual affair. I chose my brown tweed slacks and pink cowl-necked sweater. I fussed with my hair more than usual, which told me I needed to relax. Having chickened out on trying a new recipe, I'd prepared my semi-famous sweet and sour meatballs.

The drive to the Old County Road address in East Sandwich took less than ten minutes—not enough time to get that nervous. I was preoccupied with guarding the pot of meatballs balanced on the seat beside me. When I turned into the driveway, the massive front door with big wrought iron numbers assured me I had the right place.

From the porch, I heard laughter. I knocked, but no one answered, so I opened the door and stepped in. A smiling woman came right over.

"Hi, I'm Karen. You must be Annie. So happy you could join us."

"Thanks for having me."

"Here, let me help you." She reached for my slow cooker. "Sure smells good. I'll put this on the buffet table and tell Gabe you're here."

"Speaking of your husband—"

"My husband? Gabe? Oh, did you think Gabe was my husband?"

"Um, I guess I did. I don't know why ... I'm sorry."

"No reason to be sorry. I'm sure he'd make someone a great husband, but I've got one of those already. His name is Drew. He's the big hunk standing by the fireplace."

I looked his way but lost my mental foothold when Gabe walked toward me. Perhaps I didn't know as much about Captain Reilly as I thought I did—like he was single.

He reached out with both arms and gave me a hug. "Good to see you again, Annie."

"Yes … uh, you too, Gabe."

He led me into the living room and introduced me all around. "For the cops here who might not know, this is Annie, Colonel McGee's wife."

I was glad he hadn't used the word *widow*, which always evoked a certain look I didn't know how to respond to.

"Annie ran into me outside the Ebb Tide Diner recently," he said with a deadpan expression.

Hoping to keep that story between us, I changed the subject. "I've met some of you before, but it's been a long time. I hope you'll forgive me." Even those I had met, I didn't know well. Ned had outranked them, and socializing with those under his command had been discouraged.

"He was one of Massachusetts' finest," one of the men said.

"Yes, highly decorated for good reason," Drew added.

Usually, when people spoke of Ned and his numerous achievements, my protective shield went up. Staties weren't immune to professional jealousies, but I detected a fondness and respect in their comments which put me at ease.

Karen and Drew Dumont's house, an oversized Cape Cod, had the lived-in feel of an active family. Though their kids had moved out, you could tell they hadn't been gone long. Trophies still adorned the bookshelves and sports equipment hung in the mudroom. Their great room had a massive sectional and two overstuffed chairs, plenty of seating for everyone.

The menu was simple: appetizers, drinks, and conversation. I suspected the non-cops had warned their spouses because shop talk was kept to a level one misdemeanor. There was no heavy drinking—a definite change from parties I'd been to in years past. Even though there were a few in the crowd who couldn't keep "praise the Lord" or "hallelujah" out of a sentence, the others seemed normal.

Thankfully, no one went preachy on me.

As we were saying our goodbyes, Gabe pulled me aside and thanked me for coming. "I know these things can be difficult, but you fit right in. Maybe we can do it again sometime?"

"That would be nice, Gabe. Thanks."

There were ten of us in all that evening—four couples and Gabe and me.

I thought a lot about Gabe Reilly after that night. Yes, he was single, but I didn't know the details. Nobody could argue with his looks—about five-feet-eleven with black hair and steel-gray eyes. Unlike many of the local LEOs (law enforcement officers), the state police tried to stay in shape. Gabe was no exception. I wasn't sure exactly how old he was, but we were close in age. He was outgoing, with a great sense of humor and well-liked by the others.

He's certainly worth a wait-and-see.

On Monday, I called Karen to thank her for her hospitality. She suggested we get together again. I wasn't sure who she meant by *we*. All ten of us? Karen and Drew and Gabe and me? Just Karen and me? I didn't know how to ask her without sounding like a preteen. Since no specific day or time was mentioned, I'd have to wait until I heard from Gabe.

When three days passed without a call from him, I wondered why. After another three days, I reasoned: *You shouldn't get involved with one of Ned's coworkers ... and if he's this inconsiderate, why would you want to? ... Besides, isn't he kind of religious for you?*

After two full weeks, I whined. *He could have at least called. Not that I want him to call now. I couldn't care less if he calls. But why didn't he call?*

CHAPTER 9

By our seventh Party of One Friday, I counted half a dozen stories we'd already heard a dozen times. Our conversation needed some work. I waited until the following week so as not to embarrass anyone, then told them about my friend Susannah's weapon to combat repetition: "When a person realizes they've heard a story before, they simply raise their hand and keep it up. If the majority of hands go up, the storyteller knows to stop and go on to something else."

Will punched the air with a left hook. "Perfect!"

"Hey, I talk to so many people on the job every day," Vito said, "I forget who I said what to."

Since everyone agreed the idea had merit, we instituted the hands-up policy that night. During the next few Fridays, I confirmed a direct correlation between age and repetition. Kate, the youngest, never repeated herself. As a rule, neither did Lavender, unless she was lecturing us on animal rights or carbon footprints. Martina and Olene caught themselves early into a rerun, while Vito, guilty on more than one occasion, changed up the details to keep us entertained.

At first, I assumed Webster was shy. Then, I noticed he didn't talk unless he had something worth saying. Once said, he didn't repeat. Finding a quick wit under his quiet manner was like uncovering gold doubloons. He ran in and out of conversations with his clever quips—many over my head. Whenever I caught one, I felt my IQ go up a few points.

I took a long while before I felt comfortable telling stories. When I found out I could make this group laugh by relating my latest online dating disasters, I used humor to my advantage. Although I had my share of encore presentations, awareness of a possible memory lapse made me begin every story with: "Tell me if you've heard this before."

Hands down, eighty-three-year-old Will was the biggest repeat offender. The first few Fridays of our new policy, our hands went up on him so often I started to feel bad. Along about the third Friday, he began to tell a story I'm sure we all knew by heart. Without saying a word or passing a signal, not one hand went up. With the same mind, we realized the enjoyment Will got from telling a story was more important than our having heard the anecdote before.

A new strategy was needed. I came up with another conversation booster based on the "It's a Small World" theory. The gist is this: when someone has a concrete connection to a place or person someone else mentions, they jump in to explain how they're connected.

Funny thing is I can remember when that activity wasn't much of a challenge in Sandwich. When we moved here, everyone knew most everyone else in town. Even Ned and I—outsiders by all accounts—became familiar with all the old faces. The locals took their sweet time accepting newcomers, but once our children met their children, we were in.

If you stopped at McNeil's Bakery in the morning for coffee, the customers there were liable to be the same ones you'd run into later at the lunch counter at Angelo's Supermarket. Everyone knew the president of the bank and called the police chief by his first name. When you had to go to the town hall, you were "stopping in to see Virginia." There was one hardware store in town, one post office, one trash pick-up company, and one traffic light.

The population has tripled in the twenty-eight years since Ned and I made Sandwich our home. Many of those who live here now commute to jobs off Cape. We've built two new elementary schools and doubled the size of the high school. I think we're up to five traffic lights.

Gee, McGee, now who's talking like an old person?

I introduced the "It's a Small World" exercise at our next meal. "The goal is to establish a link, either primary or secondary, to a person or place someone mentions. Whoever has the closest link gets points toward a free dessert."

"What if you only know *of* them?" Martina asked.

Olene looked panicky. "Can we use fictional characters and locations?"

Vito rubbed a day's growth on his chin. "Do we have to tell you how we know them or if they're living?"

"Can we choose any dessert on the menu?" Lavender said. "Who pays?"

I sighed. How simple could this be? And they had questions? "This is a way for us to get to know each other better. Whether you're connected to a real or fictional person or place doesn't matter. As for who pays, I haven't figured that out yet. Let's see what happens, okay?"

Lavender looked suspicious.

With the loose set of guidelines in place, I started a conversation before they could question me further. "So, Kate, how's your apartment working out?"

"I love my three little rooms with the deck off the back. And my landlady, Bernice Hayden, is a sweetie."

Lavender simultaneously yelled and choked on her dinner roll, "I know her! My parents use the Haydens to pick up their trash."

"Lavender, I don't think we can count that as an 'It's a Small World' connection," I said, "since Hayden Trash Pick-up is the only trash pick-up in town."

After she had registered a formal complaint opposing my decision, we gave her a half point for being the first to respond.

When Will mentioned Clarence Nash, an old Navy buddy from Chatham, Kate spoke up. "I know an Aaron Nash, one of my professors. Maybe they're related? He's an older guy, in good shape, works out every day, around forty-five or so."

Will grabbed his chest and feigned an attack, "Old? Forty-five? What are you trying to tell me?"

Kate backpedaled over her words, trying to erase her tracks. The rest of us laughed. Often the older generation is more amused than offended by the younger generation's viewpoint. Maybe because we've experienced what they can't see coming. We also know forty-five isn't old.

Will promised to ask Clarence if he knew anyone named Aaron Nash. "At what school is *old* Nash a professor?"

Kate ignored his tone. "Brown University."

Vito raised his glass to Kate. "I'm impressed. An Ivy Leaguer, huh?" His eyes lit up. "Hey, my brother-in-law-the-mobster had a cousin at Brown—Anthony Minerella. Ring any bells?"

"No," Kate said, "but Brown's a big school."

Martina addressed Vito. "Did you say Minerella? My son used to date a girl named Tina Minerella."

Vito sang out, "Oh, yeah, baby!" He raised his hand, searching for a high-five. "I met Mineralla's daughter at a party last year. Guess what her name is? Tina! Yup, Tina! How many points do I get?"

The others cheered at the found connection, but I had my doubts. Vito remembering his brother-in-law-the-mobster's cousin's daughter's name was a stretch.

"What were you doing at a party given by a mobster?" I asked.

"For cryin' out loud, Annie. Not like mobsters were leavin' their violin cases stacked at the door at Tina's First Holy Communion celebration."

"Didn't you say *last* year"? Martina said. "Wouldn't that make her, uh, around seven years old, a little young for dating?"

"Oh, yeah, well, maybe." Vito seemed reluctant to admit his error.

He lost points for getting us all excited, but we gave them back to him for making us laugh.

Later, when Olene spoke of her Aunt Elizabeth Hanssen who volunteered at the senior center, Will said, "I know a lot of Elizabeths but don't remember their last names. Can you describe her for me?"

Olene obliged. "She's seventy-seven, slim, wears glasses. Very pretty."

Will winked at Olene. "All the Elizabeths I know fit that description! I think you need to be more specific."

She promised to bring in a picture.

When Webster mentioned one of his uncles who volunteered as a tour guide at the Strasburg Railroad Museum in Pennsylvania, Lavender shouted, "I've been there! I love model trains. My dad still has a big O-scale layout in the basement."

Later, after Will told us about a cousin who used to work for the National Weather Service in the 70s, Olene interjected, "My brother was passionate about weather. He would watch The Weather Channel all day." She stared off into the memory.

This was the first time she'd mentioned her brother since her first Friday night. I could tell she was troubled but hoped talking about him would help.

Lavender rubbed her hands together. "I've got a good one! Does anyone know Kimberly Bourne?"

None of us had heard the name before.

"Does she live in Sandwich?" Martina asked.

"Does she work for the town?" Olene guessed.

Lavender crossed her arms. "Yes, she lives in Sandwich. No, she does not work for the town."

Will's eyes brightened. "Is she related to the founders of the Town of Bourne?"

"Her ancestors are, but that's not how you'd know her."

I peered at Lavender over the rim of my glasses. "Is this some kind of reincarnation or mental telepathy thing?"

Lavender gawked at me like I had bug eyes and antennae. "Why would you think that?"

Will raised a finger in the air, looking so sure he had the right answer. "Wait. Does she work here?"

Lavender said, "Nope. Give up?"

"Not quite yet," Webster said. "Are you Kimberly?"

"Correct!" Lavender was so excited I believed she forgot she might be liable for Webster's dessert.

Vito scratched his head. "Hey, how can you be Kimberly Bourne?"

"Wow, Vito, you didn't think my parents actually named me *Lavender*, did you?"

Hmm. This game might work after all.

Getting a handle on Webster wasn't easy since he rationed crumbs of personal information over weeks of Friday dinners. So far, all I had for him was a dry wit, a big vocabulary, an interest in aircraft, trains, weather, and a preference for soup. I didn't even know what he did for a living.

I loved when Vito asked him one night, "Hey, Webbo, what's your story? Come on, give."

Finally, one of Vito's inappropriate questions for Webster. Now we'd get somewhere.

Webster shrugged. "My story isn't nearly as interesting as yours. I was at the same job for twenty-five years, then left to start a consulting business. Married once, too long ago to remember. Relocated to the Cape a few years ago. See—mundane. How about you? How are things going with your wife?"

Even though Renata was Vito's *ex*-wife, none of us ever referred to her in that way.

Vito sank into his chair. "I'm sure she hates me. I can't say I blame her. We lived in a four-thousand-square-foot home in the center of a three-acre lot with beautiful flower gardens and grape arbors all around. We had to put the house on the market last year."

"Did it sell?" I asked.

"Yeah, but not until after I buried a statue of St. Joseph upside down in the yard."

Lavender leaned forward. "Wow. Can anybody do that? Or do you have to be Catholic?"

"Anybody can," Vito said, "but you gotta know what you're doing. Make sure he goes in head first, his eyes facing the house, then cover him with six inches of dirt. I think I messed up on the prayer though, 'cause the house didn't sell for eight months, and we took a loss."

Lavender jotted notes as Vito talked.

Will asked her before I could. "Why do you ask, Lavender? Do you have a house to sell?"

"No, but I might one day." She closed her notepad. "Knowing these practices could come in handy."

Sure they could.

Webster interrupted. "Where does Renata live now, Vito?"

"In a condo in Mashpee, about one-third the size." He shook his head. "Our furniture, all imported from Italy, was too big for her new place and had to be sold. All she's got now is six small rooms and a few window boxes. I was so stubborn. I didn't think someone like me could be a drunk. I'd been drinking wine since I was a kid, so I figured giving up the hard stuff would be enough. It wasn't."

We let Vito talk. He seemed to need to.

"Not that I was abusive to Renata. No way. But I made bad decisions when I drank. She says I'd do cockamamie things. She's right. I remember some of them. If I'd given her children ... things might have been different."

Vito stopped for a few seconds before he swore under his breath. "But me? No. I hadda be a *chooch*."

My heart went out to him. He did sound sorry and was taking steps to change. He had a good job as a construction superintendent with a respected general contractor. (I had worked on their marketing plan a year back, so I knew they were solid.) He was even paying off bad debts from his bankruptcy, debts he wasn't bound by law to pay. I wondered if his ex-wife knew all that.

Wait a minute.

How had Webster answered Vito's question? Oh, yes, he'd worked at a company for years. What type of company? Now he owned a business. What kind of business? He'd been married, but for how long? When and how did the marriage end? Where did he live now?

Like a skipjack leaping along the water's surface, once again Webster managed to avoid the deep and tell us nothing.

CHAPTER 10

On more than one occasion, we had people join Party of One with ulterior motives. They didn't want a dinner club, they wanted a singles' club. I wasn't opposed to people finding romance, but that wasn't the main purpose of Party of One.

There were the young studs (originally detoured from the bar by Gracie) who angled for a seat near Kate. They showed up a few times, sometimes alone, sometimes in pairs, double-teaming her for better results. When she expressed more interest in Will than she did in them, they moved on. None of us ever encouraged Kate to give the hopeful saps a chance. I was certain she was smart enough to know when the time and person were right.

There were a few women who checked out Vito and Webster too.

As far as Vito was concerned, he was still married and told them up front. "The first time I laid eyes on my Renata, I knew she'd be my wife one day. She was seven, and I was eight. That was thirty-one years ago."

Then he would push up his right sleeve and point to his tattoo, a white ribbon across a red heart with *Renata, eterno amore mio* in script. Renata, my eternal love.

Webster was polite and kind but showed no particular interest in any of the women. At first, I wondered if he already had someone in his life. If so, then why would he need to spend time with us?

Curiosity could kill all nine lives of a cat waiting for him to tell.

A few months into Party of One, Martina announced, "I'll keep track of birthdays. We don't have to buy presents or anything, but acknowledging them would be nice."

She recorded them in her special birthday book and reminded us a week ahead. The first one we celebrated was Webster's on March 2. I can't get the night out of my head. That was the evening we met Francine Porridge. With a name like that, you'd think short hair, a brown felt hat, sensible shoes, and a wool tweed suit.

Wrong.

Francine was a minimalist, shall we say, regarding clothing. She wore halter tops and mini-skirts other women may have envied— some thirty years ago. Those same women were more apt to be a little embarrassed for her now.

The single Ms. Porridge showed up hungry, arriving early to scan the menu—and I'm not talking about the food. About as subtle as a shark at a shipwreck, she circled the table and squeezed a chair in where there wasn't room for one—right next to Webster.

She leaned so far into his personal space he had to balance on the back legs of his chair to keep a safe distance between them. She wore a Kate Moss blouse with her Dolly Parton figure, and the pressure built up behind her buttons. If one popped, someone could lose an eye. Since she pretty much ignored the rest of us, that someone would be Webster.

Francine skittered through questions for him as if a quiz show clock was ticking. I think the rapid fire format was her version of a qualifying round.

"How long have you been coming here, Webbie?" she asked.

"The name's Webster—"

"You here every week?"

"Uh, yes, most—"

"So you live nearby?"

"In the vicinity."

"Have you ever been abroad?"

"Abroad? Years ago, um, a few times on business—"

"Are you a sushi lover?"

"I'm not a big fan—"

"Have you ever danced the salsa?"

"Danced the what?"

Francine mimed the dance in her chair, her penciled eyebrows morphing into sultry seagulls.

When she got excited, her voice rose to such a shrill we expected glass to shatter. She switched on and off to a little girl voice—to which I attributed my onset of acid reflux. When we sang "Happy Birthday" to Webster, Francine giggled and clapped as if his birthday was theirs to share.

We're not sure if Webster said anything to discourage her, but after a month she stopped coming. For weeks, though, we could spook him by saying, "Is that Francine?" His head would snap in the direction of the door as we yelled "Gotcha!" He'd tell us we were mean, but he never badmouthed Francine.

Something about her scared me. Could that same desperation be buried inside me, trying to tunnel its way out? If so, what would I do if it succeeded?

After weeks of working with us, Gracie figured out a simple system to alert us to potential members. When a customer came in alone, she would announce over the intercom "Set up for a party of one, set up for a party of one." That phrase signaled us to greet the person at the lectern. We had to be sharp since we never knew what accent Gracie would be trying out or what part she'd be playing.

On the night Will's turn was to meet and greet, he led a man to the table. "Everyone, let me introduce Bogs."

Clutching a misshapen hat in both hands, Bogs cleared his throat and explained, "Name comes from my days working the bogs for Ocean Spray."

"What brought you to Sandwich?" Vito asked. "Not Ocean Spray, I bet."

Bogs rubbed his forehead. "I don't recollect, but this town's a real nice place. I got me a room not far from the tracks."

Bogs' age was hidden behind a month of salt-and-pepper stubble. All we could make out were hard lines and empty eyes. I think he'd made a patchy effort to clean himself up but had fallen short of the mark. His shabby was in no way chic. To be frank, he stank.

When he sat on the maple chair, I heard the faint sound of bone on board. His hands shook when he reached for a roll. His expression made me wonder if swallowing pained him. We kept our conversation flowing around him, pretending we didn't notice his differences.

He didn't look any of us in the eye until Webster said, "Bogs, did anyone tell you about our first-night policy? Your meal's on the house."

Bogs faced Webster to confirm what he'd heard. "On the house? Free? That right?"

First time I'd heard about the policy too.

Webster took a sip of his Pepsi. "Yes, even dessert and coffee are included."

If any of us wondered how this man of indigence planned to pay for his meal, Webster had removed our concerns. Bogs ate as much as his frail body could handle. He was almost relaxed by the time dessert was served. He shared a few stories from long ago, tales that meandered in and out of his corroded memory banks. They weren't easy to follow, but telling them seemed to comfort him.

When he got up to leave, he said, "Pleasure meetin' y'all. I'll try to get back next week, but ya know how companies are … they transfers people all the time … ya' know how that is."

We told him we did.

I don't know whether or not we fooled Bogs. Maybe knowing someone cared enough to share a meal with him under any circumstances was enough.

I saw the way the others looked at Webster that night. And I knew why.

Like siblings in any family, we checked up on each other's social or romantic life, the sole purpose being to razz each other. I went on the offensive and chose self-deprecation—my go-to method for keeping my personal life private. My dating stories were pathetic enough to squelch the others' need to rag on me. Sometimes, I exaggerated for effect, but more often than not, the truth was sufficient.

There was the old family friend my dad pushed into my path. His idea of a first date was to wash our cars together at his place because he had better water pressure. My dad was wrong, but the friend was right. My car never looked so clean.

Then I got fixed up with a coworker's brother-in-law, who spent the whole evening giving me a dissertation on his breakfast habits. "I usually have a big breakfast. Yuh, sometimes I have fruit and eggs and toast and sausage or bacon or ham. Once in a while, I'll have steak and eggs, yuh, but on a rare occasion. Hee-hee, get the pun—rare? Of course, I like my muffins and bagels and French toast and pancakes too. Yeah, I like my big breakfasts. You like breakfast?"

I believe my reply was, "Not so much."

There was Junior, the guy I met online, who charmed me into meeting him for brunch by playing the harmonica and singing to me over the phone. When my tablemates laughed, I said, "I know what you're thinking. I've been told before."

I'm not sure whether Junior was nervous or needy, but before we placed our order, he asked me if I liked jewelry. While eating our meal, he offered to take me to Paris. And over coffee, he promised to build me a home overlooking the water. Ah, but there's more …

Junior might have tipped the scales at a hundred twenty pounds—if he'd been wearing a wet wool coat with his pockets full of rocks. For our first date, he chose to wear striped overalls and a matching railroad engineer's cap.

I want to know what logic makes a grown man come to that decision. Was he wading through his wardrobe or rifling through his drawers looking for a theme? What were his other choices? Fireman? Cowboy? Was his decision a tough one? Or was finding the Choo Choo Charlie ensemble a eureka moment for him?

It was for me.

I have no regrets about Junior. Although some days I imagined a satisfied woman out there, bedecked in jewels, fresh from a month in Paris, headed to her mansion by the sea. A kind woman, perhaps one who likes to play dress-up.

After I had regaled my fellow diners with the Choo Choo Charlie misadventure and others, Webster said, "The axiom 'quantity has a quality of its own' has been attributed to Joseph Stalin. Tell me if I have this right … you've applied this principle to your dating life?"

Did he really compare me to Joseph Stalin?

I scowled at him. "I can assure you, there has been no quantity or quality to speak of."

Like WD-40, the "It's a Small World" exercise was an all-purpose lubricant for our conversation. One night, I mentioned my children Casey and Griffin. I was surprised at those who knew them. Even though Casey was employed by a good-sized marketing firm in Boston, and Griffin taught high school math in Plymouth, their syndicated column "Double Header" is what gave them local celebrity status. Since they'd been picked up by an agent, they'd done a number of interviews on local talk radio and made multiple television appearances on cable sports TV. As their mother, even I became an object of awe.

Usually, more men than women recognized their names, but this time Martina knew them from a grand opening of a sporting goods store in the mall. "You should be proud, Annie. They gave a talk to the kids about how they were able to turn their love of sports into a career because of their good education."

Since I'm more mother than sports aficionado, knowing Ned's and my investment in Casey and Griffin's education had paid off—although not ahead of the tuition loans—gave me a bit of satisfaction.

Lavender was impressed. "Cool. Are Casey and Griffin their real names?"

"Yes." I didn't bother to explain that cool didn't enter in since Ned and I had used our grandparents' surnames.

"Griffin was funny," Martina said, "and Casey is a real beauty."

Vito's brow furrowed. "Your son Casey is a beauty?"

"Casey's my daughter."

"Hey, I didn't know that," Vito said. "I've read their column. They know their stuff."

"Yes, they do. When they were little, they'd sit with their father and watch games on TV. Ned never excluded Casey because she was a girl, but he didn't demand she sit there either. She loved sports as much as they did. I was the oddball in the family."

Webster spoke softly, "I'm sure you're grateful they had those times together."

"You're right, I am."

He added, "And I bet your family never thought of you as an oddball. Besides, you know more about sports than you let on."

I could have argued, but I didn't. "Whatever I know about sports must be through osmosis. And there's a secret to avoiding the appearance of ignorance. I keep my mouth shut until I'm sure of my facts."

Now if I could only employ that methodology in other areas of my non-expertise.

CHAPTER 11

Watching the group dynamics evolve was a fundamental lesson in human behavior. For quite a while, there were only the eight of us, so we'd settled into a secure routine of sitting in the same seats at the same table. Will, the patriarch, sat at one end, and we all knew *his* end was the head. Vito sat at the other end because he needed room for his hands to talk. Lavender was between Kate and Webster with her back to the wall for the energy flow, and Martina sat between Olene and me.

We had no assigned seats. At least that's what we said. Watching what happened when a person found someone sitting in *their* seat was a curious thing.

The seat-stealer would sense someone hovering and say, "Oh, I'm sorry, am I in your seat?"

The hoverer would always say something like: "No, no, first come, first served here."

They lie. They want you out of their seat—and fast.

There were a few exceptions to the rule. Like the night the two F-15 pilots showed up. On a layover at Otis Air Force Base nearby, they'd searched out Cranberry Fare specifically for its New England clam chowder.

Seeing the uniformed officers, Will went right over and shook their hands and thanked them for their service, adding, "We'd be honored if you'd join us at our table." Immediately, both he and Webster surrendered their seats to the pilots.

On another night, a woman seated alone at a table nearby caught Vito's attention. He practically dragged her over to join us. "Hey, everyone, say hi to Yvonne."

"Hi, Yvonne," we sang out as a chorus.

"Pleasure to meet you," she said.

Yvonne tried not to let on how she knew Vito, but he blew her cover in the first few seconds. "Yvonne was my counselor at Goodale Rehab. Didn't she do a great job with me?"

Gotta love Vito.

The poor woman didn't stand a chance against his insistence, so she agreed to join us.

Vito offered her his seat at the end of the table. "Hey, Web, shove over, will ya, so I can sit near the good counselor."

I smiled at her. "So much for your quiet evening, huh?"

She shrugged. "Perhaps. But success stories like Vito's are few and far between, so I'm not about to complain."

After twelve people had shown up one Friday, Gracie shifted our table to a roomier section of the dining room the following week. Will and Martina were present when the change was made. But the rest of us went directly to *our* regular table.

When I arrived and found the table otherwise occupied, uneasiness set in. I wondered who'd canceled the dinner, and why they hadn't informed me. I was delighted when Martina waved me over to the new location.

The three of us watched the others' reactions as they arrived one by one. Olene stopped short of the table when she didn't see anyone she knew. She took a slow step backward and froze. When she pivoted, we read anxiety all over her face.

Will stood and called out, "Olene, dear, we're over here."

She put her hand over her heart and exhaled.

The sight of strangers at our old table didn't scare Vito. He marched right over. "Hey, whaddya guys doing here? Today's Friday, ain't it?"

Kate, looking poised, paused in the middle of the dining room and checked her smart phone before she noticed us. "There you are! My week's been so full I didn't know if I was a day early or late."

The funniest thing was watching Lavender negotiate for a chi-flowing chair with one of the strangers. Kate finally rescued her (and them) and guided her over to us.

Webster sauntered over like nothing had changed but later confessed, "Gracie tipped me off on my way in."

Once we settled into our new spot, Will addressed the group. "Confess. Most of you were too disappointed to look across the room."

I was the first to admit I was bummed. "I guess I've come to rely on these dinners."

"And each other," Webster added. "Which is not something to eschew."

"God bless you!" Vito said.

My, my, Webster, you've come a long way in a few short months.

Martina never tried to talk us into praying, silently or otherwise. She led by her example, but I don't think her prime motive was to lead us at all. I think she simply wanted to thank God for her food. She seemed uncomplicated and authentic. Her lack of a hidden agenda made joining her easy. Some did, out loud, others in silence. We could be spiritual or not in a natural environment with no pressure or guilt.

At first, most of us sat quietly with our heads down. I peeked but didn't pray. After a while, some tacked prayers on the end of her whispered grace. Some were never ready, but that was okay too.

Will felt comfortable enough to pray for his granddaughter's husband. "God, please protect Brian as he serves overseas and give his wife peace while he's gone."

Vito prayed, "Our Father who art in heaven, you know what my prayer is by now, but I'm asking again. Please, send my Renata back. Amen."

Olene's pose was reverent but her voice silent. Lavender prayed to an unknown female deity for her garden, the universe, and her cat, Pyewacket. Webster was hard to read. He kept his head down, and I had no clue what rolled around inside.

Once, without thinking, I prayed silently for a man—why and to whom, I don't know.

Although Webster wasn't as verbose as others, he used words most of us didn't, words like pelagic, progenitors, and penultimate. We certainly couldn't accuse him of dumbing down his language for us.

Olene commented one evening, "Webster, with your extensive vocabulary, you must excel at Scrabble."

With no trace of affectation on his part, his reply was offhanded. "Not often. In Scrabble, being somewhat of a sesquipedalian can be a hindrance."

Sesquipedalian? I couldn't resist. "Have you always talked like that?"

"I guess. My poor social skills led me to books for company. That's where the nickname came from."

I was confused. "Nickname?"

"My brother started calling me Webster when I was a little kid. The name stuck. Legally, I'm Steven Lucas Townsend— but everyone calls me Webster or Web."

Webster wasn't a know-it-all—he just knew a lot. Over time, we turned to him as a resource on a variety of topics. He didn't always know the answers, but more often he did. One day, while he was in the middle of explaining how something worked (maybe a steam engine or a musical instrument or the spawning habits of coral, I don't recall), I found myself watching him. His whole countenance changed when he spoke of something he was passionate about. I wasn't sure if he was more enthused about the topic or helping us understand.

"I bet you get a lot of answers right on *Jeopardy*," I commented.

"A few," he said, shrugging.

More than four, I bet.

No matter how deep or shallow the question, if Webster could answer, he did so with respect. One of my favorite examples of this was when he said one night, "Did anyone catch that crepuscular ray show on your way in this evening?"

Lavender scrunched up her face. "Yuck. Webster, could you please watch your language? I'm still eating."

Webster didn't laugh or explain. And to my knowledge, he never used the word *crepuscular* during dinner again. But in case he did, I wanted to be ready. Wikipedia's description was like this: "Crepuscular rays, in atmospheric optics also known as sun rays, God's rays, or the Fingers of God, are rays of sunlight that appear to radiate from a single point in the sky."

Fingers of God? I wonder if Webster believes that one.

Over the weeks, our "Small World" connections added up. When I reminisced about college one night and mentioned Andrea Segal, my old roommate from New Jersey, Webster said he knew an Andrea from New Jersey. We trod carefully, considering our past jump to conclusions with Vito.

"How old is she?" I asked.

He thought for a second. "Around fifty, I think."

"Sounds about right. How did you meet her?"

"My brother Philip brought her to a family gathering in Fairfield one Christmas."

"Christmas? I don't think we're talking about the same person. My Andrea is Jewish."

"So is mine."

"Was this in recent years?" I asked.

Webster said, "No, years ago in a galaxy far away."

"Andrea transferred at the end of her sophomore year, so we lost touch. I don't know how we'd find out for sure."

"If our Andrea is the same person, I can tell you." Webster leaned back in his chair. "She's married to Philip, and they have three kids and two grandchildren and live in Falls Church, Virginia."

"What a coincidence that would be!" Martina said.

Kate added, "Webster, when can you call your sister-in-law?"

"Is now good?" He picked up his phone. "Hi, Andrea, Web here … No, I'm looking for you. Have time for a question? … Okay, here goes. Did you have a roommate at UMass named Annie"—he turned to me—"Annie, what was your maiden name?"

"Molyneaux," I said.

"Molyneaux," he repeated.

"Molyneaux?" Vito echoed.

"You did?" He gave us a thumbs-up. "Guess what? She's here with me now. …No, we're with a group. Here, I'll let you say hi if you have a minute." He handed me his phone.

"Is this really Andrea Segal … I mean Townsend? … I can't believe I found you after all this time."

We chatted like thirty years hadn't passed, then exchanged numbers and promised to call each other soon.

Vito said, "Hey, Annie, did I hear you say Molyneaux? I worked with a subcontractor—a mason—on the Cape a few years ago named Molyneaux. Any relation?"

"If he lives in Barnstable and his first name is Leo, then he's my brother."

"He's the one!" Vito yelled and banged his hand down hard on the table.

"Way to go, Vito!" Will raised his glass. "My treat—desserts all around!"

CHAPTER 12

The following week only Lavender, Olene, and I arrived on time. As a pharmaceutical rep, Kate periodically had ride days with her district manager, and this was one of them. We didn't expect to see her tonight. Vito and Renata were going to an AA meeting. He planned to invite her for pizza afterward. Technically, Martina was in the building but covering a shift for a coworker.

This was the first Party of One Will had missed. I was a little concerned but had no idea how to contact him, or even if I should. We'd been so careful to protect our personal lives we'd never exchanged phone numbers. There was no sign of Webster either.

The three of us women scanned the room to see if we could invite others to join us. When I turned back to the table, Webster was there.

"Yikes! How do you do that? Come in without a sound?"

"Sorry, I didn't mean to make you jump. Am I that scary?"

"Not scary so much as eerie, in a Beam-me-up-Scotty sort of way."

He tried to hide his amusement but with little success.

Olene noticed a guy sitting alone at the bar sipping a beer. We overheard him talking to the bartender about the local wind farm controversy—an environmental impact issue which had pitted environmentalists against each other. He was by himself, so we sent Lavender over. He accepted her invitation with nary a question. Jeremy made five, and Lavender seemed pleased.

Lavender didn't wait long to engage him in eco-politics. "I heard you talking about the wind farm. Have you picked a side yet?"

"I'm usually on the side of the wind, but in this instance, I'm on the side of the water. Man, those huge wind turbines will ruin the sound and be dangerous for sailors too."

"I'm with you." Lavender looked excited to find someone who cared as much as she did.

Her eyes sparkled when Jeremy placed his order. "I'll have the vegetarian pocket and a side of coleslaw, please."

After she had ordered her meatless meal, Jeremy asked, "Are you vegetarian?"

"Yes ... yes, I am." She made no mention of being vegan.

Jeremy asked how often we got together. We invited him to join us whenever he was free.

He avoided looking at Lavender when he said, "Thanks, I'll keep that in mind."

We still had room at our table, so we asked Gracie to keep an eye out for unsuspecting candidates. A few minutes later, we heard her unmistakable impression of a young Katherine Hepburn: "Set up for a party of one, set up for a party of one."

Olene looked toward the podium. "I recognize that accent. What a flawless Kate Hepburn!"

As the greeter that night, I walked to the foyer where a portly, middle-aged black man, dressed in a bowtie and tweed jacket, stood, holding a book at his side. I introduced myself and made my pitch.

"What a kind invitation, Ms. McGee. Professor Oswald Whitley here."

I was surprised at his British accent. That didn't often happen in Sandwich.

When we arrived at the table, Olene was the first to speak. "Why, hello."

"Hello,"—he bowed slightly from the waist—"how splendid to see you again and so soon." He held up the book he carried. "This accommodating woman helped me navigate the stacks this afternoon. I was searching for this collection of essays by Huxley. I did not get your name. I would have remembered if I had." He offered his hand to Olene. "Professor Oswald Whitley."

She shook his hand. "Olene Hanssen."

I started, "Professor Whitley, let me ..."

"Please, call me Professor."

"Okay, Professor, let me introduce the others. Lavender, Webster Townsend, and Jeremy ... I'm sorry, Jeremy, I don't know your last name."

"Bancoski. Jeremy Bancoski. Nice to meet you, Professor."

Professor Whitley made his way around the table to an empty chair.

"What do you teach, Professor?" Webster asked.

"English *lit-truh-chure* at Harvard."

Lavender spouted, "Harvard? No way! Cool!"

Leaning on the stereotypical leather-patched elbows of his jacket, the Professor added, "Yes, I am a bit of a purist with no appetite for the proletarian works so popular in America today. A collection of penny dreadfuls, I say. I'm ashamed to think of what currently passes for literary work. Long gone is the respect for the masters."

"So, if we're to understand you correctly, Professor," Webster said, "you put American literature on the same level as British cuisine?"

"Ah, good man, you have me there!" The professor patted his ample belly, unable to conceal his mirth. "I do so enjoy American food."

"Man, Professor," Jeremy said, "must be a long drive round trip to Cambridge every day."

"Oh, that would be much too much for me. I have a townhouse in Cambridge, but I return to Sandwich each Friday after my morning class, far in advance of the masses. I lease a colleague's guest house in town where I spend most weekends enjoying the much-needed solitude."

Martina said, "No family ties in the States?"

"No, and only a few distant relations back home in England. Some have described me as *confirmed*—not in a religious sense but in my marital status. However, I have not spent much time deliberating my bachelordom."

"Do you mind if I ask why you left England?" I was curious, mainly because I dreamed of visiting one day.

"Not at all, Ms. McGee. In my earlier years, the percentage of black British accepted by the University of Cambridge was in the single digits. To gain entrance, I needed excellent grades and a list of notable accomplishments. By the grace of Providence, I achieved both. However, once I received my doctorate, there was no question of my ever becoming a member of the faculty."

The idea that Great Britain might be behind the United States in racial relations was one I'd never considered.

The term "man of letters" was an apt description of the Professor. That night he spoke of his long-dead literary heroes—Tennyson, Chaucer, and Shakespeare—as if he'd chatted with them earlier over tea.

"Once, in a university production, I had the marvelous privilege of playing the title role in Will Shakespeare's *Othello*. More recently, I resurrected my performance to commemorate the 400th anniversary of the bard's death."

Before any of us could comment, the Professor bounded into a mini theatrical performance:

By heaven, I saw my handkerchief in's hand.
O perjured woman! thou dost stone my heart,
And makest me call what I intend to do
A murder, which I thought a sacrifice:
I saw the handkerchief.

Lavender responded in a clear Shakespearean cadence:

He found it then;
I never gave it him: send for him hither;
Let him confess a truth.

Shock plastered all over his face, the Professor said, "Do you know the fair Desdemona well, Miss Lavender?"

Lavender knew Shakespeare?

"Nah, I played her in ninth grade. Can you pass the pepper, please?"

Olene came alive during their passionate discussion of books and authors. Webster held his own in their debates. The conversation made me want to read again. Like so many others, I had put down books and picked up the habit of watching TV. When the Professor spoke of Austen, James, and Hugo, the predictability of television and the slavery of the remote control seemed less and less inviting.

"Professor, you've inspired me to pay a visit to Miss Lizzy Bennet and Mr. Darcy again," I said. "*Pride and Prejudice* is one of my all-time favorites. I've often wondered how they've fared after all these years."

"Come by the library, Annie. We have a number of copies ... although one is four days past due." Olene shook her head and sighed. Addressing the Professor, she continued, "That a person who reads the classics would not honor a return-by date is an enigma to me. Even with the steep fines we impose, this heedlessness occurs more often than you might think."

Ooh, imagine such a thing. Lock 'em up, I say.

Olene's fairy tale slant on serious crime was enchanting.

The Professor gave her a corresponding head shake. "Indeed, a sad commentary on today's societal ills."

Before Webster left, I pulled him aside. "What do you think about Will not showing up tonight?"

"I wouldn't let his absence trouble you too much. Will's age may qualify him for antique plates, but his running gear certainly doesn't reflect it. He probably got a better offer."

"I suppose."

I was the last one at the table. I could hear my mother's voice in my head, "Annie, afraid you're going to miss something?"

True, I got a kick out of eavesdropping on Lavender and Jeremy and Olene and the Professor. More so, I was heartened both women had found people of like interests. Often, I fell short of relating to them. I hoped these men became regulars.

When I got up to leave, I noticed Martina exiting the kitchen.

She waved and came over. "I thought I'd missed everyone. How was dinner?"

"We ended up with four regulars and two newcomers. Will wasn't here though."

She responded exactly as I knew she would. "He wasn't? Do you think he's okay?"

I tried to reassure her. "You know Will. He has so many friends, Webster thinks he got a better offer."

"Could be."

I hadn't convinced her or myself. "I'll tell you what, when I get home, I'll search online for his phone number and call tomorrow."

Martina left the table and came back with a phone book. "Look. William Anderson. School Street, Sandwich. Here's the number. Do you have your phone?"

"Yes." I punched in his number. Anyone other than Will, and I would have hesitated, thinking calling might be against the Fourth Amendment to the Constitution.

"Hello," said a man's voice.

"Is this Will?"

"Yes. May I ask who's calling?"

"Annie and Martina."

"Oh, my, I'm so sorry if I worried you girls. My grandson Ethan came by to introduce me to his new pup Roscoe, a rambunctious yellow lab. In all the excitement, I forgot about the supper."

"You're forgiven as long as we know you're okay. Please! Don't ever do that to us again!"

"Thank the good Lord!" Martina said. "Now I can relax. Annie, do you have time for a cup of decaf?"

After I had consented, she poured us each a cup. "I don't know what I'd do without my Friday touchstone."

I asked what she meant exactly.

"Party of One is a constant, a place where I belong. After my children grew up and moved out, I lost my purpose for a while—along with my family. I felt so alone, the same way I felt when my husband left me. But my God is a faithful God! He gave me the gift of this wonderful Friday night family. I'm so blessed."

I thanked her though I had a hard time swallowing the idea. But if believing we were an answer to prayer or a gift from God helped Martina, I wouldn't argue the point.

I remembered the quote she'd shared at an earlier dinner and asked her if she still had the clipping with her. She reached in her wallet.

The truth is I could have recited most of it word for word. I asked her where it came from.

"Psalm 31. Why do you ask?"

"Well, I guess the verse sounds a bit like my life too, so I was curious."

"Do you have a Bible at home?" she asked.

"Uh, I think so." Did I? Whatever happened to that Holy Bible we had when I was a kid, the one we kept on the dining room buffet? Did I take the big white tome or did it disappear in my parents' last move?

"I'll bring one in for you next week," she said. "Then you can read the whole Psalm."

I dribbled my sip of coffee. Party of One was not the place to be handing out Bibles. "Uh, that's okay. I don't want you to go to any trouble. I can always search online."

"No trouble at all. Besides, you may not have the version called *The Message*."

The Message? I had no clue what she was talking about.

On my drive home, I thought about that big white book again, the one with *Holy Bible* embossed in gold on its cover. Once upon a time, I believed that book held power and secrets and answers. As a preteen, I was the one who decided to keep the book open in a place of prominence on the mahogany buffet in our unused formal dining room. I remember turning the translucent pages, studying the colorful holy pictures between the chapters, and marking the location of the Ten Commandments with the red silk ribbon.

However, when I tried reading the words, I didn't understand them. I wondered if I was supposed to read this book at all, or if that was a job best left to the pope and the priests. All I know is, when I polished the furniture for my mother, I judged the book's padded leatherette cover worthy of a soft wipe with Pledge.

As promised, the next week Martina remembered to bring *The Message,* a modern-day version of the Bible. I told her I'd read Psalm 31 and return the book the following week.

"Please keep it, Annie. I've got another copy at home."

Martina seemed elated when I relented. Doesn't take much for some people. Besides, I reasoned, since the BIBLE category wasn't going away anytime soon on *Jeopardy,* thumbing through the book might help me get a couple more answers right.

CHAPTER 13

For the last few years, my life had resembled a strange game of Boggle. With lettered dice scattered around me, I scrambled against an invisible hourglass to put them in an order that made sense. No matter how hard I tried or how fast I went, I felt like a q without a u.

Was the missing piece syndrome due solely to losing Ned? I sensed my longing was more, but what? Was that missing piece faith? Did I believe in God after all these years of being away from him? If not faith, what was I searching for? Love? Fulfillment? Purpose? Or the happily-ever-after formula to life?

Or maybe I had too much time to think.

I conducted my search for the ultimate missing piece on a path of conformity. I had a respectable job, decent income, conservative wardrobe, nothing that would cause me to stand out in a crowd. I was more concerned about fitting in than being a rebel. I had enough common sense to avoid going too far and wide of acceptable standards. Although I never asked whose standards I followed, I was sure they were right nonetheless.

I often reflected on the other Party of One-ers. Were any of them searching? Had anyone found the real truth?

Lavender's path of nonconformity, with her stones, crystals, stars, and moons included one goddess today and another one tomorrow. These fickle gods of her own making didn't convince me she had the answer.

Kate fretted more about her physical body and career goals than she did about religion. When Martina asked her if she attended church, Kate said, "My parents took me when I was young. If I ever have kids, I'll do the same. It's important to raise children with strong values and good morals."

If Kate's church was such a great place, why didn't she still go?

Vito prayed and went to Mass every week. I believed he was sincere, but his practice of his religion seemed mottled with habit, superstition, and guilt.

"I gotta pay the price for my past sins. I only hope my penance isn't losing Renata for good."

When I asked Vito if his religion gave him hope, he said, "Hey, I do what I know to do until God shows me somethin' better."

Not exactly the rousing endorsement I expected.

The Professor and Olene seemed to search for their spiritual answers in knowledge. Sometimes, I wanted to point out that the PhDs and philosophers they quoted were not much different than the rest of us. They were just bright enough to come up with better questions. And even *they* disagreed with each other on the answers.

Will and Webster didn't act embarrassed when the topic of God or religion came up. I believed Will had a good heart and a strong moral compass but did these character traits earn him credit toward heaven—if there was such a place? As with most personal issues, Webster kept his holy cards close to his chest.

Martina's questions had more to do with *how* she could serve God better, not if he existed. More than once, she told us, "Every day I pray for him to show me how to live my life, and he does."

This energetic wrestling [with God?] wore me out. Or down. I wasn't sure which. "Oh, God, help me to stop thinking about this!"

Great. Now I'm praying to a God I'm not sure exists and asking him to help me stop thinking about him.

During a slowdown in our conversation one night, we explained the "It's a Small World" exercise to the Professor and Jeremy, hoping to get them involved.

Soon after, Will reported, "By the way, Kate, my grandson Ethan took me over to see my friend Clarence. Turns out he doesn't know your *old* professor, Aaron Nash."

Olene repositioned herself in her chair and folded her hands in front of her. "I am well acquainted with a number of Ethans. Ethan Allen, of course, the American Revolutionary War patriot. *Ethan Frome,* the Pulitzer Prize-winning novel by Edith Wharton. More recently, author William Dietrich's popular Ethan Gage historical suspense series."

Huh? What did that have to do with Will's grandson?

Will was more gracious than I. "My, what a quick response, Olene. My grandson's full name is Ethan Harte."

At breakneck speed, Kate demanded of Will. "Did you say Harte?"

Something was up. Did she know the name?

"Yes. He's my eldest daughter's son."

"Where does he live?" Olene said.

"Is he a student?" the Professor asked.

Martina teased, "Is he as handsome as you, Will?"

"One at a time!" Will chuckled. "He lives in Weymouth. He's a cabinetmaker and—"

The Professor interrupted. "A cabinetmaker? I jolly well hope he plans to further his education. He can hardly support a family—"

Will ignored him and finished his sentence. "And he's more handsome than I ever was!"

"I doubt that." Kate's response had an edge. "Uh, I mean, how could anyone be more handsome than you, Will?"

Too late, I caught her slip. So, she did know the name and didn't want to tell us how. I glanced around the table to see if anyone else noticed Kate's telltale reaction. When I got to Webster, he read my face and nodded once, but nothing was said.

The following week, Will brought a guest—his grandson, Ethan. He was a little taller than his grandfather, with sandy-colored hair and sky-blue eyes. He was Matt Damon good-looking with a slighter build. When Will introduced him, I glanced at Webster. He knew what I was thinking. There was nothing we could do except wait for Kate to get there. We weren't even certain there was a connection.

About ten minutes later, Kate rushed in apologizing as usual for her tardiness. She slowed when she saw Ethan.

When Will introduced them, Ethan stretched out his hand. "It's a pleasure to meet you, Kate. I've heard a lot about this group, and now I've met you all."

Kate shook his hand before resuming normal speed. When she reached her seat, she snapped her napkin open, then placed it on her lap. "You must be proud to have a man like Will as your grandfather."

I was surprised but relieved there was no problem. Still, Kate's mannerisms seemed more deliberate than usual.

During our meal, Vito told Ethan about our successful "It's a Small World" exercise.

"Sounds interesting," Ethan said.

"You've never dated a Tina Mineralla, have you?" Vito said. "Cause if so, you'd be in big trouble!"

Our laughter told Ethan he'd missed something.

The Professor lit up. "Smashing! Let us continue our dialog."

Martina asked, "Where did your grandfather say you lived?"

"In Weymouth. About forty minutes north of the Sagamore Bridge."

"A close friend of mine lives in Weymouth." Kate's voice was steady. "Her name is Heather Underhill."

Ethan looked at Kate. "I know a Heather Underhill! I did some work for her a while back. Do you think she could be the same person?"

"How many Heather Underhills could there be in Weymouth?" Kate said. "What did you do for her?"

"Some kitchen cabinets and some built-ins."

Kate put her fork down. "Remember anything else about her?"

"Uh, I met her fiancé, Kent, too. They were good people."

"Were?"

"Well, I mean *are*. We were going to get together but never did."

The rest of us felt like we were at a tennis match. Before we could ask Ethan a question, Kate backhanded another one to him.

"Why didn't you get together?"

"Uh, well, I don't know. Um, they wanted to fix me up, I think."

"You think?" Kate countered.

"Yeah, for a wedding or something," Ethan mumbled.

"Or something?"

"Yes, well, actually, the blind date was for their wedding … with a bridesmaid, no less." Ethan forced a chuckle. "Can you imagine what that would've been like?"

We could see the train wreck coming, but he had no clue.

"No, I can't imagine," said Kate. "Funny, the last wedding I went to was theirs."

"Really?" Ethan's mind was running but not quite fast enough.

"As I recall, I went alone."

We waited.

"Is that right?" Ethan looked confused.

"Yes, their cabinetmaker agreed to escort me, but he backed out at the last minute."

Game, set, match. The paralyzed look on Ethan's face told us he finally got the message.

Webster said, "Connection made. Ethan, I do believe you owe Kate a dessert."

We waited for Ethan and Kate's next move.

Ethan stood and faced her. "Kate, I apologize for any embarrassment I may have caused you. I acted selfishly; no, cowardly. Please forgive me."

What could the girl say? Yup, he was a charmer like his grandfather.

CHAPTER 14

I had this need to label Webster as I'd done everyone else. But my limited experience with men—whether in my family, marriage, or workplace—had been with tradesmen, jocks, policemen, or corporate suits. Webster didn't fit those molds. Although intelligent, he wasn't an academic like the Professor. He was more geek or nerd. Since I'd never had close contact with either one, I wasn't sure which.

I actually googled the phrase "the difference between geek and nerd." I came up with these so-called facts:

> A nerd is an intelligent person fascinated by knowledge and learning. A geek is a person often obsessed with a certain subject. A typical nerd's brain has an extremely active logic center but an underperforming imagination center. A geek's brain has both active logic and imagination centers. A nerd might be the smarter of the two. A geek doesn't have to be smart. He can just do strange things. A geek can be cool, a nerd can't. A geek might have more social contacts than a nerd, but they both have poor social skills.

After reviewing the subtleties of both geek and nerd, I still didn't know which tag to stick on Webster. Either way, considering his social skills deficit, I was surprised he showed up every week. (Of course, spending my time googling nonsense like that might raise some questions about me too.)

Another not-so-good thing about me is my mind gets lost in thoughts that shouldn't concern me, thoughts that don't amount to an ounce of lint. One night at Party of One, I observed how our style of dress was as different as our upbringing, personalities, and jobs.

Will dressed like a man whose wife hadn't been around to help him for a long time. His clothes were soft and durable, made in America back in the days when Sears was with Roebuck, and Abercrombie & Fitch sold quality to adults, not junk to teens. Of course, plaid was his staple, especially in winter. All the clan tartans were represented—often three or four at a time.

Kate, in her classic professional wardrobe, exuded confidence and success. She came directly from work in her tailored suits of neutral shades and white blouses, still crisp at day's end. Her quality accessories were understated. I don't think the word *fad* was part of her shopping experience.

Even when Martina came straight from her shift in the kitchen, she always changed out of her uniform and freshened up. She considered this night special and reflected that sentiment through neatly pressed clothes in cheery colors. As always, her smile was her best accessory.

Olene's wardrobe was the color of a dreary day. Whatever the outfit, her gray-streaked mousy-brown hair was always pulled back at the nape of her neck and tied with a dark grosgrain ribbon. Twenty years ago, her parents had died and left her to care for her disabled brother. Her style had not changed in the years since.

Over a starched oxford shirt, the Professor wore one of his many cardigans or jackets. He wore trousers, never jeans. And when he crossed his legs, you could catch the scent of the fresh paste polish on his English cap-toe oxfords.

Lavender's job as a research assistant had a similar dress code to Jeremy's job as an environmental engineer. Often, they dressed alike in jeans, tees, and cotton flannel shirts. Recyclers at heart, neither one of them were likely to discard an article of clothing before its time.

As for me, I was no fashionista. Corporate casual with little jewelry, I reserved my heels and suits for the days I met with clients. Mail-order catalogs were my favorite places to shop for current, neat, and comfortable clothing. I dressed sensibly because I was sensible.

As for Webster, he made the practical choice of short-sleeved polo shirts and added fleece pullovers as needed. His footwear was constant—brown leather boat shoes. I think he owned three pairs of the same shoes all at various stages of wear. Weird.

And weirder that I noticed.

Over weeks of observing the interaction of our group, a theory began to take shape regarding Webster. I believe his genius was compromised by his choice to wear light blue, flared, stretch-denim Wrangler jeans.

I'm not a brand-name snob or a fashion expert, but that's my point. If even *I* know light blue, flared, stretch-denim Wrangler jeans are not *in*, then they've been out for a while—a long while.

I ascertained this much about Webster and maybe others with high IQs. They don't give a hoot about the latest trends. Webster and his compatriots believe judging a person based on their clothing is illogical and bowing to fashion gods is hypocritical.

I agree—to an extent.

All the Websters of the world listen up. Here's my theory: Those of you who snub style are often some of the most intelligent, knowledgeable, and witty people. You are the very ones most likely to say something worth hearing.

However, I conclude, the masses aren't listening, because they're distracted by your fashion illiteracy and/or offended by your flaunting indifference. This may be a shallow philosophy but no less valid. Many of the people who are led solely by fashion and fads *are* shallow. Therefore, we can assume they are also the ones who would benefit most from the wisdom you might impart.

Now I'm not asking for Armani or Gucci, but in general, if you care about humanity as a whole and want to do something philanthropically for the masses, a trip to the Gap will do.

Enough said. I have dismounted my high horse.

CHAPTER 15

A few of us women noticed something one night. We usually had as many men as women. That surprised us, considering the normal ratio of single women to single men in any age bracket is usually seven to one. We wondered aloud how this group managed to beat the odds.

Vito guffawed. "Easy—da food."

I looked around the table at the other men. "Is food the reason all you men are here?"

Webster answered. "Speaking for myself, if you'll remember, I got tangled in your web when I came in for dinner."

Jeremy pointed his thumb at the bar. "I was at the bar getting ready to order my supper when Lavender came over."

"I was here to dine with a good book the night of your delightful invitation," the Professor said.

Ethan shrugged. "Gramps was treating."

Will admitted, "Since I was a regular at Cranberry Fare, dropping by the Party of One table on a Friday night wasn't such a stretch—especially with Gracie prodding me."

"Okay, let me ask you this," I said, "if you'd read an announcement in the paper for another kind of singles' gathering, would you have come?"

In one way or another, they all said, "No."

Webster followed up, "Annie, let me be clear about this. The food got us in the door. The company kept us coming back."

I realized then Webster wore kindness well—if not the latest style in jeans.

Like any real woman would do (and an honest one would admit), I mentally paired Party of One-ers like a junior-high girl making a list for a boy-girl party. Under probable matches, I had Ethan with Kate and Jeremy with Lavender. Under possibles, I had Vito with Renata and the Professor with Olene. Then there were four: Will, Webster, Martina, and me. I believed finding a match for Will would be easiest.

That reminded me. "Olene, did you remember the picture of your aunt?"

"Yes, I did." She reached into her bag, pulled out a three-by-five photo, and passed the picture down to Will.

He adjusted his glasses before holding the photograph up to the light. "If I'd met this lovely lady before, I certainly would have remembered." He took another long look before returning the picture to Olene.

With an ulterior motive the size of the Trojan Horse, I said, "Have you invited your aunt to join us? She's always welcome, you know."

"Yes, but I will ask her again," Olene said. "Aunt Elizabeth and I have grown closer since her retirement. I would love her to meet you all."

That was easy. Now perhaps I could move on to Martina and Webster. I caught myself. I had no idea whether either of them was interested in having a relationship at all. They'd never said. Lavender, however, was not shy about admitting her needs—at least her sexual ones. I wasn't sure if she thrived on the shock value or just stated the facts as she saw them.

And as for you, McGee, you talk a good game, but are you sure you want a man at this stage in your life?

In the end, I decided Friday night with Party of One-ers was not the time or place to entertain romantic fantasies for others or myself. I had other nights for that.

I hoped.

The next week Olene arrived with a guest, Miss Elizabeth Hanssen, who looked like a 1940s Swedish model still entertaining job offers. This was Olene's old maiden aunt? Tall and slim, she wore tailored wool slacks, an ivory silk blouse, and an aqua pashmina. She was as fashionable as Olene was not.

Miss Elizabeth was not pretty-for-her-age but pretty—period. Her eyes were teal blue, her complexion fair with few lines, and her smile inviting. Her still golden hair framed her face in soft swirls—unlike many women her age who preferred a tight set that would last a week.

Before Olene could begin the introductions, Vito blurted out, "Miss Elizabeth! Nice to have you join us!" He gaped at Olene. "*This* is your famous Aunt Elizabeth?"

Elizabeth surprised us when she said, "Hello, Vito, will I be seeing you again next week?"

"Auntie, how do you know Vito?" Olene was as out-of-the-loop as the rest of us.

Elizabeth winked. "Our little secret. Right, Vito?"

He kidded back. "Yeah, but the news will make the papers soon, so we might as well tell 'em."

Elizabeth threw her hands up. "Oh, well, if we must."

"The company I work for is the general contractor for the elderly housing complex addition," Vito said. "I'm the super on the job. Miss Elizabeth takes very good care of us."

"You know the ladies are pleased to spoil you and your men," she said.

Will asked, "Miss Elizabeth, have you lived at the complex long?"

"Oh, I don't live there, Mr. Anderson. A few years back, I offered to transport a friend to her various appointments. Before I knew what she had done, she'd bamboozled me into a three-day-a-week stint helping other residents. Friday is my busiest day—the all-important hair appointments. After a year of volunteering, they made me an honorary resident. That's how I met Vito."

I suspected Elizabeth's outgoing personality had made her a shoo-in for the position of liaison between the residents and the construction crew.

"The job end is in sight, less than a month away," Vito said. "We're gonna miss you."

"Now don't forget the special picnic lunch the residents have planned for you all. They've been pulling recipes and writing shopping lists."

"Are you kidding? My guys won't let me forget! I'll make sure to leave my rosary beads out the night before for good weather."

Lavender's head popped up. "Cool. I got some rosary beads at a yard sale. Now I know what to do with them."

Vito looked askance at her but made no effort to explain the main role of the beads.

The only hint of the aging process having set in was a hearing loss to which Elizabeth openly admitted. I moved down a few seats so she could sit near Will. My gesture wasn't so much about my matchmaking as about Elizabeth having a better chance of hearing him if she was seated nearby.

Okay, so maybe my move was a little bit about matchmaking.

When Gracie came by the table a few minutes later, she addressed our newcomer. "Miss Elizabeth! Do you remember me?" She got into character as Ethel played by Katharine Hepburn in *On Golden Pond.*

"How could I ever forget? If I recall correctly, we gave you a standing ovation."

Gracie bowed. "Yes, you did, and I thank you."

"Another case of 'It's a Small World!'" Will said. "Miss Elizabeth, I believe you're entitled to a free dessert—maybe even two!"

In mid-July, Party of One would celebrate its six-month anniversary. With the exception of Martina and me calling Will that one time, we stuck to our unspoken rule of limiting our social interactions to Cranberry Fare. Work was work, friends were friends, Party of One was Party of One, and never the twain shall meet (or something like that). We simply showed up on Fridays—no questions asked, no contact information shared.

I liked the way things were. I adhered to the if-it-ain't-broke-don't-fix-it philosophy. Maybe I didn't like change because being widowed had brought so much. Besides, hadn't I already colored way outside the lines by starting this dinner club? Why take the risk we wouldn't have enough in common to sustain a relationship outside of this venue?

Will was kind, so was Elizabeth, and Vito was a trip but one night a week was sufficient. Webster seemed at home in his reclusiveness, and I was sure Kate's concession to spending time with us older people was limited to Friday nights. I didn't want to mix Martina's religion with my life any more than necessary. Given the chance to get to know me better, the Professor and Olene might find me every bit as proletarian as the authors they didn't read. And could I picture myself hanging out with Lavender and Jeremy at a global warming bonfire or medieval fair?

With some contemplation, I convinced myself expanding by adding more people like Elizabeth was fine, but the best situation for us all was if Party of One stayed contained within the walls of Cranberry Fare.

Then why, oh why, did I have to ask, "Does anyone know what's coming up in two weeks?" No one knew, so I answered myself. "Our twenty-fifth Party of One dinner."

Before I could stop them, my tablemates suggested ways to celebrate. Most of their ideas involved leaving the confines of the restaurant: bike riding and a picnic along the canal; going to a fancy restaurant (which I thought was a bit disloyal); and having a cookout at someone's home.

What happened to the keep-it-separate-stupid theory everyone liked so much? Was I the only one with common sense? What was wrong with acknowledging the night at our table at Cranberry Fare at the usual day and time?

Against my better judgment and before I could do anything to prevent them, Party of One-ers exchanged phone numbers and email addresses and vowed to call each other. They talked about a menu and wondered about inviting guests. A few wanted to decorate and have prizes.

"Prizes for what?" I asked. "Cleaning your plate?"

Things got out of hand. I either had to give them my phone number or be labeled a big fat spoilsport. My only hope was sometime during the next week, they would all come to their senses and realize this was a mistake. That did not happen. I got a call from Martina on Tuesday asking me if I agreed with the idea of a progressive dinner. I couldn't say because I didn't know what a progressive dinner was.

She explained in detail. "Since four of us volunteered our homes for the silver anniversary dinner, we'll go house to house for each course. See? That's where the word progressive comes in. The others in the group will serve as co-hosts. What do you think?"

What I thought had nothing to do with what I said. "Um, yes, I guess, if that's what you all want to do. Who are the hosts? Do they live near each other? Won't there be a lot of driving?"

"Not really. I live in South Sandwich. Vito lives in East Sandwich. And Olene and Webster live in the center of town. With a little gerrymandering of the route, we were able to accommodate the menu."

Did I hear her correctly? Olene and Webster had volunteered to be hosts? The skittish librarian and Mr. Social Skills himself?

Martina continued, "We start at my house for appetizers, then we go to Vito's for pasta, then onto Olene's for salad. We end at Webster's for dessert and coffee. Sounds great, huh?"

"Yeah, great," I lied. "Wait, wouldn't salad come before pasta?"

"Not according to Vito. Being Italian, I guess he'd know."

During our next dinner, they made the anniversary party official. I still hoped someone would speak up and say what was on my mind, but they all seemed pretty pleased with themselves.

"My mother has a great recipe for stuffed mushrooms," Kate said. "I'll make them."

Will said, "Vito, how about I bring some bread and butter to go with the pasta?"

Vito raised his glass. "Make the bread Italian and add garlic butter and you got a deal."

Lavender and Jeremy offered fresh produce from their communal garden for Olene's salad. The Professor was assigned to salad dressing. Ethan and I were left to help Webster with dessert and coffee.

I still couldn't believe this was happening.

When I called my friend Maddie to complain about this latest turn of events, she responded in her usual manner, "What's your problem, Annie?"

"What do you mean?"

"You like these people, don't you? You said so yourself."

"Yes, but—"

"What are you afraid of? Getting too close? Losing control?"

"No. I don't know."

"Well, suck it up, cupcake, because they're not going to change their plans for you."

CHAPTER 16

The twenty-fifth Friday arrived. With directions in hand, I set out to find Martina's condo. I got there a few minutes early. Kate pulled up as I was getting out of my car. She had a sheet pan covered with aluminum foil.

"Mm, smells delicious," I said.

"I hope they taste as good. I haven't made them for a while."

Soon after we got inside, Webster showed up, followed by Will and Ethan. After I had greeted them, Ethan made his way into the kitchen toward Kate. One by one the rest of the group arrived.

Webster had a camera with him and clicked away.

The total opposite of Gracie. He seems more comfortable behind the lens.

I reassured Webster I'd remembered to bring dessert.

"Great. I need something sweet to offset my coffee."

Then I remembered Webster didn't drink coffee, so he had no reason to know how to brew the beverage. Boy, this whole night was a stretch for him.

Martina's dining room was open to the living room, giving the area a spacious appearance. Layers of bright colors atop a neutral palette brought the generic condo to life. Curtains, blanket throws, pillows, and art all spoke of a colorful heritage.

Her décor was filled with evidence of her faith and family: a simple wooden cross, framed Bible verses, and baby and graduation pictures of her children. The bookshelves held various versions of the Bible along with other books. From the titles, I gathered many were religious. A worn burgundy-colored Bible imprinted with her name in gold lay on a side table near an upholstered chair, well-lit by a wrought iron floor lamp.

I don't know why, but I was pleased Martina's home was just as I'd imagined.

We tried to pace ourselves during this first course, not an easy task. We'd arrived hungry and were met by mouthwatering aromas. In the end, we finished all of Kate's mushrooms and Martina's tortilla chips and mango salsa.

Before we needed to leave for Vito's, Will called for everyone's attention. "With pleasure, I present this token of our appreciation to our founder, Annie McGee. Thank you, Annie. Without you, we would have missed out on meeting each other."

They gave me a deep-pink potted orchid and a funny card they'd all signed.

My conscience blushed when I thought of how I'd resisted this idea. And when I attempted to thank them, my words stuck on the lump in my throat, totally surprising me.

"I smile when I think of that first Party of One," Kate said. "My first day in Sandwich and my first day in my first apartment. I'll never forget how kind you all were!"

"Were? That's not a goodbye speech, is it?" Ethan asked, perhaps a little too quickly.

"No goodbyes yet—unless I don't meet my sales quota!"

I whispered to Martina, "I bet she could sell Ethan something."

Martina hid a giggle with her hand.

Olene held tight to her glass of ginger ale. "Because of Party of One, my Friday nights are no longer lonely."

"You can say that again!" Will said.

The Professor stepped forward. "Yes, we have all benefited from Annie's start of something brave and new."

The accolades had officially become maudlin. I raised my hand. "Okay, I hear you. I'm wonderful. Now stop!"

When we arrived at Vito's, a surprise guest met us at the door—Renata. At least, we were surprised. We found out later Vito had convinced her to come because he needed her meatballs to go with his gravy. Or so he said.

I wasn't sure exactly what to say to her. Should I acknowledge I knew her? Should I pretend he never talked about her? Should I refer to her as his ex-wife?

Vito helped me out by saying, "Hey, everyone, this is Renata. Didn't I tell you she was gorgeous?"

The beauty Vito saw in her was all natural: olive complexion, almond-shaped brown eyes, warm smile, and curves in places most men appreciate.

Renata blushed and shook her head at Vito. "I hope I'm not intruding. Vitorio assured me I'd be welcomed."

Will said, "Of course you're welcome! We've heard so much about you."

I winked. "All good too."

"I think Vitorio is prone to exaggeration," she said.

Vito interrupted her. "Maybe, but not when describing you, my love!"

No surprise, our forty-five minutes at Vito's was loud and fun and filled with a lot of food. He had made true Sicilian gravy and pasta to go with Renata's meatballs. He even had a chunky garden version for Lavender and Jeremy.

"Mangia bene!" Vito talked with his hands. "Enjoy!"

His apartment was decorated by a man who had no intention of taking up permanent residence. The three rooms served a practical purpose—a holding cell for a repentant prisoner waiting to be remanded to the custody of a forgiving ex-spouse. The space was clean and orderly but lacked personal touches. The only exception was a large oil painting of Tuscany.

"Wonderful how the artist captured the true feel of the Tuscan hills," the Professor said. "An old classmate at Cambridge summered there one year as a young man. I was privileged to see his slides."

Webster studied the painting. "Sure is impressive."

"Did you buy the painting in Italy?" I asked, thinking of their original imported furnishings.

"Not exactly," Vito said.

Renata fingered the gilding on the frame. "He *painted* this scene in Italy."

"Vito's the artist?" I sounded as dumbstruck as I was.

Renata smiled. "Vitorio has many hidden talents."

Ethan held up a forkful of pasta. "Yes, like this sauce."

"*Gravy,*" Vito corrected.

"Gravy, sauce, whatever," Ethan said. "All I know is you and Renata make a good team."

Ethan's comment might have made someone else uneasy, but not Vito. He cajoled Renata, "See, they all agree with me! Now, will you listen?"

Everyone laughed—even Renata. "Vitorio paints his best when he listens to opera. He says Pavarotti and Bocelli inspire him. He has some vintage Caruso albums too."

"Ah, Pavarotti was my favorite," Will said.

Vito shook his head. "Such a shame to lose him so early."

The quixotic Vito loves to cook, listen to opera, and paint Tuscan landscapes. So maybe that box I put him in wasn't quite big enough.

We arrived at Olene's for the third course. The poor woman's attempts at being gracious only accentuated her awkwardness. Next to Webster, I thought her offering to host this event was odd. Apparently, as I discovered, she'd been *encouraged* by Lavender and Jeremy.

"We would've offered our apartments ..." Lavender said.

Jeremy finished, "Yeah, man, but even if you put both our places together, we wouldn't have enough room."

The house where Olene lived had been passed down through four generations. Outside, the signs of age were prevalent: chipped paint, torn shutters, and overgrown shrubbery. Inside, most of the furnishings—faded upholstery, threadbare rugs, and tattered drapes—were in dire need of attention. There was no life inside the musty walls. The place needed air—and sun.

But the Professor thought otherwise. With his hand on Olene's elbow, he led her through the large rooms of the old home as if on a grand tour of Buckingham Palace. "My, my, imagine the wealth of family history contained behind these walls. Of course, their years are brief compared to homes in Europe. Yet the tales this house could tell! Do share with us, Olene."

For Olene's sake, I wanted to believe what he said was true, but I only saw a sad, old house with sad, old memories that needed a complete overhaul. Though, I admired the Professor for his grand optimism.

Olene confessed, "For lack of funds, time, and ability, the place has deteriorated over the years. Any projects my parents began, such as replacing the clapboard and rebuilding the brick steps, were left to molder half done after they died."

Miss Elizabeth arrived without fanfare. "That's not your fault, dear. You were not raised to be a carpenter or a mason."

"Why, hello!" Will said. "You decided to join us after all, Miss Elizabeth."

"Thankfully, Mr. Anderson, my condo meeting adjourned early. As for this house, Professor, my grandparents were the builders, and they passed it down to my parents, who passed the place on to my brother and me. I didn't want to stay any longer than I had to. The house was too big and needed a lot of attention. I had other plans for my life. My brother and his family made a home here."

Will tilted his head. "Miss Elizabeth, do you mind my asking what those other plans were?"

"Not at all. Since I was a little girl, I dreamed of traveling to faraway places. Soon after college, I gained employment as a tour guide with an international company. For over forty-five years, I was privileged to visit almost every country on this good earth—many twice. I stashed away more memories than money, but I have no regrets."

Olene spoke up, "My attic has the proof. How many boxes of memories do you own?"

"Can never have enough good memories—the memorabilia is the problem." She laughed. "If your family hadn't let me use that space, I don't know what I would've done. My condo's bursting at the seams!"

Jeremy and Lavender had gathered enough organic produce from their garden to create a salad and a vegetable medley. The Professor had taken his salad dressing duties seriously. I heard the two gardeners teasing him in the kitchen as he unpacked his sack.

Lavender placed the salad on the table. "Pick your poison. I think the Professor brought a bottle of dressing for each of us."

The Professor laughed. "Perhaps I went a bit overboard—but I have never seen such a marvelous variety. The display was dizzying."

"But nine bottles?" Jeremy said. "Man, you're not at home in the kitchen or the food store, are you Professor?"

"You are correct in your assessment. I much prefer dining out."

Vito took a spoonful of the vegetable medley. I heard Renata whisper, "Vitorio, leave the broccoli. It doesn't agree with you." She patted his arm.

I suspected she might not hate him as much as he feared she did.

Will walked around Olene's home, taking in the dilapidated condition. "Olene, this home's a lot for you to care for on your own."

"Yes, and I have no idea where or how to begin."

"Well, maybe we can find you some help," he said. "Let me do some thinking."

When Jeremy wandered over to where we were standing, I asked him how long he'd been on the Cape.

"Close to seven years. I studied oceanography, but I couldn't find a job where I grew up."

"Where was that?" Webster asked.

"Alford, a small town in the Berkshires, where the anchor stores in the only strip mall are a Dollar Tree and a Suburban Auto & Truck Parts. Not much there and nowhere near the ocean."

"Though," Webster said, "the Berkshires do sound nice and serene."

"I know, right? I used to hike the mountain trails and fish and sail on the lakes growing up. But I found it harder and harder to watch the locals strip the forests, contaminate the air with their gas guzzling trucks, and pollute the water with their big boy toys. I decided to move to the Cape where I could at least put my degree to work and try to make a difference."

"How's that going?" Webster asked.

Jeremy paused before he answered. "Come to think, man, my degree and I are working harder than ever."

I was full and tired at the end of this course, but as a dessert co-host, I had no choice but to meet my obligation to Webster. Who was I kidding? I couldn't wait to see this guy's place.

CHAPTER 17

The cavalcade of cars trailed behind Webster's SUV down a dark road, winding behind the old Dexter Grist Mill. As he promised, he drove slowly so none of us would lose our way. After a half mile or so, he rounded a bend and took a right into a wide driveway, where we all had room to park.

The group hadn't lost anyone in the final transition. We'd tried to stay only thirty minutes at each house, but we'd run over all three times. Now, at nine thirty, we still had all the regulars and Renata and Elizabeth too. I had to admit full attendance was a nice testimony to the evening.

Webster's driveway and back deck were well-lit. We entered the house through a set of French doors leading into a spacious kitchen. The travertine tile on the floor complemented the granite countertop's variegated shades of gray. The kitchen cabinets were custom. I loved the two-tone finish—white on top, warm gray on the bottom.

"Very nice," I said, impressed with what I saw.

Ethan checked out the kitchen. "Good work. Who did your cabinets?"

Webster put his camera down. "I can't take any credit. Bought the place like this."

There was room enough to walk around the island, so we set the desserts out there. Webster turned the gas burner under the tea kettle to high. Two coffee machines were on the counter, all loaded and ready to go—one decaf, one regular. He double-checked his coffee-water ratio with me before he turned the knobs to brew.

"For someone who doesn't drink coffee," I said, "I'm surprised you own one coffeemaker, never mind two."

"I confess I bought a second machine and googled how to make good coffee."

"Smart. I'm a big Google fan myself," I said, remembering my recent geek/nerd search.

I'd had a hard time imagining what Webster's home would be like since he spoke so little about where he lived. The main structure was Colonial-style, but a newer addition looked designed by an architect rather than a cookie-cutter contractor. Though a two-story home, the feel was that of a loft because of the high ceilings and open rafters in half the first floor. The traditional lines combined with contemporary details gave the place more character.

Webster's decorating style seemed more about function than fad. Warm earth tones and comfortable furniture softened the clean lines. He had a few interesting art pieces displayed but no extraneous junk. There was very little surface clutter—not a Christmas Tree Shop knickknack in sight.

A collection of sepia print sailboats with their sails in various positions hung in the living room. A pond yacht was suspended from the rafter above the fireplace hearth. On my way to the powder room, I passed a trio of framed black-and-white steam locomotive photographs hanging in the hallway. From there, I saw a collage of World War II fighter planes above his desk in his office.

Lavender stopped in front of the sailing prints. "Webster, do you sail?"

"Used to, years ago."

"Oh. How about the rest of you?" Lavender looked from one face to another. "I need someone who belongs to a yacht club."

Kate took a sip of her water. "May I ask why?"

"When I get my massage therapy certificate, I want to offer massages on the beach—you know like they do in those cruise commercials. I figured a private yacht club would be a good source of rich people."

Kate, always polite, responded, "My parents belong to one in Newport, but I'm sure that wouldn't work, being so far away."

"Wow! I'd drive to Newport. Do they know the Commodore? Do you think your parents could give me a recommendation?"

"Um … well … I don't know." Kate looked like she wished she had kept her mouth shut.

Lavender turned to me. "Annie, I've even come up with a slogan. Tell me what you think. 'It's nice to be kneaded.'"

"Makes me smile," I said. "That's a good start."

Vito couldn't help himself. "If that's your slogan, what's your logo gonna be? A person rising into a big ball of dough?"

Lavender remained oblivious. "Logo? I haven't figured that out yet. Annie, maybe you could help me write a letter, you know, introducing me. You can tell the Commodore I'm certified, and all I need is a six-by-eight room with an 110 outlet."

Webster managed to keep a straight face. "Well, Annie, if you open with that line, I bet they'll read the rest of the letter."

I threw him my best do-not-encourage-her look. I mentally shook my head at Lavender and her ridiculous dreams.

"Don't ever stop dreaming, Lavender," Will said. "Dreaming keeps you young."

Elizabeth added, "That's so true."

When had I stopped dreaming?

I confess to peeking at Webster's bookshelves as I had Martina's. What a person reads reveals a lot. His shelves held a variety of subjects, including astronomy, oceanography, geology, computer technology, photography, theology, sailing, steam trains, the works of Tolkien, and the latest DVDs by Pixar.

Is there no end to this guy's interests?

I made sure to tell Webster his coffee was excellent. He believed me, yet stuck to his Pepsi. The cinnamon chip brownies I brought disappeared, either eaten or taken home for later. Elizabeth had brought lemon squares baked by a friend. She wrapped some up for Will.

Will thanked her. "With all the leftovers and goodies everyone has given me, I'll have enough for three days of luppers!"

Lupper was Will's term for a meal between lunch and supper.

That night, upon hearing of Elizabeth's organizational skills and baking connections, Will talked her into helping out with the next Sandwich Senior Center fundraiser. "I'll be there handling the cash box at the baked-goods table and eating all the broken cookies."

Elizabeth put her hands on her hips. "You have your duties all mapped out, don't you, Mr. Anderson?"

"That I do, Miss Elizabeth, that I do."

Everyone had left Webster's by ten thirty except for me and Vito and Renata—who were huddled in the den. When guests bade them goodnight, they waved but didn't get up. After I had helped Webster clean up the kitchen, we joined them. Blind and deaf to our presence, they kept talking as if they would turn into toads if they stopped.

When Vito pulled a gold chain out from under his shirt to show Renata where he wore his wedding band, I felt like an intruder. Webster signaled toward the door. We got up and returned to the kitchen. At this point, we were whispering—not wanting to break the spell for the couple.

Back at the counter, I asked Webster about his impressive collection of old cameras I'd noticed in a corner curio.

"I inherited most of them from my uncle. He's the one who got me interested in photography. To me, their value is more historical and sentimental than monetary."

"From what I saw on your bookshelves, photography isn't your only interest."

"So, you've noticed I'm a bit of a geek, huh?"

"Oh, no, I don't think that." *Liar, liar, pants on fire.*

"I know I'm an anomaly, living in Red Sox country, not knowing who's on the pitcher's mound. As for the Patriots, don't ask me to name more than a few players. I don't have a clue."

"Well, at least you're honest." I sensed Webster was almost apologizing for being different. I wondered who'd made him feel like being different was a bad thing.

Probably someone like you, Annie.

To combat my conscience, I said, "I find you quite interesting, Webster. We all do." I'm not sure if he believed me. I decided to change the subject. "Classy lounge chair. An Eames?

"Yes. A parting gift from my former employer."

"A pricey designer chair is a pretty good gift. They must have thought a lot of you."

"I guess. I still do some consulting for them, but I much prefer working from home doing what I do now."

I finally had the chance to ask. "What exactly is that?"

"Website development, design, and management."

"So, you're creative and tech savvy too. Fine combo."

"Speaking of work, I've been meaning to ask you if you'd be interested in meeting with some of my clients. They need a good marketing consultant."

"My boss is always interested in new clients. What type of business?"

"The Artisan House in Orleans. Sol and Dodi Jacobson are the proprietors."

"I've heard of them and their excellent reputation. What do you have in mind?"

"Well, we could meet here first, so I could show you what I've done on their website, then drive to their place. I'll get in touch with them, then give you a call."

Having a one-on-one conversation with Webster seemed odd, especially about something outside of Party of One. I was flattered he asked me to work with his clients. To keep the conversation going, I questioned him about his collection of land, sea, air, and rail prints.

"Some kids like sports. Me, I preferred planes, trains, boats, and automobiles."

One thing for certain, this was the home of a man. There wasn't a single trace of a female in the place.

Trust me, I'm a woman. We snoop.

Around eleven thirty, Vito and Renata walked into the kitchen, looking a little sheepish for having kept us so long. Webster waved off their apology, "No problem. We found a lot to talk about ourselves."

Renata put her sweater over her shoulders. "Thank you for letting me join you. I so enjoyed meeting Vitorio's friends."

I shook her hand. "You're too sweet, Renata."

"Yeah, this was a great night." Vito gazed at Renata, then turned to us. "I guess I'll see you guys next week."

We watched as they walked down the driveway. Vito reached for Renata's hand, which slipped effortlessly into his.

My eyes snapped to Webster. "Did you see that?"

He smiled. "Yes, I sure did."

CHAPTER 18

Spending time in the homes of my tablemates affected me. I could no longer picture them as one-dimensional cast members from my personal Friday night sit-com. I found myself eating my own words and enjoying them. Any doubts I had about starting Party of One had been swallowed up by their enjoyment of each other.

These people added interest and depth to each other's life—and mine too. They taught me lessons, the major one being I needed to change the narrow lens through which I viewed them and others. I had glimpsed their lives outside of the restaurant and had been surprised by some and fascinated by others.

I was disconcerted at first when the labels I tried so hard to stick to these people wouldn't stay stuck, going against everything I believed. The truth opened my eyes and also brought me to another question: *What else don't I know?*

This *new* ignorance didn't disappoint me as much as excite me; I wasn't discouraged as much as encouraged. I anticipated this new education like a five-year-old girl on her first day of kindergarten. I remember clearly the moment I realized my life could move beyond the status quo.

Hope is a good thing to have at any age—especially when one is over fifty.

I discovered another thing about being a member of Party of One. I was Annie McGee in this group, not Ned's wife. Since Ned died, my friends Maddie, Susannah, Robin, and others had gone out of their way to invite me to join them for meals and all kinds of events. I appreciated their efforts and thoughtfulness, but sometimes we seemed to all be trying a bit too hard. Instead of blending in, I felt like I'd been colored with a yellow highlighter. This Friday group never knew Ned. Therefore, they didn't miss him or feel they had to distract me from grief.

After two-plus years of being a widow, I finally felt like a whole person—not a half a couple.

The Friday after the progressive dinner, only a few of us were there when Vito arrived. He was quiet—and Vito is never quiet.

I tried to draw him out. "Meeting Renata last week was a treat! I have a feeling she doesn't dislike you as much as you think."

He missed my wink.

"Maybe. Sorry we kept you guys so late."

Webster backhanded his concern. "No problem. Hope you two had a good night."

"Well, I thought so. Then I did something half-baked when I took her home."

"Vito, whatever you did couldn't have been that bad," I said.

"I spent the night." His tone challenged us to argue.

"Oh ..." I didn't know how to respond to his confession.

"In the name of the Father, the Son, and the Holy Ghost,"— Vito made an abbreviated sign of the cross—"in my heart and in the eyes of the Church, Renata will always be my wife. I didn't believe we were doing anything wrong. But the next morning, she was so quiet, and she hasn't returned my calls. I ruined everything—again."

"You don't know that," Will said. "I bet she just needs time to think things over. Women are like that."

"Maybe." His shoulders slumped. "Why do I keep doing such dumb stuff?"

Nothing we said seemed to help.

That same night, Gracie announced she had won a starring role in a local production of *The Dining Room*, a play by A.R. Gurney. She passed out playbills to all us regulars—and, lest we think we were special, to everyone else in the restaurant. The production was to run for two weeks in August.

"You've got to come!" she said. "The play is set around a dining room table, and all the action takes place right there. Sort of like Party of One—but not."

I asked about her part.

"I play nine different characters."

Will sat up straight. "Nine characters? Only you, Gracie!"

"Is this a one-woman show?" Kate asked.

"No, there are three other actors, and we all have multiple parts."

As a group, we agreed seeing Gracie perform in a venue other than the restaurant would be a treat. Though we'd only been her trial audience, we felt we'd played a small part in catapulting her career in local theater. Before the meal was over, we decided to make opening night and the final curtain.

At home afterward, exhausted from a hectic week, I settled in for a night of TV, hoping to find a sappy movie. I pushed the Bible Martina had lent me aside to make room for my cup of tea. I grabbed the remote just as the phone rang.

I dragged myself out of my chair and checked the caller ID. My parents. "Bonjour, Mama."

Mom chuckled. "Bueñas noches yourself, Annie. Checking to see if I can bring anything tomorrow?"

Eek! How did I forget I'd invited them for lunch? "Uh, just Dad will do." I was pleased with my clever recovery.

I hung up, then flew through the house with my vacuum. Would I ever reach the age when my mother's housekeeping prowess didn't intimidate me? While I balked at a set schedule for household chores, she performed them with military precision. Laundry was done on Mondays. Tuesday, the bathrooms. And Wednesday was for windows. (Who washes their windows every Wednesday?) She vacuumed and polished on Thursday, shopped on Friday, and changed sheets every Saturday.

I put the vacuum away and grabbed my dust cloth and Pledge. I started in the living room, removing everything from the tables—as she'd taught me. I'd save my shortcut dusting for the rooms she wouldn't go in. In my hurry, I almost spilled my tea, now cold, on the borrowed Bible.

After an hour and a half of frantic cleaning, I resumed my position on the couch. Reaching for the remote, I picked up the Bible instead. The book fell open to a section called Galatians. I found this near the end of Chapter 5:

> *But what happens when we live God's way? He brings gifts into our lives, much the same way that fruit appears in an orchard—things like affection for others, exuberance about life, serenity. We develop a willingness to stick with things, a sense of compassion in the heart, and a conviction that a basic holiness permeates things and people. We find ourselves involved in loyal commitments, not needing to force our way in life, able to marshal and direct our energies wisely.*

Sounded like an abridged profile of Martina.

I put the book down and pondered the spiritual. I thought about those split-second flashes of enlightenment I periodically experience, when all of reason lines up with the universe. When the revelation is over, why can't I remember what I learned? Are human brains not sophisticated enough? Are they too underdeveloped to comprehend or too weak to hold onto something new for long? What are these short-lived epiphanies? Are they mini brain spasms or quirky seizures? Could a higher intelligence be trying to communicate with us? Could that higher intelligence be God?

All I know is Martina seemed to carry some sort of *knowing* with her and exude peace. She never appeared frazzled or fed-up despite her long hours at a tough job. She brought joy to the table each week—a joy I confess I didn't always welcome. Sometimes I wanted to wallow in my grouchiness, and her cheerfulness aggravated me.

She wasn't touchy about her religion either. If someone made a sarcastic remark about a Christian personality or controversial issue, she'd just smile like she knew something we didn't. I don't know if I envied Martina, or if I thought she was naïve.

When I asked myself what I stood for, I couldn't say for sure. Maybe because my beliefs kept shifting, and that shook me. Like I had a Harry & David's cause-of-the-month: green living, global warming, diet and exercise crazes, new age, old age, this movement, and that.

And where did God fit in all this?

I was impressed with Martina. I didn't comprehend how this woman with little formal education could speak with common sense that bordered on wisdom. Seemingly, she never slacked in her purpose or faith. When we pressed her on how she knew what she believed was right, she tapped her heart and said, "I know that I know that I know. That knowing is called blessed assurance. I wish I could give you the same, but you have to get that directly from God—in his time, not mine or yours."

Martina often referred to her religion as having a "personal relationship with Jesus." To me, following a carefully thought-out doctrine seemed more reasonable and believable than having a personal relationship with a God you couldn't see.

Yet did I really want another set of rules?

And if I were to seek that elusive relationship with God, what exactly could I expect? If I were to take a step in his direction, would he show me more?

I tried to drown a question, but it surfaced, gasping for an answer: *Are you afraid to accept God or afraid he won't accept you?*

CHAPTER 19

A few months had passed since Webster and I had discovered I knew his sister-in-law. Andrea and I had played a few rounds of phone tag but hadn't yet connected. I decided to try one more time.

She answered. "Perfect night to call! My husband and our youngest are at baseball playoffs, and there's not a grandchild in sight. I'm alone and free!"

"Good," I said. "Now, let's not waste any time. Tell me everything!"

She told me where she'd gone after she left UMass, the jobs she'd held, where she'd met Philip, and about the Christmas in Fairfield when she'd been introduced to his family. We exchanged the vital statistics of our children and her grandchildren.

She shared how much she and Philip were still in love after all these years. "We've had a glimpse of what empty-nesting will be like, and we like what we see ... Oh, Annie, I didn't mean to ... Webster mentioned you were widowed. I'm so insensitive."

"You're not insensitive. You're happy. That's a good thing."

"I'm sorry about your loss. I wish I'd been around to help you."

I opened my mouth. A question was about to come out but changed its mind. She caught my brief intake.

"Annie, what were you going to say?"

"Uh, nothing."

"I heard you. You were about to say something."

"Well, I wanted to ask you about your brother-in-law …"

Before I could finish, she pounced on my words. "Why? Are you interested?"

"Don't get all excited. I'm only asking because Webster wants me to collaborate with him on a project for one of his clients. And,"—I planted my tongue firmly in my cheek—"since he's so forthcoming, I could use some insight into his personality."

"Are you sure that's all?"

"Andrea, you know me. Seriously, do you think Webster's my type?"

She paused. "Guess not."

Andrea proceeded to tell me all she knew about him. He was fifty-three, two years younger than her husband. Born in Stonington, Connecticut, his family moved to Fairfield when the brothers were in their early teens. He graduated magna cum laude from UConn.

Her tone changed when she talked about Webster and his postgraduate studies at George Washington University in DC. "That's where he met Nieka—a gold-digging foreign exchange student prospecting for a green card. She talked Webster into eloping before any of us met her. Less than a year later, she left him for a man twice her age with ten times the money. Web was devastated."

"Ouch! That had to hurt." I had a better understanding why Webster was so reticent. "She sounds like a user, and you still sound angry."

"I am. Web's a good guy—and terrific with my kids. He deserved better."

"Well, sounds like he's done well for himself career-wise since then."

"Yes, he has. He worked for a major IT company in Boston for years, then started his own business. A few years ago, he sold his condo in Back Bay and bought the house in Sandwich. However, in the romance department—zilch."

"Well, now I've got enough information to put him on eHarmony. I'll do you one better, Andrea. I'll keep an eye out for a suitable wife for him, and I'll even play *shadchen*."

"A Jewish matchmaker? You would do that for him?"

"I would do that for *you*." We closed the call with Andrea telling me she and Philip were thinking about coming up in August. "My in-laws haven't visited Webster since his move to the Cape. They don't drive long distances anymore, so we're trying to work out a plan so the four of us can make the trip together. We'd love to see you, Annie."

The following Friday, Webster told me Philip and Andrea and his parents were coming for a week in mid-August. "Why don't you come by? You can see Andrea and meet the rest of the family. Maybe Sunday afternoon?"

"Sounds like fun. Thanks for thinking of me, Webster."

Or should I say Andrea?

One Friday evening, before everyone arrived, Martina, Kate, and I talked about our favorite personal makeover reality show. We commented on the changes we saw in the women who endured the process to the end.

Kate said, "When they dress for their body type, they look thinner."

"And not just clothes and makeup," Martina said. "They're renewed on the inside too."

"Yes," I added, "the self-confidence they find in the process always gets to me."

As if on cue, Olene walked in. The three of us looked up at her but avoided looking at each other.

The next day, Martina called me, and I called Kate. We'd all spent the night imagining how we could accomplish a makeover for Olene, without putting her on national television.

We strategized. According to a remark made by Elizabeth, we knew Olene had a little inheritance from her brother's estate which she hadn't touched. With a bit of connivance, we might get her to spend some of the money on clothes. Kate would be our fashion consultant and expert shopper. I would line up my friend Maddie, who was a hair and makeup specialist. And Martina knew a manicurist at her church. We also put Martina in charge of encouragement. We needed someone to convince Olene to take the risk. Her self-worth was in a fragile state, and we didn't want to break her.

"Should we enlist Elizabeth's help?" I asked. "She certainly has excellent taste."

Kate pushed her bangs to the side. "I thought of that too, so I called her. She thinks the suggestion would mean more coming from us as her friends."

We discussed how we would approach the subject with Olene. Then, ignoring my own rules *again* about mixing my personal life with Party of One, I invited Kate, Martina, and Olene over to my house for Sunday afternoon tea.

Once they'd all arrived, Martina started, "Olene, please forgive us. We had a special reason for inviting you here today. We want to do something for you."

Olene's brow furrowed. "You do?"

That's where I picked up. "Yes, we want to help you reach your full potential. Please hear us out, okay?"

Kate spoke next. "Olene, from what you've shared over dinner, you've never had much time or money to spend on clothes for yourself over the years. Are we wrong?"

"You are correct. I commuted to Bridgewater State because, after my classes, I had to relieve my mother in caring for my brother. With not much of a social life, I never had the need for fancy clothes."

Kate pushed her sweater sleeves up. "Have you ever had anyone offer to show you the ins and outs of fashion and makeup?"

"No, never." Olene's eyes, now big and round, glistened.

"If Martina, Annie, and I offered to help you with a personal makeover, would you be opposed?"

Olene pressed her palms together like she was praying. "Not at all!" Her fingers bounced off each other in mini claps.

As we knew she would, Kate closed the deal. "Is there any reason we can't get started right away?"

"None!" Olene jumped up. "You cannot imagine how long I have dreamed of this. I had no idea how to proceed. How will I ever repay you?"

Poof! Any misgivings we had disappeared.

Our goal was to get the makeover done by the next Party of One. Since time was short, Martina took Olene clothes shopping the next day, and Kate joined them after work.

Martina called me to report in. "Kate and I were pleasantly surprised to find a nice figure under her shapeless clothing. She tried on clothes in at least ten different stores."

I was almost afraid to ask, "But did she buy anything?"

"Ha! As soon as those purse strings were loosened, there was no holding her back!"

I joined them Wednesday night for the visit to the manicurist, who gave Olene her first ever manicure and pedicure. Maddie couldn't do her hair and makeup until Friday, but Olene had that whole day off.

Kate, Martina, and I got to Cranberry Fare early that Friday. We were anxious to see Olene's big reveal. None of us had talked to her that day. One by one, the rest of our group came in. No sign of Olene. We worried ourselves with second-guessing and whispered with each other.

"What if she's sorry she let us talk her into this whole makeover thing?" Martina asked.

I sighed. "What if she doesn't like the way she looks?"

Kate said. "Or worse, what if she backed out?"

Will turned his head toward the entrance, then back to the table. "Miss Elizabeth, do you know where Olene might be? She's usually on time. I hope she didn't have trouble with that old car of hers."

Elizabeth, privy to the weeklong events, patted his hand. "I'm sure she'll be along soon, Mr. Anderson. No need to fret."

We were interrupted by Gracie doing an excellent rendition of Humphrey Bogart as Rick Blaine. "Of all the family-style restaurants in all the towns in all the world, she walks into mine. Set up for a party of one, set up for a party of one."

"Ah, *Casablanca*, one of the all-time greats." Will grinned. "My wife always accused me of having a crush on Ingrid Bergman. I can't honestly say she was wrong."

Elizabeth rolled her eyes. "You and every other man, Mr. Anderson."

"Darn," I said under my breath. Being my turn to greet, I hurried to meet the newcomer because I didn't want to miss Olene's arrival. When I got to the hostess station, there was a well-dressed, attractive woman with short hair, mid-thirties or so, standing near Gracie. I approached her and spoke as fast as I could without being rude. "Hi, my name is Annie. If you're dining alone tonight, I would like to invite you to join our Party of One table."

She leaned toward me and whispered, "Annie! It's me— Olene."

My mouth dropped open and stayed that way until she told me to close up before someone called 9-1-1. I couldn't believe my eyes. She was a different person—taller, prettier, and ten years younger. With no trace of heavy makeup, her face glowed. Her hair had been cut, colored, and highlighted. The style was casual, and the short layers gave way to her natural curl.

When Olene spoke to me, she made eye contact for the first time ever. Her smile told us she was pleased. Dressed in the color of the sun, she shone. When she walked to the table, she took long strides and held her head high.

"Everyone, I'd like to introduce the updated Ms. Olene Hanssen!"

The expressions around the table told us no one had guessed.

Olene was gracious as she accepted the many compliments, giving all the credit to Martina, Kate, and me. Although her confidence level was high, she was humble, making her even more attractive.

The men had always treated Olene like a lady, affording her the same courtesy they might reserve for a frail old woman. That night, however, they seemed flustered by the change, acting like seventh-grade boys having their first conversation with a girl. Webster pulled out her chair and helped her with her jacket. Will whistled while the Professor was at a loss for words. That alone was worth the price of admission.

Martina looked like she would cry. "Such a pretty shade of yellow! So beautiful on you."

"My Olene has always been beautiful," Elizabeth said. "You've just enhanced her natural good looks."

"Aunt Elizabeth, please," Olene said, blushing.

"Yes, quite lovely indeed." The Professor didn't take his eyes off her.

Webster raised his glass. "A toast to Olene's new confident self!"

CHAPTER 20

That Friday, two in our group were celebrating their birthdays: the Professor and Lavender, the professing pagan. As far as I was concerned, that pretty much shot the whole theory of astrological signs dictating how you would turn out. If there were ever two people so totally different, just consider these fellow Leos.

To commemorate his fifty-eighth birthday, the Professor had made a head start on his syllabus for the fall semester, and for relaxation, he'd re-read *Beowulf*. I knew we were in for a lecture when I saw him position both hands on the edge of the table, extend his arms, and inhale like he was preparing to blow up an inflatable podium.

"*Beowulf* is most fascinating," he said. "With over 3,100 long alliterative lines, this Anglo-Saxon epic poem can be studied as often as one has time."

Are you kidding? Who would know this stuff?

"Yes, a daunting read but well worth the effort," added Olene.

The Professor continued to no one in particular. "This account of the Anglo-Saxon fifth century migration and settlement in England takes place prior to Saxon's relationship with their Germanic kinsmen."

Webster commented, "Ah, Beowulf, the hero of the Geats, who battles a dragon and Grendel and his mother."

Oh, for crying out loud, et tu, Webster?

Elizabeth leaned in. "Professor, do you think your ability to speak so fluidly is one of the qualities that make you such an excellent professor?"

He paused to reflect. "That is an intriguing concept, Elizabeth. Perhaps you have stumbled upon a truth I had not previously recognized. Let me tell you about this one particular class …"

I caught Will winking at Elizabeth while covering a grin with his hand.

Lavender had celebrated her thirty-fourth birthday by taking a trip to Maine for some fresh mountain air. She'd driven her new, used, smokin' (literally) VW diesel Rabbit, which she'd bought from her Reiki instructor for $400.

"I had a great time." Lavender interrupted herself to blow her nose. "I spent a day and a half hiking in mountain caves, searching for chrysoberyl cat's eye."

Vito looked puzzled. "What in the world is … what you said?"

"It's a rare gemstone known to protect people from evil spirits, illness, and poverty." She muffled a cough in the crook of her elbow.

"Does the stone work?" Vito asked.

"Oh, yes," she said, "and it's so pretty."

Lavender had taken two unpaid days off work for the trip, choked on fumes to and from the mountain of clean air, and caught a nasty cold. Once again, the irony had escaped her.

As always in the summer on the Cape, the conversation turned to traffic. The Professor asked Ethan, "Young man, why would you choose Friday night to visit your grandfather? The traffic is beastly coming over the bridge at that time of day. Surely another night would be more convenient."

I couldn't believe he said that. He truly had no clue.

Ethan shrugged. "Traffic's not that bad." He looked down at his plate, pushing French fries around with his fork.

Why Ethan visited his grandfather on Fridays was obvious to me—and to all the other women. Ethan came to see Kate. But until those two were ready to move forward in their relationship, we pretended we didn't know.

To watch them was a treat. We'd catch Ethan peeking at Kate when she wasn't looking at him. Then we'd catch Kate looking at Ethan when his head was turned. When they'd catch each other staring, they'd pretend they didn't notice. I often wondered if these mating rituals were recorded in some anthropological textbook somewhere, for their existence was hard to deny.

The Friday after the Professor asked Ethan about the traffic, Ethan didn't seem to be coming. Every few minutes for almost an hour, Kate stretched her neck and looked toward the entrance. More than once, she mumbled to herself, "I wonder where he is."

After an hour had passed, she pressed Will. "So, I guess Ethan's not coming tonight?"

Before Will could answer, Jeremy arrived. "Sorry, I'm so late. On my way back to the Cape, I got hung up behind a bad accident on Route 3. Looked serious, man … cops, fire trucks, ambulances. A red pickup was upside down off the road."

Will's eyes narrowed. "A red pickup truck? You didn't see a yellow lab puppy running around, did you?"

Ethan didn't go anywhere without Roscoe.

"No, I didn't see any dogs."

Kate sat at attention. "Did you catch the make of the truck, Jeremy?"

"Toyota, I think."

Kate blanched. We all knew Ethan came that way. We also knew his pickup was a red Toyota.

"But you're not sure, Jeremy, right?" Will said. "And you saw no dog?"

I think Jeremy caught on. "You know, I can't be positive. There was a lot going on."

When Will got no answer on Ethan's phone, he tried to keep his fear hidden behind a feeble smile, but his eyes told another story. Our attempts to distract him and Kate with chitchat failed. Neither could focus long enough to contribute to the conversation. And every minute that passed, Kate looked closer to falling apart.

I was trying to think of something more to say when Ethan showed up. "Sorry. I witnessed an accident and had to stay and talk to the police. I would've called, but my phone was dead." The quiver in his voice told us he was still shaken.

"Young man, you must keep your phone properly charged!" the Professor said. "Your grandfather was on tenterhooks waiting on you."

Kate's voice seesawed from panic to calm. "You're all right, aren't you?"

Will stood and put his hand on his grandson's shoulder. "You weren't injured, were you, son?"

"No, Gramps, I'm fine. But seeing a tragic event like that does make a person realize how short life is." He paused for a second. "Uh ... Kate, may I speak with you for a minute ... in private?"

"Me? Um, sure," she said in a tone that raised my matchmaking radar.

From the looks I saw around the table, I wasn't alone.

She got up to join Ethan. He walked alongside her with his hand at the small of her back and guided her into the foyer.

When they were out of earshot, Will said, "Oh, please, let those two get their feelings out in the open. I'm too old for this much suspense!"

From that first night, sparks had flown between Ethan and Kate; their mutual attraction was clear. Like a regular Ken and Barbie, they were made for each other. To watch them struggle with their emotions week after week had become almost painful. Was it fear? Doubt? Stubbornness? Pride? I worried they'd wait too long, but I had no choice but to wait with them.

Fifteen minutes later, Ethan and Kate returned hand-in-hand and faces flushed. Their eyes, shining like Sirius siblings in the northern sky, told us the wait was over.

Before they could sit, Gracie, who'd watched them the whole time from the lectern, sashayed around Kate, paraphrasing Sandra Bullock's lines from *Miss Congeniality*, "You both are gorgeous, you want to kiss …"

Kate giggled, then wiggled her eyebrows at Ethan. "Well, do you?"

Ethan played to his audience, wrapped Kate in his arms and kissed her like he'd been dying to for months.

After Ethan and Kate's feelings for each other were out in the open, I was aware if this trend continued some singles could become couples and not have a need for Party of One. If there was ever a group less likely to coalesce, it was us. Yet, we'd become close, and this new development awakened concerns about the changes romance could bring.

Vito said, "Hey, you kids gonna dump us now that you're seeing each other?"

"Of course not," Kate said.

Ethan looked puzzled. "Why would we do that?"

Lavender said, "Yeah, it's bad karma."

"Why would any of us want to give up such delightful company?" added the Professor.

"Well, there's no rule that says you have to be single to attend," I said. "We've had a few couples show up, haven't we?"

"Yes, that's true," Martina said, "but they didn't become regulars. This situation is different."

Vito said, "I'm back on Renata's good side again. Who knows? If I stay away from stupid, I could be the next Party of One dropout."

Martina caught his eye. "Why don't you ask her to join us instead?"

"We've always had a no-show-no-guilt policy," I said, "so nothing will change." Plop. The words fell right out of my mouth onto the floor. As soon as I said them, I knew they weren't true. Good things never last.

Webster leaned back in his chair. "There's one thing that scares me more than change."

"I'll bite. What?" I asked.

"Everything staying exactly the same."

Vito said, "Hey, Webster, we boring you?"

"No, but just think." Webster rested his arms on the table. "Do you see yourself sitting at this same table with the same people talking about the same things ten years from now?"

"No, I guess that would be like stunting your growth," Lavender said, "which restricts a healthy energy flow."

"Being a little sad about change is a good thing," Will added. "Just means we're enjoying each other at this time in our lives. There's nothing wrong with that."

"You're right, Will," Webster said. "When the right time comes to move on, we'll know."

I got what he was saying. So why did I want to stand up and shout, "Okay, everybody, put your hands up and keep your mouths shut! Nobody's going anywhere!"?

CHAPTER 21

When Webster's family got to town, Andrea called to remind me about Sunday dinner. Although I'd consented, part of me thought meeting her at my house would be better. How were we supposed to talk about our college days with her husband and his family there? No matter, I was looking forward to seeing her after so many years.

I pulled into Webster's driveway around noon, and Andrea came running out to greet me. We hugged, then leaned back to survey each other. We'd both gone up a size since college, but we were thirty years older, after all. In some ways, we looked better.

She read my thoughts. "We look great, don't we?"

I laughed. "Still humble, I see."

"That's me! Before we go in, let's plan to get some private time after dinner, okay?"

"I had the same thought on my way over."

"Wait until you meet Philip. He's the complete opposite of Webster and their dad. He'll chew your ear off!"

Andrea wasn't exaggerating. Philip streamed live on his job, his house, his children, and most especially his grandchildren. He had more pictures stuffed in his wallet than was rational, and he made sure I saw them all. I liked him. Andrea had made a good choice.

Mrs. Townsend, or Helen, as she insisted I call her, had made Webster's favorites—chicken and dumplings and blueberry pie.

"Glad I skipped breakfast, Mom," Webster said. "Everything was delicious. Hope we've got leftovers."

Helen beamed like her son had awarded her a Pulitzer Prize. When she was safely out of earshot, Andrea called Webster a kiss-butt. He threw a roll at her, and Philip laughed.

Andrea and I helped clear the table. Despite our offer to do the dishes, Helen shooed us out of the kitchen. We joined the men in the living room, where they'd settled their overstuffed bodies on the overstuffed sofa.

Andrea began reminiscing. "Annie, do you remember the professor—I can't think of his name—who incited us to protest the protesters?"

"Oh, yes," I said, "and how about the freshman class president who streaked during the lacrosse match?"

"And the big Halloween party at the campus hall?"

I laughed. "How could I forget? We went as Raggedy Ann and Raggedy Andy. As I recall, the nicknames stuck for a while—and not to your liking."

"Oh, I can well imagine my Andrea wouldn't like being called raggedy anything," Philip said. "She's pretty finicky about clothes."

"I wouldn't say finicky," she said. "I *care* about what I wear. There's a difference."

Philip's eyes widened. "*Care?* Andrea, you practically lay out my clothes for me each night."

"I have to or there's a good chance you'd dress all in green."

Helen joined us. "Philip, all men need a little help in that area."

Mr. Townsend piped up. "I don't have anyone pick out my clothes."

"No, that's right, Richard. But after fifty-eight years of marriage, I know you pretty well. You take the first shirt hanging to the right in the closet, and whatever pants are on top in your drawer. Who do you think puts them there?" Helen winked at the rest of us.

Richard's face registered surprise, then affection.

Webster looked smug. "Well, well, I seem to be the only Townsend man who dresses himself successfully each day."

Andrea and I caught each other glancing at his signature flared, stretch-denim Wrangler jeans. We tried not to laugh but didn't succeed.

"What?" Webster looked at us. "What's so funny?"

Andrea saved the moment. "Annie, how about a walk?" She looked at the others. "And, no, you can't come with us. We have a lot of catching up to do. Besides, we may want to talk about one or all of you, maybe an old boyfriend, so don't even think about tagging along."

Instead of trying to stick to the edge of Webster's winding road, I suggested we take the five-minute drive to the Cape Cod Canal. The wide blacktop pathway that ran alongside the waterway was a popular attraction to walk, run, bike, and rollerblade. Locals and tourists alike focused on the scenic views while ignoring the elephant in the room—the mammoth, oil-burning power plant.

People were always friendly down by the canal. They waved, said hello, or slowed to comment on the weather or scenery. They let their pets nose each other and their children play together. Canal etiquette. However, if you ran into the same person in the grocery store aisle a half mile away, neither of you would say a word to the other. All perfectly acceptable.

Dry, cool pockets of air rippled through August heat waves, making the temperature bearable. People marched by and nodded hello but didn't infringe on our space or conversation.

"You're right, Andrea. As far as I can see, Philip and Webster are nothing alike."

"Told you. That's why they get along so well."

"Your in-laws seem nice. And I like Philip a lot."

"Yes, but the real question is do you like Webster?"

"Don't start. We agreed he's not my type, remember?"

"I know, sorry. Just wish he'd find someone."

"I'm trying." I thought of Olene and how Webster had reacted to her makeover.

"Got a live one?"

"Could be, we'll see. I don't wanna jinx my next move."

"Proceed with caution. Philip told me his family always compared Webster to him. Philip was outgoing and athletic. Webster was not. Philip had a girlfriend. Webster did not. His family thought Web needed a push in social situations.

"Helen confided in me they may have pushed too hard. Webster was insecure enough to think since his family wanted marriage for him, getting married was the next step. His self-worth took a hit when Neika the barracuda did what she did."

"That was so many years ago. You'd think he would've recovered by now."

"I know, but he was torn up. I think he wants to avoid being that hurt again."

"Maybe he just hasn't found the right one yet," I offered.

"I'm not sure he's searching. An extra special person will be needed to change his mind." She tilted her head and smiled, trying for angelic but failing.

"Keep teasing, Andrea, and I'll see you get a sister-in-law named Francine Porridge. Mention her name to Webster if you want to see abject terror."

Near the end of our walk, I spotted Jeremy and Lavender and three others sitting on a blanket on the grass adjacent to the blacktop. I stopped to say hi, and introduced Andrea, reminding them about the "It's a Small World" connection between Webster and me.

"I remember!" Lavender said. "That was so cool."

Jeremy leaped to his feet. "Nice to meet you." He introduced the others. "We were at my place holding a little strategy session, but, man, the weather's so nice we brought the meeting outside."

"Yes, perfect day today." I noticed the Stop the Wind Farm brochures on the blanket.

Jeremy grabbed a few. "Please, take a couple of these and pass 'em around. We're in favor of wind farms in general, of course, just opposed to this location."

Andrea and I left them to their meeting and headed for the car. I glanced back at the five eco-advocates, heads together in the shadow of a pollution-belching power plant, planning a wind farm protest.

Opening night had arrived for Gracie in *The Dining Room*. At one point, I'd thought about a girls' night out with Mom, Casey, and my daughter-in-law, Jillian. Or maybe with Maddie, Susannah, and Robin. But mixing my people groups could get complicated. Besides, when I finally told Casey about Party of One, her many questions revealed her disapproval of this singles' group. I didn't need her attitude. When would my daughter grow up? (Of course, some might ask the same thing about me.)

One by one, Party of One members showed up at the entrance to the theater. We'd bought our tickets in advance to make sure we could sit together. There were fourteen of us in all, including Elizabeth, Ian, and Renata. We were a lively bunch but did our best to behave after the curtain went up.

Gracie's performance surpassed our highest expectations. She would've received a standing ovation even if no Party of One-ers had been there. The other three actors were commendable, but Gracie was clearly the pro.

We hung around after the curtain to congratulate her. We chose Will to present her with the bouquet of roses. Teary-eyed, she hugged every one of us and thanked us for coming.

I wiped a tear off her cheek with my thumb. "Watch out world! Gracie, your talent's too big for Cape Cod!"

CHAPTER 22

I still missed Ned. Sometimes I felt he'd been gone longer because the grief began when the cancer came back about three years before his death. We were thankful we had time to say goodbye. I wouldn't call cancer a silver lining, but the time we had was something.

After the initial shock of his death passed, there was nothing to do but ache and wait. The canonization of Ned by loved ones ran its course over a few years. I missed the imperfect man I'd loved for thirty years. I felt disloyal turning him into a person he wasn't, as if the person he *was* wasn't enough.

As I'd been married right out of college, I'd never lived on my own before. With no choice but to move on, I returned to work full-time with renewed focus and pursued outside interests which had lain dormant under my family's preferences. I chose historical documentaries over sports, artsy films instead of sci-fi thrillers, and opted for simple quiet.

I started to believe my life would be better one day. Then one day it was.

Unlike some, the idea of remarrying doesn't scare me—perhaps because my experience with marriage had been a good one. Not mountaintop-high good every day, but the kind of good that's worth the climb out of a few marital valleys. I didn't have any set plan to remarry. I was merely leaving marriage open as an option. I was smart enough to know being alone is easier than being with the wrong person. I didn't expect someone else to bring me happiness.

There was one thing though. Sex. Even though I'd learned to live capably on my own, *if* there was a God out there, and *if* he planned to send a man my way, I'd like him to send one soon. I'd never been in my fifties before, so I didn't know what to expect. Occasionally I'd have these mini anxiety attacks, thinking Mr. Perfect would propose one day after Ms. Libido expired.

Webster called me at home on Saturday. I was surprised to hear his voice. He'd finally put his material together for the Artisan House and wanted to schedule a marketing consultation with the owners and me. I agreed to meet him Thursday morning at eight-thirty at his home office and leave for Orleans from there.

Almost six weeks had elapsed since the progressive dinner when we discussed working together. Of course, I'd immediately updated my marketing survey in anticipation of his call. When so much time passed, I thought he'd forgotten, so I'd filed the papers away. I dug them out and reviewed them.

Doubt nipped at my confidence. Would Webster and his clients think the survey was too long? Would they understand why I needed to know all about the parties involved, including owners, artisans, and customers? Would they like my relational approach?

I loved my work because good marketing was all about creating good relationships—between my clients and me and between my clients and their customers. If we all did our jobs with the other's best interest at heart, the relationships grew stronger. If the parties involved didn't understand this basic principle, then I'd be feeding my best efforts and ideas to a shredder.

One more thing worried me: Sandwich to Orleans was a long trip. What would he and I talk about all the way there and back? As Andrea said, he was no Philip.

On Thursday, I got to Webster's house a little before eight-thirty. I found him out back, filling his bird feeders. When I was there before, I hadn't seen the spacious backyard. Beautiful, old, maple trees with large, vibrant green leaves stood tall among some healthy oaks. A dry-stacked stone wall separated his yard from the neighbor's. A colorful variety of summer flowers was planted along the base.

"Good morning, Mr. Audubon."

"Right on time. Let me finish picking up this mess. The squirrels did a job on this feeder. Someday, I'm going to get one they can't get at."

I noticed his dark-washed jeans. They looked new ... like Levi's. The moss green polo shirt and khaki ball cap were pure Cape Cod.

"I like your jeans." I regretted the words the minute they left my mouth.

"Philip and Andrea sent them as a thank you of sorts. I think my sister-in-law is trying to tell me something."

"Well, they're nice anyway."

"Thanks." He put the broken pieces of the feeder in the trash barrel. "Come on in. I told Sol and Dodi we'd be there about ten thirty. That'll give me time to tell you what I know about their business and show you the progress I've made on their website. I even made coffee." He grinned, looking all proud of himself.

I accepted a mug of black coffee—he remembered?—and followed him to his office. He had the client's website up on his oversized screen. The Artisan House was more art studio than gift shop and featured the work of juried artisans from all over New England. The studio even had a special section devoted to those from the Cape and Islands. The site was modern and crisp, and the photos did justice to the artwork, pottery, and stained glass.

"Wonderful design, Webster. Did you do the photography?"

"Think so? I wanted to make sure visitors to the website could see the detail and colors."

We went through each page. His design was simple yet sophisticated enough for this high-end studio, and the site was easy to navigate. What he and the clients needed was help with the product descriptions, artists' profiles, website copy, and an overall marketing plan.

"I'm sure I can help. Between you, the owners, and the artists, I have a lot to work with already. Makes my job easier."

We climbed into Webster's SUV and decided to take Old King's Highway. I didn't often take the time for this more scenic route. The historic homes and well-maintained-yet-informal gardens along the winding road reminded me why Ned and I had moved to the Cape in the first place. On the way, I asked Webster to tell me more about Sol and Dodi Jacobson and the Artisan House. The conversation flowed better than I'd imagined.

With early fall tourists going slower than the speed limit, we took almost an hour to get there.

Sol, in his late sixties, had a strong handshake and a big smile. His booming voice made you want to listen, and his laugh was infectious. He clearly adored Dodi. Her orange curls framed her face, offsetting her green tourmaline eyes. She wore a multi-colored, pleated peasant skirt and a hot-pink linen blouse embroidered with wild flowers and butterflies. Their back-and-forth bantering was like an old vaudeville routine developed over forty-five years of marriage. They were each other's best audience.

Many of the artists wandered in and out of the shop while we were there, like the place was home, and Sol and Dodi were their parents. Meeting them and hearing about their work was a bonus I hadn't expected. I knew watching each of them work—or rather create—in their own environment would be a big part of my research. I even scheduled a few visits that day.

Morning with Sol and Dodi turned into afternoon. When Dodi noticed the time, she said, "Oh, my, you dears must be starving. I've got a pot of homemade soup simmering on the stove. Won't you join us?"

I glanced at Webster, and he nodded.

"Sounds great …" My words trailed off when I noticed Sol shaking his head and waving his hands behind Dodi's back.

I wasn't sure what message he was sending, so I added, "I mean, unless our staying isn't convenient, for you, Sol?"

Dodi looked back at her husband. "We don't have any plans, do we?"

"No, dear."

I caught a hint of resignation.

After she was in the kitchen, he slapped his forehead and mumbled, "Ay, ay, ay."

Before too long, Dodi called us to lunch. The table was set with deep bowls of steaming soup. By each bowl sat a plate with a single slice of bread. "Dig in!" she said. "And don't be shy. There's more in the pot."

I dunked my spoon in and came up with a mouthful. The flavor took my taste buds for a rollercoaster ride—a polite way of saying the soup turned my stomach. I took a bite of the bread to offset the spoonful of nasty. In self-preservation mode, I calculated the ratio of soup to bread, which didn't look good.

When I caught Sol's eye, he shrugged as if to say, "I tried to warn you."

I couldn't look at Webster when we all turned down seconds.

Dodi said, "Looks like we'll have leftovers, Sol!"

When Webster and I were about to leave, Sol excused himself. He returned minutes later with a plastic container. "Here, I want you to have the rest of Dodi's soup."

"Oh, I couldn't,"—Webster raised a hand—"but I'm sure Annie would love having leftovers."

Sol handed me the container and begged with his eyes. He turned to his wife. "What? I should be so selfish?"

Dodi patted his back. "Such a mensch, my Solly."

As soon as we were out on the road, the plastic container safe in my lap, I mimicked Webster's comment to Sol in a sing-song voice: "I'm sure Annie would love having leftovers."

He laughed so hard he could hardly get the words out. "What ingredients do you suppose were in that culinary concoction?"

"My guess is catnip, shoe leather, and liver."

In a voice like a *Bon Appétit* food critic, Webster said, "With a hint of OxiClean. One teaspoon will clean the whole Super Dome."

The one redeeming quality of Dodi's soup was it made us laugh, which led the way for more relaxed conversation on the drive home. I talked about my work and my desire to change the perception of the term *marketing* from hard sell to relational. Webster talked about his goal to keep his business small to bypass overload and stress and give him time to enjoy clients like Sol and Dodi. We discussed the serious talent we'd seen at the Artisan House.

"Did you catch what Sol said about a refining fire?" I asked.

"Yes. Sol often refers to difficult times as being in God's refining fires. He says they're the proof God is working in his life, still molding, still polishing."

"If you don't mind my asking, do you have a *higher power* like Sol or Vito or Martina?"

"If you're asking me if I believe in God, my answer's yes. And what you saw today is God-given talent."

Clarice G. James

"I'm sure these artists have studied for years to get where they are now," I said. "Don't they deserve some of the credit?"

"Although I credit natural talent to God, I believe we're responsible for developing what he gives us to our fullest potential."

"So, we all have God-given talents?"

"I believe so. Sometimes we have trouble recognizing them. We discount the gifts God has given us, thinking they're insignificant. We have this bad habit of always thinking others are more talented."

Was he talking about someone he knew or himself?

We got back to Sandwich around four thirty. I thanked Webster for the referral. "I know I'll love working with Sol and Dodi."

"I knew you'd hit it off with them." He glanced at the soup and smirked.

Not knowing what else to do, I'd kept the stinky soup on my lap the whole way back. I held up the container and said with mock evil intent, "You do know you'll have to pay for this, don't you?"

"Do what you must, Annie. Just don't spill that stuff in my car. That broth could burn a hole in the floorboard."

I knew precisely what I would do with the soup. I just needed to figure out when.

143

CHAPTER 23

Maybe due to my God conversation with Webster, that night I picked up the Bible and flipped through the pages, landing in a book called Isaiah. Verse 11 in Chapter 7 stopped me: *Ask for a sign from your God. Ask anything. Be extravagant. Ask for the moon!*

A sign? Anything? Whoever this Isaiah was said to ask—so I did. I fell asleep soon after.

I awoke at dawn with the verse on my mind, wondering what kind of sign God would send me to show he was real. After climbing out of bed, I walked over and opened the window. I stuck my head out and peered at the sky. Would there be a rainbow or maybe a miraculous cloud formation? Perhaps thunder would clap or lightning would strike?

Nah, too mundane.

Having fun in my fanciful world, I threw my sweats on and walked the mile to the beach. The verse wouldn't leave my mind. I kept my eyes down. *Why?* Was I hoping to find a message in a bottle or a talking conch shell? Then I looked up. While an angel might be a stretch, maybe a dove or a seagull would sweep by and tilt its wings?

Coming up with all these silly notions and farfetched ideas was fun. As the morning sun shone brighter, one thing became clear to me. I *wanted* there to be a God, one who would give me a sign.

How about that?

So, I waited and continued to wonder. Would I lose ten pounds overnight? Would a stranger appear out of nowhere to hand me a secret message? Or would I finally win the Publisher's Clearinghouse Sweepstakes?

Eventually, like a kid who tires of waiting for the cereal box-top toy to come in the mail, I forgot about my request.

Word-of-mouth and local reviews assured closing night of Gracie's play was packed. After the final curtain fell, the cast members came out for their bows, introduced in the order of their appearance. Gracie was the second one out. The audience went wild. When the remaining actors walked out, even they turned to applaud the young star. This was the first time I'd seen Gracie lose her poise—but not for long. She curtsied and applauded her co-stars as well as the audience. And when she saw the group of Party of One-ers—all fourteen of us again—she waved and blew kisses.

Reports of her talent had reached the ears of playhouse directors from all over the Cape and Islands. They sought her out and offered her roles in upcoming productions. We knew the next time we saw a performance by Gracie Camden, third row center tickets would cost way more than eight dollars.

My boss was as excited as I was to have the Artisan House as a client. We always preferred doing business with companies we respected. I was given all the time I needed to work on the account. To be trusted this way by my employer was a high compliment, one I valued.

I'd already made appointments to visit some of the artists at work in their studios. Even though I utilized the resources of the local library and the internet in my research, I knew there was no substitute for my senses. The purpose of these site visits was to see, hear, smell, and touch as much as I could, so I could best express the creative process to the customer and art collector.

I narrowed my first trip to the Lower Cape to see a stained-glass artist, a jewelry designer, and a painter who specialized in Cape landscapes. In preparation for my visit the next day, I put my notebook, handheld digital recorder, and camera case in front of the door so I wouldn't forget all I needed.

Wanting to capture the detail, I wished I was a better photographer like Webster. Then inspiration hit me. *I wonder if he has any photos I could use?*

I left him a message. "Annie, here. I'm visiting some of Sol and Dodi's artists tomorrow in their natural habitat, so to speak. I hope to get some good pictures of them during their creative processes, but I thought I'd see what you had first. Call me back, okay?"

He returned my call soon after. He invited me to go through his stock but admitted the majority of his photos were of the finished product not the process.

"I could come along and take some shots if you want—unless I'd be interfering with what you had in mind."

"Not at all. I'm a lousy picture taker. Awfully short notice though. Are you free tomorrow?"

"Well, I'm not free, but I can be bought cheap. Might cost you lunch."

When we walked into the stained-glass studio the next day, the first thing I noticed was color and light. Stained-glass pieces, some old, some new, hung throughout the shop in front of every window and on rafters above. A large church window rested on a long table. The artist had fans running and windows open for ventilation. The studio was hot. I asked what the odor was. He told me the fumes from flux, always evident during soldering.

Racks held pieces of glass and copper sheets. One long shelf was filled with flux, patina in black, and copper for soldered lead. The shelf above held finishing compound, wax, polymer, glass cleaner, and orange oil for cutting glass. I wrote the names down and opened the containers to smell the contents. He explained how each item was used.

Webster circled the room, unobtrusively taking pictures. "I've always wanted to try my hand at stained glass," he said. "I'd like to create a piece to hang in front of the octagonal window in my house."

From the little I knew about him so far, I surmised he'd tackle the project one day.

The next Artisan House artist on our tour had a place on the water. He liked to paint outside, and fortunately for us, the temps were cooler by the ocean. The smell of Cape Cod air cannot be replicated, but his paintings came close. And despite his broad strokes with oil, his attention to detail was remarkable.

"I learned to paint in oil from my grandmother," he told us. "After I was hooked, I studied at the Boston Museum of Fine Arts."

He was also an accomplished boat builder. We visited his art studio, which was an addition off a large red barn where he worked on his latest slipper launch. The scent of wood shavings and oil paints mixed with the salt air.

I was amused as I watched Webster aim his camera again and again at the boat. Mischief got the best of me. I tossed a pine cone at him, which bounced off his shoulder.

Caught off guard, he stumbled. "What was that for?"

I laughed. "For taking more pictures of that boat than you have anything else today! And since the Artisan House doesn't sell boats, I can only assume these pictures will be hanging on the walls in your house. Am I right?"

"Guess you'll have to break in to find out."

The jewelry designer's shop was our last stop. She was excited to talk about her craft. "Plain and simple, I'm blessed to be doing what I've wanted to do since I was a child—design and make jewelry. I even refine my own gold and silver."

There's that word again—refine.

As she was known for her variety, she had collections of cloisonné enamel, turquoise mixed with sterling silver, and fine gold and platinum paired with cut stones and pearls. Her creations were distinct, either made from her original designs or by updating a vintage piece.

I whispered to Webster, "I've never thought much about jewelry, but watching her work has given me a new appreciation for this art form. Like this enamel brooch—not only beautiful but different from any piece I've ever seen."

As I browsed a few more glass display cases, a sapphire ring stood out amid diamonds.

"Would you like to try the ring on?" she said.

"Sure, all in the name of research, of course." I tilted my hand under the light to watch the gem sparkle. "Is this one of your designs too?"

"Yes, the white-gold scrolls give the emerald-cut sapphire a vintage feel with a modern touch. No two are alike."

"Exquisite." I handed the ring back.

Webster whispered to me, "That's the God-given part."

I nodded. "I think you're onto something. The level of talent these artisans possess has to be innate, inbred, God-given, whatever you want to call it. Maybe this talent *can't* be taught."

I took extensive notes and verbally recorded my first impressions before they got lost in the jumble of the day. Webster understood why I needed to see them at work. And I was certain his eye and camera had captured the essence of their gifts better than I would have.

Since we forgot about lunch, on the way home we stopped for dinner. When I said, "My treat," Webster knew by the tone in my voice not to argue.

"This is becoming a habit," he said, "us eating together."

"Habit, maybe. Bad habit, no. As the saying goes, 'All things in moderation and moderation in all things.'"

"I like Mark Twain's version better. 'All things in moderation, including moderation.'"

"Ooh. Does that mean we can order dessert?"

Energized by the successful day, we spent an hour talking over dinner, going from one subject to another—our friends, our families, our work. We talked about his family's recent visit and the pros and cons of living alone.

I confessed my initial reservations about Party of One. "Doing something like that was so unlike me. I had second thoughts about the whole thing."

"I thought you people were a little bizarre—especially Gracie, playing Scarlett O'Hara."

"Well, all in all, I'm pleased by the way everything turned out."

"I agree, Annie. We're all glad you ignored your doubts."

While I had him in a vulnerable place, I treaded lightly. "So, what do you think about Olene's new look?"

"Stunning. She seems to have brightened on the inside too."

I filed his comment away, not sure how or if his observation would come into play.

CHAPTER 24

Over the months at Cranberry Fare, both Ian and Sarge got to know our likes and dislikes. Ian reflected that well when he approached the table on Friday. "Pot roast, Mr. Anderson?"

"Yes, indeed. Always done to a turn and the best meal of the week."

"Of your *every* week," Ethan teased.

"Make fun all you want, but the portion always gives me enough for —"

"Lupper the next day. Yes, Gramps, we know."

Ian interjected, "I've got my next question for you, sir."

"Shoot!" Will said. "I get more respect from you than my own grandson!"

"What is the most important aspect of a business?" Ian asked. "I'll be back around for my answer in a few."

He moved to the next person at the table. "Miss Kate, have you chosen your salad tonight?"

"Yes, the Cobb salad—but no onions and low-fat Italian on the side, please?"

Ethan was ready. "I'll have a cheeseburger, medium, and fries."

Per his usual, Webster asked, "What's the soup du jour?"

"Chunky cream of tomato," Ian said. "I had a bowl before my shift today. Never knew tomato soup could be so tasty."

"Sold," Webster said. "Can I get a half of a BLT too?"

When Ian got to Lavender and Jeremy, he said, "Chef has prepared some long grain wild rice and beans. He also made ratatouille, all organic. How does that sound?"

Jeremy handed Ian his menu. "Sounds perfect."

Lavender added, "Tell Chef he's the coolest."

Like Will, Lavender always had leftovers, although her meatless tidbits were usually earmarked for her cat, Pyewacket. To date, her efforts at converting the cat had failed—Pyewacket remained a devout carnivore and expert mouser.

Out of respect for Lavender's beliefs—or maybe because we didn't want to listen to her preach again—no one ordered veal. Others assuaged their guilt by dubbing free-range chicken the lesser of two evils. And there were still those who ate whatever they wanted with neither compromise nor malice.

Occasionally, when we'd let her, Lavender would lecture us on the virtues of organic vegetables and the use of chemicals in foods. Then, after her meal, she'd join Vito out back by the dumpster for a cigarette.

Ian took everyone's orders and ended with me. He added a little tune to his question. "Annie McGee, what would you like, my Annie McGee?"

I loved that kid. "I'll have whatever fresh veggie you have and the grilled swordfish ... extra lemon, please."

"Ian, before you leave," Will said, "I have my answer for you, if you have a second?"

"Yes, sir, I do."

"The most important part of any business is its employees. Train them well and treat them better, because without good people, you've got nothing—including customers."

CHAPTER 25

A new Party of One guest arrived the next Friday. In less than a minute, we knew her profession. Dressed in a charcoal gray tailored suit and carrying an expensive-looking leather handbag, she approached the table and said, "Tanya-Lotner-Attorney-at-Law," as if her name and profession were all one word.

I thought she was serving us papers.

Attorney Lotner tried to sit at the head of the table. Olene told her that seat was taken by Vito, who was parking his car. We knew there was no chance he'd move, since Renata had finally accepted his invitation and was in the chair next to his.

Kate said, "There's a vacancy near me, if you like, Tanya."

"Thank you." Tanya removed her suit jacket, then held the tailored garment off to the side and shook it—somewhat like a matador—before she hung the jacket on the back of her chair.

The suit screamed expensive. I wondered if our seeing the label was important. I chuckled to myself because Lavender had done the same thing the week before to show off the *new* thread-pulled, pink-and-purple-flowered jacket she'd snagged from a lost-and-found bin somewhere.

Kate commented, "Love your suit, Tanya. Kay Unger is one of my favorite designers."

"Mine, too!" Tanya seemed pleased that Kate noticed, then took a minute to scrutinize the rest of the group. "Am I mistaken? I thought Party of One was a club for professionals."

Having joined them, Vito replied, "Depends on what you mean by *professional*."

"I meant, um ... I thought I'd have more in common with you."

The Professor folded his hands. "My dear counselor, do you have reason to believe you do not?"

"No ... no ... I meant ... well, you know what I mean."

"No, do tell us," Vito continued.

Webster broke in. "Tanya, is your law practice located in town?"

"Yes, but I have an office in the city too."

"You mean Brockton?" Vito looked way too innocent after he brought up the name of this blue-collar city.

Tanya looked horrified at the suggestion. "No, *Boston*."

"I used to live in the city," Webster said. "Mind my asking where in Boston?"

Lavender jumped in. "Hey, do you do pro bono work? We need legal help with—"

Tanya ignored Lavender's question and answered Webster's. "My satellite office is actually located south of the city, in Quincy. I have a suite in one of the upscale hotels."

"What a coincidence," Renata said. "My friend used to rent one of those hotel suites for her Mary Kay meetings."

Tanya turned on Renata. "I hardly think renting a room for a makeup party is the same thing!"

Vito was about to react until Renata placed a firm hold on his arm.

Will clasped his hands together. "Smart renting in Quincy, Tanya. I bet you save a lot of valuable time not having to go into the heart of the city."

"Waiter! Waiter!" Tanya shouted across the room. "What does one have to do to get service around here?"

"Our waiter's name is Ian," Martina said. "I'm sure he'll be here as soon as he's finished serving that table." She motioned in his direction.

When Ian arrived, Tanya ordered an extra dry Grey Goose martini and asked if they could do something about the air conditioning. "In my profession, I cannot afford to get sick," she said, as if the rest of us could. "I'm definitely getting a draft on my neck."

Ian stood poised with his pen and pad. "I'm sorry, miss; we don't carry Grey Goose."

"I should have known from the décor of this place. Then use Stoli—and do something about that draft!"

When he returned with her martini, Tanya handed the drink right back to him. "An olive? I asked for a lemon twist."

"I'm so sorry, miss. I'll be right back with a fresh one. With a twist."

The next few minutes were strained and silent. We bent our heads and pretended to study the menu. I think our collective thought was, maybe if we're good, Mommy Dearest won't come out again.

Tanya didn't make our efforts easy. "This is all they have on the menu? Not exactly haute cuisine."

Unclenching my teeth, I said, "Perhaps finding haute cuisine at a restaurant called Cranberry Fare might be an unrealistic expectation."

Webster spoke clearly despite his tongue tucked in his cheek. "Yes, this night is about simpler food and complex people. Our palates would be spoiled otherwise, and we wouldn't be able to appreciate the subtle differences."

What did that even mean?

Tanya took a sip of her cocktail. "You might be right. In my profession, it's easy to be spoiled by fine dining."

"I can tell you about fine dining," Vito said, "which, by the way, has nothing to do with your profession."

With years of practice only a wife would have, Renata gave him a sharp elbow to the ribs.

That first week with Tanya was rough. Her lips were either pursed or spewing disparagement. Her eyes were alternately rolling or staring down her nose at someone. Some were able to overlook her arrogant air; others failed to do so. Tanya seemed to have one interest in life—herself.

While listening to her self-important babble, I recalled an old psych class where we'd discussed the theory that braggarts may be more insecure and less confident than we think. The class theorized sometimes the best way to combat a blowhard's obnoxious behavior is to praise them before they felt the need to boast about themselves.

The next week, I came prepared for Tanya with my Psych 101 theory. I opened with, "We're surprised you could join us again, Tanya, especially considering how full your schedule must be."

She smiled. "Yes, I'm inundated, but we all have to eat sometime, don't we?"

Score one for Psych 101.

A few of the others caught on, I think, because some came up with nice things to say over the next few weeks. Kate commented on Tanya's Coach bag and Prada shoes—name brands most of us knew but didn't recognize. Lavender and Jeremy asked her opinion on the contested wind farm case. Will and the Professor talked to her about her love of law. Webster, Martina, and I lauded her for her commitment to her profession and good work ethic.

Our strategy worked. Tanya's self-esteem seemed to rise like the red on the thermometer on a Beverly Hills fundraising poster. The idea was to gradually reach a goal, not to have her zoom by us, leaving us in the dust. Our compliments seemed to infuse her ego with rocket fuel.

She snapped at Ian one night. "Take this back to the cook and tell him I've had better tasting food in a county hospital cafeteria!"

"Try to remember to put the dressing on the side this time, won't you, dear?" she told Sarge.

And every week we heard, "Make sure my martini is dry."

When Tanya spoke, everyone within a thirty-foot radius heard her vitriolic remarks. All around us, we'd see heads shake and eyebrows arch. We pleaded wordlessly with the fellow patrons we heard muttering, hoping they could read the disclaimer in our eyes: *The views expressed here are those of Tanya-Lotner-Attorney-at-Law and are not necessarily those of any other members of Party of One. Any and all offenses are the sole responsibility of the maligning mouthpiece.*

Sarge was off one Friday night, so she decided to join us. When Tanya got there, she had a fit when she saw Sarge seated at the table. "Excuse me? What are you doing here? I don't think the management would appreciate the help sitting with their clientele."

Will spoke up, "Tanya, Sarge is a member of our group. She's welcome to join us whenever she's able."

"Oh. Well, I suppose that's acceptable," she said. "As long as you're here, would you mind getting me a seltzer with a lemon wedge? I'm parched, and that Irish immigrant takes forever."

Sarge steadied her voice. "His name is Ian." She turned away and continued talking to Martina.

When Tanya finished her meal, she said to Martina, "Would you be a dear and pack a take home container for me?"

"I'm not on the clock tonight," Martina said, "but I'm sure Ian won't mind."

Tanya ignored her response. "Now I don't want to open the box and find goulash when I get home, so be a good girl and wrap each item individually."

Martina's resolve faltered and she slid her chair back.

Sarge grabbed hold of her arm. "Martina! Stay where you are. Ian will deal with her leftovers."

Tanya's petty tyranny ended on her fifth Friday when she did the unthinkable. In her attempt to get quicker service, she shouted "Waitress!" and snapped her fingers at Sarge.

One did not snap their fingers at Sarge—not if one valued one's life.

Sarge put her heavy tray down nearby and faced our table. In unison, we froze mid-cringe. Oblivious, Tanya kept talking. She had no clue a sentence was about to be pronounced on her. We prayed the punishment would be quick and painless—for us.

Sarge approached the table "Was someone snapping her fingers at me?"

"Yes, it was I," said Tanya, the unrepentant prisoner.

"Mind telling me why?" asked Sarge, the guard holding all the power.

"You were taking so long, I thought you went home," said the smug inmate.

"Is that so?" The warden was planning for the prisoner's final meal.

"Where is our food?" said the dead man walking.

"Your dinners are right here." The smiling executioner pointed to the tray.

None of us spoke a word as Sarge calmly served everyone at the table. To add to the suspense, she saved the lawyer's meal for last. She walked to the tray and picked up the remaining plate. Taking quick, terse steps toward Tanya's side of the table, Sarge stubbed her toe on the attorney's oversized bag as she rounded the corner. In doing so, she achieved the ideal combination of lift and thrust to propel the order of chicken Marsala over Tanya's shoulder, down the front of her blouse, and into her lap.

Before Tanya could finish convulsing, Sarge spoke. "I'm sorry Tanya-Lotner-Attorney-at-Law. Let me help you pick the chicken out of your hair."

Some of the nearby customers clapped and cheered while a number of employees scurried into the kitchen so they wouldn't get caught laughing. The rest of us stared and waited. Tanya had no choice but to retreat. She tiptoed through the morsels of her meal until she reached the host station. Once there, she flung epithets (garnished with mushrooms) and threatened to sue everyone.

After the hubbub died down, Sarge confessed, "Truth be told, that was an accident."

Vito didn't look convinced. "You sure 'bout that?"

"Sure, I'm sure," Sarge said. "My plans for Tanya were way more creative. They involved itching powder and ancient curses."

CHAPTER 26

For the next few days, I tried not to laugh every time I replayed that scene in the restaurant between Tanya and Sarge. Though Tanya brought retribution on herself, somewhere deep inside me, I felt sorry for her. She'd spent the past five weeks with people she didn't seem to like, which told me she had no better place to go. How sad.

Thinking about Tanya reminded me how grateful I should be for my family, my health, my home, my friends, and my job. I thought about thanking God, but since we weren't on regular speaking terms, I felt that might be too presumptuous on my part.

I thanked him anyway, relieved there was no smiting.

Lately, when I thought about God and religion, my fallback excuse that the church was full of hypocrites sounded hackneyed. That rant didn't deliver the same self-righteous punch it once had. I was as much a hypocrite as those I accused. I doubted others would accept me as I was, so I presented myself the way I wanted to be seen. I wanted to fit in rather than be myself.

Many of the moral convictions I once held had long ago given way to public opinion and political correctness. I made sure others expressed their point of view *first*, before I jumped in to agree. I was afraid to be different, afraid to appear foolish. I wanted to be on the side of cool, whatever or whoever that was today. And talking about God wasn't cool.

I had a collection of masks. A smart and efficient one for the workplace. A calm and confident one for my friends. A clown one suitable for avoiding intimacy. And a strong, non-grieving one for my family. The masks weighed heavily as the years passed.

Why did I care what others thought? What was I afraid of? Did Hollywood stars and talk show hosts care about me? Did the pope or the president have my personal interests on their agendas? Did politicians make decisions based on my opinion?

Talk about self-centeredness.

My labeling, prejudices, failures, fears, and needs were all based on rickety convictions. I thought what others expected me to think. A picture stuck in my brain of a popular TV psychologist sitting beside me saying, "And how's it working for you, Annie?"

So, my life might not be going the way I planned, but did I need a full-time god? If so, what kind of a god? A holiday god dressed up for Easter and Christmas? An in-case-of-emergency-pull-this-lever god? Or a god of weddings and funerals? How about a closet god I could put away when my god-unfriendly friends were around? A don't-call-me-I'll-call-you god, so I wouldn't be inconvenienced or embarrassed?

Would I want to follow a god I could totally understand and manipulate? And what would be the point of having a god at all if I was on the same level as he or she? If I didn't even want to be chairman of the businesswomen's club, why would I want to be god? Finally, I ran out of questions—or did I run out of answers?

I'd come across something in *The Message* that troubled me, from 1 Corinthians 1:8-19:

The Message that points to Christ on the Cross seems like sheer silliness to those hellbent on destruction, but for those on the way of salvation it makes perfect sense. This is the way God works, and most powerfully as it turns out. It's written,

I'll turn conventional wisdom on its head, I'll expose so-called experts as crackpots.

God dying on a cross to save my life didn't make sense to me. But was I really "hellbent on destruction"? I wanted to understand the cross and all it meant. But how?

And another thing, God, where is that sign you promised me?

On Saturday, I went to my parents' home to help them with their fall cleaning. My mother was one of the few people I knew who still adhered to those old-fashioned practices. Her fall cleaning always had to be done by the end of September—first week in October at the latest.

Though they hadn't asked me, I was determined to help. I didn't want them climbing on ladders to wash windows or going to the attic to get winter linens. By the time I arrived, they'd already retrieved a few boxes. I scolded them with the full knowledge they would pay no attention.

Mom sighed, "Oh, please, they weren't heavy. By the way, we found something we meant to give you years ago. Don't know how we misplaced that box."

"For our Annie" was written in black marker on the top of the cardboard carton. I smiled, wondering what family *heirloom* was being pawned off on me. I opened the flaps and peeked inside. I removed the item, large and heavy, wrapped in tissue paper. I folded back the paper … and stared … at the big, white, Holy Bible of my childhood. I pressed my face against the cover. The slight scent of Pledge shook me. My hands trembled. I choked up.

I knew, I just knew. This was my sign.

I pulled myself together. To reassure my parents, I credited my emotional reaction to some menopausal malfunction or other. Physically, I worked with them the rest of the afternoon, but mentally, I was somewhere else. I couldn't wait to get back home alone. I needed to think about what this all meant.

Later, in the quiet of my own house, I sat in my reading chair and opened the book by its worn cover. I found my young handwriting on the ornate family history pages. I remembered secretly filling out this record for God. The many errors and misspellings were witness to my youth.

I ran my hand across the print of a time long gone by, then again over the colorful photo plates of the Virgin and Child and the saints by the old art masters. The wonder and awe returned. I believed once again these words held power and truth.

Between the back page and cover, I found two old letters. I turned the envelopes over. The childlike printing read:

> From Annie Molyneaux
> 18 First Street
> Quincy, Mass.
> To God
> Heaven
> USA, The World

I had stuck four five-cent stamps on the envelope. Maybe because I thought heaven needed more postage than did my grandparents in New Hampshire. I opened the letter.

> March 3, 1973
>
> Daer God,
>
> My name is Anne Marie Molyneaux. I am 8. I live with my mom and dad and my 2 brthers in a house

in Quincy near A+P. My mother is a real good mom. My father works at Bethelhem Steel. I think it is near where baby Jesus was born.

We have a big Holy Bible in our house. I try to keep it clean for you. Sister Alberta told me you love me. She is a nun. She can't lie. Father Bernard said you love me becuase you sent your son Jesus to die for my sins. I dont think he lies. Not Jesus. Father Bernard. I wanted to right to tell you I love you to. Say hi to Jesus.

Your friend,

Annie Molyneaux

PS Please right back.

I had to reach far back in my vault of memories to remember the day I wrote that. The second letter was from me too.

April 29, 1973

Dear God,

I told Sister A you did not send me a letter. She told me you have a lot of stuff to do. It is ok if you don't right back. Sometimes I pray and I feel like you are hear. That is funner than getting mail anyway. If you finish your work early one day, my addres is the same as it was before.

Your best freind,

Annie M.

xoxoxox

PS One time my big brother wanted to let my little brother sit on our Holy Bible so he could reach the supper tabel. I didn't let him. We used 2 telephone books.

When I returned to the pages of the Holy Bible and began to read, I realized I'd received my letter from God after all these years.

As I prepared for bed, I got my keepsake box out of the closet to add my two letters to my collection. On the first anniversary of Ned's death, I'd tied my wedding band and Ned's together with a red ribbon. They lay on top. Now, bow and all, I placed them on my left ring finger.

I remembered the booklet Gabe had given Ned just before he died. Though I'd never read the contents, I knew the message had been important to Ned. I found the booklet under a stack of sympathy cards. That night, I read every word.

There was a prayer for salvation on the last few pages with a place for the date and your signature. I found Ned's weak scribble. He'd signed his name and written the date. He'd also added "Annie, find your way to Jesus. I'll be waiting."

Although the prayer wasn't too formal, I decided to talk to God from my heart, in my own words, for the first time since I wrote those letters as a child. I didn't want to use someone else's prayer.

I confessed as many sins as I could remember and asked God to forgive me. I told him I still had doubts and was worried what others might think. He already knew anyway. I admitted I'd been angry with him a lot, especially about Ned. I told him I was afraid and lonely at times and missed having someone to love and to be with.

"Lord, my faith is weak, but I'm willing to try. I need your help. There's so much about you I don't understand. I want to know you better, but you have to show me how."

I went to my knees, put my head in my hands, and released the tears I'd been holding back for years. I needed God; I wanted God, pure and simple. Without pretense or fear, I gave myself to him.

The reality of God's presence is difficult to describe but harder to dismiss. I felt the Holy Spirit all around me. At my moment of surrender, I'm not sure whether I couldn't move or didn't want to. Gently, firmly, God's peace and love took hold of me. Somehow, I knew when I chose to follow the Lord, his was not the easy way—but the only way. This spiritual experience, this renewal was not the culmination of my life but the beginning of a new one.

"Jesus." Saying his name sounded different.

As soon as I could, I returned to my chair and picked up the booklet and signed my name under Ned's. I smiled. "Can you believe it, Ned? When I couldn't find God, he found me."

CHAPTER 27

The next day I wanted to tell someone who would understand. I tried Martina but got no answer. Ironically, Gabe—the guy I hoped would call me back but didn't—was the only other person I could think of who might want to know. And because of him, Ned was at peace when he died. I owed Gabe a huge thank you for that. I picked up the phone.

He answered after the second ring. "Hello."

"Hi, Gabe."

"Annie? This is an unexpected pleasure."

I got right to the point. I recounted his last visit with Ned and told him how I'd kept the booklet he'd left behind. "I didn't understand what Ned was trying to tell me before he died. I do now. I also wanted to thank you for being there for my husband."

"I considered it a privilege to lead Ned to Christ, Annie. After he died, I had such peace knowing my friend was in a better place."

"Gabe, I have that same peace now too."

"Praise God! Then my prayers for you have been answered."

"You've been praying for me?"

"Yes, Annie. A lot of people have." He promised to check his schedule so we could get together. "This news is something to celebrate!"

I wanted, no needed, to be among others who believed as I now did. That meant connecting with a church—but which one? I was afraid I'd get trapped in tradition again, so I ruled out the church of my childhood. I wanted a new beginning with God. To me, that meant a new church.

Martina went to a large church a good forty-five minutes from Sandwich. If her church was like her, I knew I'd be welcomed. Yet, I wanted something smaller and more local. I checked the paper but couldn't decide. Figuring God was good for at least one more sign, I asked him where he wanted me to go.

A few days later on my way to work, I drove by a quaint church a few miles from my house. I had often wondered what the church was like inside. They always had the same message on their sign: "Jesus saves." I used to think they were consistent if not original. From the looks of the plain white building, I wasn't worried so much about finding aging hippie Jesus freaks inside as I was about finding a *Little House on the Prairie* congregation.

"Well, I won't know till I go." I decided to attend the next Sunday.

I entered the little white church on creaking floors and sat on the end of a pew. The wooden seat felt worn to fit me. The idea this old church building had been home to so many before me was reassuring. Somehow, I knew I belonged in this place at this time. Other than weddings, funerals, and baptisms, I hadn't been to a regular Sunday service in years. This was different. I was different. I was here because of a decision made by *me*, not by others or by a misplaced sense of obligation. My new walk was a personal experience, more intimate, between God and me.

The piano music began softly. I closed my eyes and listened. My heart swelled. I'd never known what that expression meant before, but I did now. The minister, a robust, gray-haired man in his mid-sixties, beamed at the rows filled with people. He welcomed us and began to sing along with the music. The people reached for hymnals and joined in reverent yet celebratory worship. I heard a few off-key voices and flat notes (mostly my own), but I imagined God heard a purer sound.

Prayers were offered and announcements made. When the pastor instructed us to greet one another, acting out of my newfound boldness, I stretched over pews in front and behind me and shook hands, young and old, light and dark, large and small. When people said, "Nice to meet you," I believed them.

The pastor's message of God's grace versus man's law was one I needed to hear. I didn't think I deserved grace. I expected judgment. The message of grace was fertile soil for hope to thrive in, and hope grew exponentially with each point the pastor made. I planned to return the next week.

As for sharing my new faith with others, I didn't expect my family or friends, especially the Party of One-ers, to understand. Other than Martina, whom I'd been unable to reach thus far, I had no plans to tell them. I needed to protect my new relationship with God, and I feared my infant faith wasn't strong enough to withstand criticism or ridicule.

But they kept at me.

"Hey, what's up with you, Annie?" Vito said. "You're acting strange."

Lavender lifted her arms together above her head, then let them fall open like a fan. "Your aura's different."

"Have you met someone?" Martina asked.

"You could put it that way," I answered with no intention of going any further.

Kate sang a ditty. "Annie's in love."

"Tell us what's going on, Annie." Webster sounded like I paid him $150 an hour to listen.

When their pestering didn't cease, I answered with a simple statement. "I've become a Christian."

Martina raised her head and hands. "Praise the Lord!"

"Whaddaya mean a Christian? Were you Jewish before?" asked Vito as if those were the only options.

"No, but I guess you could say I'm following a Jewish man."

"You converted to Judaism?" Lavender looked impressed. "Cool."

"No, but—"

Olene faced me. "So what religion are you now?"

"It's not so much a religion as a relationship—"

The Professor scowled. "Oh, dear! Tell me you have not joined one of those heinous cults."

"Annie? A cult? I doubt that," Jeremy said. "Man, she wouldn't even go to the psychic fair with Lavender and me."

Will held his hand up. "Let Annie speak."

"Thank you, Will. I'll tell you my story, but you have to let me finish with no more interruptions. Promise?"

They agreed.

"First of all, let me say this decision is the most important one I've ever made in my life. The term 'spiritual rebirth' says everything. I feel like a baby in many ways—like I have so much to learn. All I know is God loves me and Jesus is alive. I know you might not fully comprehend—because I don't know if I do yet. So, don't ask me a lot of questions, because odds are I won't know the answers."

I knew I sounded weird to them, but suddenly, I didn't care because I knew what had happened to me was real. A few raised their eyebrows, and some turned aside. I think they were trying to get me to stop embarrassing them—or myself.

Where had I seen that look before? Oh, yes, in the mirror on my face.

I continued. "I know you might think I'm wacko, and that's okay. I've thought the same about Christians too. Even you, Martina. Now I care more about what God thinks. I don't have to know everything. God has the answers, and that's good enough for me."

From their reaction, I decided I'd said enough for one night. Although I wanted them to understand the great release I felt, something kept me from going any further. I had to trust God to show me the right place and time. And to show them.

The Party of One-ers were a little subdued that night. They changed the subject the first chance they got. I wasn't offended. After we said grace, Martina smiled and gave me a thumbs-up. Webster kept his head bowed longer than usual.

I wondered if I'd made a mistake trying to explain my new faith to them. Had I essentially intimated that God loves me more because of the experience I'd had? I didn't want them to think I thought I was better than they were. Well, too late now.

Lord, help me. Show me what to do, tell me what to say.

I sensed some of them were keeping the same watchful eye on me as I had kept on Martina. I didn't want them to feel differently about me, but I knew they would—if they were anything like I used to be.

Used to be. I liked the sound of that.

Little by little, I found meaning in my Bible readings that week. I remembered some passages like the Psalms from my childhood. Back then they had seemed like nice poetry, but now the words leaped off the page, reaching my soul with clarity.

When I walked into church on the second Sunday, the sanctuary felt like a place I'd been coming for years. I sat in the same pew—fifth row from the back on the center aisle. I knew where to find the hymnal, and this time I had my Bible with me. Although I struggled to find all the chapters and verses the pastor mentioned, when he told us to turn to the Gospel of John, I found the book right away.

When time came to greet one another, I shook hands with a couple and their teenage daughter in front of me. I reached behind me and found the same couples from last week along with some new faces. I reached for a hand that appeared on my right from the aisle. Tilting my head back, I stared.

Then I looked down at my hand—in Webster's.

CHAPTER 28

"Where did you come ... why are ... uh, I mean, do you come here?"

He grinned, then sat down next to me and whispered, "I'll talk to you after the service."

Seated next to Webster, I had a hard time concentrating on the message. What had I missed? Why was he here? When he got up to take the offering, one question was answered. This was his church. How could I have possibly known that?

Sheesh. I hope he doesn't think I'm spying on him.

After the service ended, Webster walked me out and introduced me to a few people. One woman gave me a welcome packet. A few others eyeballed Webster and me as if waiting for further explanation. He didn't seem to notice, of course. I was caught off guard again when Karen and Drew, the couple whose house I'd been to with Gabe, approached me.

"What a surprise to have you join us, Annie! Gabe told us the good news."

"He did? Gee, I'm bumping into all kinds of people I know today. Webster, here, for instance. I imagine you've already met."

Drew stuck out his hand. "Drew Dumont and this is my wife, Karen. I don't believe we've been formally introduced."

While the guys exchanged a few courteous comments on weather and traffic, Karen pulled me aside. "Annie, I wish we had more time to chat, but we've got family coming for

Sunday dinner. I'll call you and Gabe soon so we can plan that get-together, okay?"

On the way to my car, Webster mentioned he'd seen me the Sunday before.

"Why didn't you say something to me then ... or on Friday?"

"I thought your first visit should be an unencumbered one."

An unencumbered one. That was Webster. In a way, I was glad he'd let me have that first week to myself. He was right. Seeing him that Sunday might have affected my decision to return one way or the other, and I wasn't sure which.

Gabe called me early the next week to invite me to join him for dinner with Karen and Drew.

I chuckled. "Karen didn't waste any time contacting you."

"Calling you was my idea, but she did tell me about seeing you at church. How about this Friday?"

"Um, did you say Friday?" I would have to miss my first Party of One dinner—not like that night was a special occasion. After all, others missed all the time.

"We could make it another day if you have plans that night."

"No, Friday's good," I said, scrapping my perfect attendance record.

"If I pick you up around six thirty, will that give you enough time after work?"

"That'll be fine."

Well, you waited long enough, McGee, but things are finally looking up.

On Friday, Gabe was prompt, and I was ready. For our first date, I chose my dark-blue jeans, white blouse, and mulberry and gold paisley tapestry jacket to dress up the outfit. I hadn't bothered to ask where we were going, so I assumed the rules of engagement were the same as they had been thirty-some years ago: casual attire for a Friday night date and dressier for Saturdays. I was right. Gabe showed up wearing jeans, a polo shirt, and a leather sports jacket.

He didn't seem nervous at all—but I was. I didn't know if I should invite him in for a few minutes or not. I asked when we were meeting Karen and Drew. By his answer, I knew we didn't have much time. We chatted on the way to the restaurant. He told me about the class he was teaching at the police academy, and I told him about my latest project at work. He asked me how I was enjoying my new church, then told me about his.

I became more comfortable as the minutes flew by. *Easy-peasy, I can do this.*

"The restaurant's not fancy," he said, "but Drew says the food is real good."

We'd arrived—at Cranberry Fare!

Gabe went around the car to open the door for me—since he saw I wasn't moving. Should I say something? What was I supposed to say? *I eat here every Friday, so I don't want to come here again.* Or, *I don't want my friends to see me with you because I didn't tell them I had a date.* Everything I thought to say smacked of a teenage girl's objection.

In the end, I squared my shoulders and stepped in the door. Cranberry Fare usually felt like a second home to me. But being here with Gabe on a date, the place seemed new and strange. I wasn't sure how I should act. All I knew was, I hoped the hostess—who I prayed was not Gracie—would seat us in the small separate dining room off to the side. I felt immediate relief when I saw a new face at the lectern. When Gabe gave the host his name, he led us to where Karen and Drew were sitting—in the dining room off to the side.

Phew. So far, so good.

I had a lot in common with Karen, who confessed she loved being a housewife and mother when her children were young.

"Not that I want to go back to those days," she chuckled, "but I did enjoy them."

I agreed. "Yes, while other women marched for equal rights and broke through glass ceilings, I counted on Tupperware and closet organizers to make my life better. Is that lame or what?"

"What is lame is us not realizing that once we finally gained the freedom to work full-time *outside* the home, we'd still had to work full-time *inside* too!"

I sighed. "What were we thinking?"

Other than the fear of being spotted by Party of One people, the evening went well. I could finally say I had a good first date. I hoped Gabe felt the same. When Drew and Karen invited us back to their house for coffee, Gabe deferred to me. I said yes.

When we stood to leave, Gabe held my coat up for me. I slipped my arm in one sleeve and turned—just in time to see Martina, Olene, and Webster on their way to the door. Martina and Olene didn't see me, but Webster gave me a chin-up nod. I acknowledged him with a wave as my hand exited my sleeve.

We stayed about an hour and a half at Karen and Drew's. The men against the women, we played Trivial Pursuit. I think Karen and I won, but I'm not sure. On the way back to my house, I wondered what would happen at the front door. Gabe made things easy.

He walked me up the steps and gave me a hug. "I'll be in touch, okay?"

The night was nice, very nice. So was he.

CHAPTER 29

I dropped my car off Friday morning for its yearly once-over and took the dealer's shuttle to work. Later in the day, the service manager called to tell me he had to wait on a part that wouldn't be in until Monday.

I called Martina to tell her I would have to miss another Party of One. "They'll get me home, eventually, but I'm stuck after that."

"I'm off today. Forget the shuttle. I'll pick you up at work. We'll have a chance to talk in private too."

And talk we did—well, mostly me asking questions. "Are there any sins God won't forgive?"

Martina looked both ways at a stop sign. "All your sins are forgiven—past, present, and future—the moment you believe Jesus died on the cross to pay the full price for them."

"How do I tell Casey and Griffin about all this without them thinking I've gone off the deep end?"

She laughed. "I have no idea, but let me know if you find out. My son still thinks I've been brainwashed."

More questions popped into my head. "I read somewhere some Christians don't play cards or dance either. How about drinking? Is birth control okay in the Protestant church?"

"Annie, try not to focus so much on what you can or cannot do as a Christian."

"That doesn't make sense. How will I know what to do?"

"Following Jesus is not about rules and regulations but more about having a personal relationship with the Lord. You'll grow closer when you spend time together. Read your Bible. Talk to the Lord. And ask the Holy Spirit to lead you."

"I'm such a list person. Without rules and regulations, I'm afraid I'll get lost."

Martina shrugged. "And, what? You think God can't find you?"

Her remark made my concern seem kind of ridiculous.

Before we got out of the car, I enlisted Martina's help in the practical joke I wanted to pull on Webster that night. I'd let the Dodi soup incident simmer purposely for weeks to lull him into forgetfulness.

"I'll give you the signal—but, remember, only if he orders soup."

"Got it," she said.

As we walked toward the restaurant, Martina stopped and grabbed my arm. "Wait a minute. What made you ask me about birth control, of all things? Is there a wedding in the near future for you and your old flame, Choo Choo Charlie?"

"So not funny, Martina."

"Not funny? Then the relationship is serious?"

"Still not funny."

Our discussion provided a perfect opening to tell her about Gabe, but I didn't and wondered why.

Later, when Webster heard my car was in the shop, he asked how long I'd be without a vehicle.

"Until Monday afternoon—if the part comes in."

"Monday, huh? Need a ride to church? I could swing by."

"Thanks, that'd be great." I felt a little guilty about what I had in store for him but not enough to give up my payback.

Olene caught Webster's attention with a little wave. "I have something for you." She handed him a gift-wrapped package.

"For me?" He looked confused.

She blushed. "I hope you will not think me too forward, but when I saw this at the store, I thought of you."

Webster tore the wrapping. "Tolkien's *Children of Húrin.* Thank you, Olene. How did you know I wanted this one?"

"A while back you mentioned wanting to add Tolkien's last book to your collection."

"But, Olene, isn't today *your* birthday?" It was his turn to look a shade embarrassed. "You should be the one getting gifts."

Olene smiled, obviously pleased with herself. "Perhaps my new tradition is giving gifts on my birthday instead of receiving them."

While I was mildly surprised that Olene remembered Webster's comment about a book, I was shocked that Webster remembered her birthday. Though Martina gave us a week's notice, the men seldom remembered until they saw the dessert with a lit candle placed in front of the person.

Olene and Webster? Maybe my radar had picked up signals after all.

When the time came to order, I waited to see what Webster would do. As I expected, he said, "What's the soup today, Ian?"

Ian kept his eyes on his order pad. "Lentil, from scratch."

"Hmm, sounds good, give me a bowl. And could I get some extra rolls and butter too?"

Bingo! I cued Martina. She excused herself for a moment and went into the kitchen—where Dodi's plastic container of soup had been safely stored.

After Ian had served everyone else at the table, he put the bowl of soup down in front of Webster. I sat back to enjoy the show, not wanting to miss his first bite.

Before the spoon was out of his mouth, he made a face like a baby tasting his first bite of strained liver after a diet of rice cereal and peaches. He caught my guilty grin before washing the soup down with Pepsi. "Diabolical, Annie! And Martina and Ian, shame on you for acting as her accomplices.

I'm appalled." Webster glared at me. "Fair warning, Annie McGee—"

"Un-uh," I protested. "This makes us even, remember?"

"Ha! If I were you, I would be vigilant. You'll never know how or when I will strike."

CHAPTER 30

As our conversation continued that night, Olene and I discussed our need for a dependable handyman.

I began. "I wish I were more of a modern Ms. Fix-it, but growing up in my house, the women handled the housecleaning while the men took care of the maintenance and yard work. Between my dad and my brothers, then my husband and son, I confess I've never mowed a lawn in my life."

Olene added, "Not all men are handy like all women are not good cooks, but my mother and father were neither. And the little time my father had outside of his full-time job, he spent relieving Mom to care for my brother."

"My problem's been getting people to finish the job." I sighed. "The first time I hired an electrician after my husband died, I trusted the guy to do what he contracted to do. When he was just about done, I paid him the balance. He never returned. The embarrassing thing is I made the same mistake with a tile man and a plumber."

Will shook his head. "I don't understand how people can do that to a widow—or anyone—and feel good about themselves."

"Man, you must've been mad," Jeremy said. "Did you take 'em to court?"

"No. I was angrier with myself for being so gullible—and I didn't want to go public with my stupidity."

Olene shrugged. "My house needs so much work. I have no idea where to start."

"Well, you know where *not* to start ..." Webster cracked, "with Annie's tradesmen."

"I guess I won't complain the next time I have to call the maintenance supervisor," Martina said. "That's one advantage of condo living."

"Olene and Annie, what are some of the important things you need done?" Will asked. "I've been giving this some thought. I'm sure we could help you. I'm a pretty good painter and a fair carpenter, if I do say so myself."

Will was my hero all over again. "I'm in!"

"Why don't you two make a list," Webster said, "and we can check a few things off over time."

Elizabeth added, "Maybe those of us with no handyman skills can provide refreshments for the workers."

Before long, Will, Webster, Vito, Lavender, and Jeremy teamed up to help Olene and me with odd jobs. Even the Professor agreed to pitch in when he could—which, I admit, was a scary thought.

When we sang "Happy Birthday" to Olene that night, she looked like she would cry.

"Because of you all, this is the best birthday I have ever had," she said. "Thank you so much—not only for the offer to help but for everything!"

I got up early Saturday. As a treat, I planned to fix myself a nice breakfast and linger over a second cup of coffee. I didn't often take time to do that.

Maybe some bacon and eggs ... yes, sounds good.

I checked the freezer, sure I'd find bacon. Nope. I looked in the egg carton and wondered how long the single egg had been there.

Okay, so I won't have bacon and eggs. Plan B—coffee, juice, and cereal. I opened the refrigerator. No milk, no juice. And no car. I was stuck. Plan C—black coffee.

Without a car or an excuse, I decided to get my laundry and housework done. I stripped my bed and emptied my hamper. I had enough for three loads. I reached for the laundry detergent above the washer. There was none.

Duh, that's why you have so much dirty laundry, remember?

While deciding what to do next, the phone rang.

"Hi. Web here. Checking to see if you need anything at the store."

"At the store?"

"Yes, you know the place where you buy food and other essentials?"

"I was out of everything I reached for this morning. How did you know?"

"A little birdie must have told me. On second thought, from the condition of my feeders, the town crier may have been a squirrel. A fat one."

"When do you need me ready?"

"Is a half hour too soon?"

"I can do that."

I scribbled a short shopping list on the back of an envelope, then threw on an outfit more appropriate for public viewing. I dampened my hair and blow-dried the bed-head out, then added some color to my cheeks and lips. With such short notice, this mock makeover was the best I could do.

Webster was at my door in thirty minutes. Ten minutes later, we were at the store. On our way in, he grabbed a hand basket, and I took a cart. In an instant, I felt unsure of what to do next. I never thought of grocery shopping as that personal a task, but once I was in the store with him, I felt self-conscious. Like picking out bacon or laundry detergent was such a private act? I was grateful I brought my list because, all of a sudden, I couldn't remember one thing I needed. Was I supposed to walk through the store with him or go my own way?

What was I? Five?

Webster handled my shopping conundrum succinctly. "I only need a few things. Take your time, Annie. I'll meet you back at the car. Remember where we parked?"

"Pretty sure I do."

I didn't want to hold him up, so I rushed through the store and got only what was on my list. We were back at my house in a half hour.

He helped carry my bags into the house. "There you go, all set."

"Thanks so much. This was huge." Before I thought too long, I asked, "Did you eat breakfast this morning? I'm starving. How about I cook us some bacon and eggs?"

"Are you sure you feel like doing that?"

"I felt like cooking a couple of hours ago. Thanks to you, now I have food."

I pulled out my pans and got the bacon started. I told him to grab a stool at the counter and gave him a glass of juice. I scrambled some eggs, stood the bread in the toaster, and put the jam out. Somewhere in the middle of the flurry, I realized my old habits had kicked in. How many times had I done this with Ned and the kids at that same counter? Cooking for Webster seemed strange yet not unpleasant.

We finished our breakfast and managed a decent conversation which defaulted several times to our work on the Jacobson account. Nonetheless, I was impressed with our social strides.

"You have a lovely place, Annie. Very welcoming. Have you got plans for this afternoon?"

Huh? I wondered why he asked and paused before I answered. "Uh, no."

"As long as I'm here, why not get started on your to-do list? The others are over at Olene's today."

"Oh, sure. Uh, let me see … my list, yes. Where did I put that pad?"

As promised, Webster picked me up for church the next morning. I thanked him again for the ride to the store as well as for fixing my leaky faucet and caulking my drafty windows. "Have you heard how the others made out at Olene's?"

"Yes, Olene told me Jeremy and Lavender made substantial progress in removing the dead shrubbery around the house. Kate and the Professor helped her prepare the interior walls for paint. Will plans to start painting mid-week."

"I hope he's not going to paint by himself. Those ceilings are high and—"

He finished my thought. "Yes, he shouldn't be climbing ladders. The women came up with a plan to keep an eye on him. If he picks a day to paint when Olene's at work, then either Elizabeth or Sarge will drop by. Vito and Jeremy promised they'd paint the ceilings, the crown molding, and the high spots at night."

"So … the Professor showed up, huh? How'd that go?"

He knew full well what I meant. "Olene told me she stocked up on books on tape. Her exact words were, 'He may not have accomplished much work, but the recordings kept him listening instead of talking.'"

Hmm, sounds like Webster and Olene had quite the little chat.

Since I was unable to apply the brakes, Party of One continued to evolve. Ethan and Kate had already missed a few nights. Their relationship was growing; they needed time alone. Lavender had signed up for an impromptu Reiki class (scheduled as her instructor *felt led*), so she was absent some Fridays. And whenever the opportunity presented itself, Vito plied Renata with AA meetings and pizza.

When someone commented that change wasn't on the horizon but already here, Sarge quoted her favorite soap opera philosophy: "'Like sands through the hourglass, so are the days of our lives.'"

Will chuckled. "My wife used to watch soap operas when they were live TV."

Sarge said, "We can do what the soaps used to do when a cast member was absent back then. We'll have Gracie announce, 'Today, the part of Vito Falconara will be played by Stanley Tucci.'"

Vito laughed and countered, "Or 'And the part of Sarge Pappas will be played by Olympia Dukakis.'"

Will added, "Today the part of Miss Elizabeth Hanssen will be played by Miss Ingrid Bergman."

"Casting couldn't be easier," Martina said. "Gracie can play us all!"

"You know, Mr. Anderson," Elizabeth said folding her arms on the table, "your mention of Ingrid Bergman reminds me of the tour to Morocco I led years ago, arranged for people for whom money was no object. Of course, when we arrived in Morocco, everyone wanted to see Casablanca."

Lavender sighed. "Wow. That sounds so cool."

"Morocco was more hot and dusty than cool. Although Casablanca was special, Marrakesh was much more interesting. I could take you all on a tour, if you like."

"Sure, if you're paying, Miss Elizabeth," Vito said. "Otherwise, I may have to wait until I hit the lottery."

"Well, the tour would be a virtual one—at no cost. My company videotaped most of my later trips. I have a library from around the world. All you'd have to do is dim the lights, watch the video, and imagine yourself walking through Morocco."

Will chuckled. "Miss Elizabeth, at my age when someone dims the lights, I fall asleep."

"Oh, I'm sure you could handle this trip, Mr. Anderson. Give me a few weeks to gather my materials, then we'll be off to the Casbah!"

CHAPTER 31

A few weeks later, Elizabeth took us on a tour of Morocco. We should have guessed what was happening when Gracie greeted us wearing a sparkly, purple belly dancer outfit— or *bedleh*, as she called the garb. Even though a fairly conservative bedleh, I couldn't imagine anyone but her (or a professional belly dancer) wearing such a thing to work. She jiggled her hips and twirled as she led us to the private dining room Elizabeth had reserved.

With Olene and Gracie's help, Elizabeth had transformed the room into half Moroccan home, half marketplace. The tables were covered with embroidered linens and set with intricately patterned pottery and jewel-toned stemware. Small dishes filled with cones of pungent spices were arranged between the place settings. Berber weavings covered the floor, and large satin pillows in royal colors brightened the corners. Adding to the ambiance, ornate brass lanterns were lit and positioned around the room.

Will didn't withhold his feelings at his first sight of Elizabeth and Olene. "Look at you two! How beautiful!"

The two women were stunning—Olene in a blue and green print kaftan and Elizabeth in an embroidered, pale-pink, two-piece dress called a *takshita*. Both wore matching sequined slippers.

Martina looked around the room. "I'd never guess this was Cranberry Fare."

Lavender picked up a purple-and-red satin pillow. "Is all this stuff yours? I love the colors and textures. Cool! Do I smell incense?"

I took in the smiles on everyone's faces. How had my tiny seed of an idea—of not eating alone—blossomed into this happy gathering? Webster caught my eye. He nodded and winked, almost as if he knew what I was thinking.

Elizabeth asked us to be seated and face the large flat screen on the hutch. She dimmed the lights and reached for the remote. "Are we ready to embark on our journey?"

The soundtrack took over with Elizabeth's voice transporting us with its mesmerizing tone and colorful narrative: "The Mediterranean Sea is to its north. The vast open Sahara Desert is south. And the Atlas mountain range is at the center. Morocco is a country of diverse and complex cultures. We'll be landing in Casablanca in a few minutes. The first thing you'll notice upon disembarking the plane is the heat. I recommend you wear a wide-brimmed hat."

Over the next forty-five minutes, we followed Elizabeth through the streets and sounds of Morocco. Exotic birds chirped and screeched. Clothed Barbary Macaque monkeys somersaulted for treats. Charmers played *punjis* to hypnotize snakes. Storytellers and French street vendors called out to us. Even the sandstorms of the Sahara and the waves of the Atlantic coast played their own tunes.

As our group *boarded* the train to Marrakesh, Crosby, Stills & Nash sang a few verses of their "Marrakesh Express." The last stop on the tour was Rick's Café Américain in Casablanca. The familiar piano and voice of Dooley Wilson singing "As Time Goes By" was a first-class way to end the trip.

As the sentimental song faded, the video ended with Elizabeth's last lines: "Ladies and gentlemen, thank you for traveling with me. Until our next journey ..."

Once the lights were turned back up, we noticed Will had his arms folded and his chin resting on his chest.

Elizabeth touched his shoulder and whispered, "Mr. Anderson, Mr. Anderson, you can wake up now."

Will kept his eyes closed and his head down. "Why would I want to do that? I'm in exotic Casablanca with someone who resembles Miss Ingrid Bergman." He opened his eyes and looked at Elizabeth. "No, wait … she's even prettier!"

Elizabeth waved him off. "Oh, you old tease."

Will raised his water glass. "Here's looking at you, Elizabeth."

Ethan toasted Will. "Smooth one, Gramps, smooth."

"You are one talented tour guide, Miss Elizabeth!" Martina said.

Webster agreed. "As good as being there."

"Have you ever considered taking your virtual tours on the road?" I said. "Perhaps to senior centers, over fifty-five communities, or retirement homes?"

"Why, no, I haven't."

I encouraged her to think about the idea. "For some people, your tours might be the only chance they'll ever have to travel."

The Professor commented, "That's a splendid idea! Your presentation was superb and your elocution flawless."

Vito galumphed in. "Hey, and you talked real good too."

Bored and antsy a few nights later, I decided to check the online singles' site and give the powers-that-be one last chance at redemption before my membership expired. Besides, I reasoned, one date with Gabe did not a relationship make.

In my earlier, more panicky single's site days, I'd adjust my search criteria until I found a match. All my maneuvering got me was more men to reject and more men to reject *me*. Needy people do weird things. I soon learned the truth was less painful, even if the results were less satisfying.

Attraction isn't easy to explain. Sometimes, all you need is one look to know he's not a match. Sounds shallow, I know, but true. If the looks turn you on, sometimes the profile turns you off. And if you find the right look and the right profile, you still need chemistry. If there's no chemistry in the first few weeks, how do you expect the relationship to last a lifetime?

I had a message waiting when I logged in. "Dear Just Wondering, I believe we have a lot in common. Please check my profile. PS: For personal reasons, I prefer not to post a photo at this time. Sincerely, Save Face."

No photo? I wondered what he was hiding. (Even though the one I used was eight years old and an unrecognizable better version of me.) I clicked open his profile. "Male, forty-nine to fifty-five, single, no children, some college, Christian, lives within twenty-five miles of Sandwich." His other profile particulars included "self-employed and height-weight proportionate." The fill-in-the-blank data sounded fine, but the real test was the essay. "I recently moved to the Cape from a condo in the city. I used to work for a large company until I started my own business."

Have I read this one before?

"I'm shy, I guess, because my family didn't socialize much when I was young. I don't have children, but my brother's kids say I'm a fun uncle. I like to travel."

Shy? A fun uncle? Why does this sound familiar?

I re-read the profile.

Oh, my goodness ... could this be Webster? Nah, couldn't be.

I went back over every detail slowly. I found nothing to contradict what I already knew about him. As for the "like to travel" answer, I remembered when Webster told Francine he'd traveled overseas years ago. I noticed he'd checked "some college," which sure sounded like Mr. Humility-Masters-Degree himself.

The last line in the essay got to me: "I promised Mother I'd be careful, so I want to take things slow."

I mumbled. "Sure sounds like his quirky sense of humor."

His membership was only a week old. Why didn't he tell me he'd joined? He knew I was a member because he'd heard all my horror stories. His message sounded like he didn't know he was writing to me.

Or did he?

Two can play at this game.

I wrote back: "Yes, I do see we have quite a bit in common. I live in Sandwich, work in marketing, and have two married children. I've recently started attending church. Does any of this sound familiar to you? Sincerely, Just Wondering."

I felt like Meg Ryan in *You've Got Mail.* Except this time, Meg-as-Kathleen knew who she was emailing instead of Tom-Hanks-as-Joe-Fox.

Sheesh. Now I sound like Annie-as-Gracie.

Later that night, I got a response from Save Face. "Your profile might sound familiar to me because I know a lot of people who have children. I like children. Your job sounds like fun. Do you work at one market or go around to them all? Maybe I will see you in the Stop & Shop someday."

Do you work at one market or go around to them all? Okay, so Webster wanted to play too.

This foolishness went on without a break for the next few days. We came up with one silly question and answer after another.

Me as Just Wondering: "Yes, to market, to market, to buy a fat pig; home again, home again, dancing a jig. My days are exhausting."

Webster as Save Face: "I don't go to the market every day, but I do like pork. I don't dance, but I like to take long walks on the beach."

Me: "How unique."

Webster: "Yes, Mother says I'm one of a kind."

Me: "What's your sign?"

Webster: "I'm not sure, but I think I'm a Vertigo."

Oh, brother.

Renewing my membership only to see if Webster would confess his identity didn't make sense, but I re-upped anyway. Since Webster had a Mensa wit, being silly with him felt good for a change.

And having a male friend at my age made me feel—dare I say it? Cool.

CHAPTER 32

Webster called early Saturday morning to remind me of our plan to clean my gutters and to stop by the Sandwich Senior Center fundraiser later that day.

While he was on the ladder, scooping gunk out of my gutters, I thought of our online tête-à-tête and tried to make him crack. "I'm *Just Wondering* if you think you have to be here every Saturday."

"What? No, these chores are on *my* list now. I enjoy checking them off."

"You've done so much already, there's no need to *Save Face* with me."

"Huh? Save face? No, but all the others are over helping Olene again, so I'm all you've got." He kept his eyes on his task.

"I'm *Just Wondering* if I'm taking advantage of you."

He stopped to look down at me. "Annie, I'm sorry. Am I becoming a nuisance?"

"Not at all." I turned to hide my smile.

"I'll tell you what; I'll trade my handyman skills for your cooking. Deal?"

"Deal."

Will beamed when Webster and I showed up for the Senior Center Fundraiser—which made me feel guilty because I didn't want to go. Between the progressive dinner, Gracie's play, and having Webster as a professional colleague, handyman, and fellow pew-sitter, I wondered if I was getting too involved with these people.

I have to draw the line somewhere, don't I?

The senior center was packed. Before we had the chance to ask him, Will reported the fundraiser had been a huge success thus far—financially and otherwise. "And much of the credit goes to Miss Elizabeth. Her auction ideas turned out to be the highest moneymakers ever! She even stepped in without ruffling the feathers of the other hens in the house. And, believe me, that's no easy feat."

Elizabeth had convinced some friends to donate a three-day weekend at their ski lodge in Vermont. She'd also coaxed the local arts council into giving up the national award-winning quilt they had on display. One of her more creative ideas included home-cooked meals provided by women from the elderly housing complex. Each of the women was asked to stand and describe their entrée, while a volunteer walked through the audience carrying the dish, leaving a fragrant trail. Since food was the prize, most of the bidders were single men. Along with the ladies' self-worth, a total of $475 was raised on their meals alone.

Olene spotted us. "Annie! Webster! Just in time to catch the Bachelor's Catwalk." She nudged Will. "Better hurry. My aunt is waiting for you."

Somehow Elizabeth had charmed twelve old men, including Will, into putting themselves on the auction block. The winning bidder would receive "A Day on the Town with a Bachelor." (The auctioneer made clear this was not to be confused with a *night* on the town.) Men, ages seventy to eighty-seven, hammed it up in colorful outfits. One sported a

1930s bathing suit, another tried to squeeze into an old tuxedo, and one showed up wearing a white Elvis jumpsuit. They strutted, pranced, and wheeled across the stage to whistles, catcalls, and applause. Those bachelors who couldn't see well had to be led on stage, and those who couldn't hear well had to be told when the bidding had ended. The few who didn't want to leave the limelight had to be escorted off.

When the event ended, Will rejoined us still sporting his red velvet smoking jacket, ascot, and patent leather slippers.

Elizabeth found us soon after. "My, my, is this Cary Grant or Will Anderson?" She took his arm. "So, did we raise any money today—or merely eyebrows?"

Will's face lit up. "On the last-minute auctions you orchestrated, we earned over half of our total take. And Olene is still counting the receipts from the Bachelor's Catwalk."

"From the reaction of the audience," I said, "that might be your most popular event of the day."

Webster looked at Will from head to toe. "So, this is how you dress at home?"

"Not usually. Gracie borrowed these items from the theater." He ran his hands down the front of the jacket and adjusted the ascot. "But I might have to keep them."

Olene came by holding a clipboard. "I have the tally. Considering the fixed income of the bachelorette bidders, most of the bids averaged twenty-five dollars. However, A Day on the Town with Bachelor Will Anderson went for $500 to an anonymous call-in bidder!"

Will blushed. "Who would do such a thing? Even for a good cause?"

Elizabeth smiled. "Someone who knows a good value."

"Speaking of value, Miss Elizabeth," Will said, "After seeing what you accomplished today, I'm quite certain you have the spunk to build a successful virtual travel business. I'd like to offer my services."

"Funny you should say that. Ever since Annie's suggestion, I haven't been able to think of anything else. Let's talk later."

"Count me in!" I said. "Marketing campaigns have been filling my head since I mentioned the idea."

What were you saying about drawing the line?

On my way home from the senior center, I thought back over the event, picturing those tempting dishes prepared by all those sweet old ladies. For some odd reason, Dodi's soup popped into my head. I chuckled. If she'd been among the cooks, the Board of Health would've closed the auction down.

What on earth made you think of that?

In seconds, I made a fuzzy connection between Dodi's soup and Webster … and Save Face and me. What had Webster said after I pulled that prank on him with the soup? "Remain vigilant. You never know how or when I will strike."

I pulled into the garage and shut the engine. The ruse became clearer. This whole Save Face, singles'site thing was his payback! I couldn't believe I'd almost missed the charade.

You're good, Webster. Too bad I'm better.

Pleased I'd avoided making a fool of myself, I decided to speed up the pace and call his bluff. I went to my laptop and wrote: "Dear Save Face, We should meet so we can move on to the next stage of our relationship. Please join me next Friday night at six o'clock at the Party of One table at Cranberry Fare."

No surprise, he accepted: "I am glad you feel the same way. With much pleasure, I anticipate our long-awaited rendezvous."

I just bet you do.

Gabe called Sunday afternoon mainly to tell me he'd be in DC for a Homeland Security conference the following week. "I caught a break. Enrollment was closed within twenty-four hours after registration began. When a slot opened up, I was offered a chance and accepted."

"Sounds like quite a privilege."

"The Chief put a good word in for me. There'll be Staties there from all over the country. And since 'iron sharpens iron,' we can learn a lot from each other. I'll touch base when I get back, okay?"

Gabe's call revealed a consideration not all men possessed. And that pleased me. Yet I sensed some relief on my part. *You might want to ratchet back a little on the relationship. You don't want anything to happen too fast. A short break won't kill you.*

Ratchet back? A short break? After one date? And a good date at that? What is your problem?

Immediately, the word *FEAR* came to mind.

I'd been in the market, so to speak, for a relationship for a while. Why was I afraid all of a sudden? I'd dated a few times, so what was the big deal? The answer snuck up on me: Gabe Reilly was my first and only viable candidate. None of the others fell into that category.

Breathe, McGee. Whatever you do, don't blow this.

CHAPTER 33

On the Friday Just Wondering and Save Face were to meet at Cranberry Fare, I fixed my hair differently and dressed up more than usual. I wondered if Webster would show up as Save Face or his regular old self.

Ridiculous, I know.

Oddly, playing this silly role brought tension and excitement I hadn't expected. Had Webster figured out I'd called his bluff? Or did he still think he'd be the surprise? I decided to get there late to make a grand entrance.

Oh, the subtleties of the stage—especially when you're the star.

Once I'd arrived, I positioned myself off stage in the foyer, making sure to have a clear view of our table. Nerves made me giggle like a school girl. I could see the backs of two newcomers, one in my usual place, the other in the adjacent chair. But the seat next to Webster was vacant.

Perfect.

I strode to the table with Broadway flair and circled around to Webster's side. I leaned in to catch his attention. In a melodramatic tone, I projected my voice. "So, Save Face, finally we meet."

Webster glanced up at me, speaking in a cool-as-iced-tea tone, "Hi, Annie. I'm sorry, what did you say?"

Before I could respond, a large, middle-aged man seated across the table stood. "Hello. I'm Save Face. I'm here to meet Just Wondering. *Annie*—is that your name? Are you her?"

I glanced at him, then back at Webster, asking myself how this guy could know about Just Wondering. I searched for an answer, found one fast, and forged ahead. "Oh, you're good. Did Gracie help you get this actor?"

"Huh?" Webster played dumb smartly.

How do I describe the man purporting to be Save Face? He was over six feet tall and huge—sort of a non-Incredible Hulk. There wasn't a trace of hair on his head *or* his round pink face. He was sweating profusely, and with no eyebrows, there was nothing to divert the flow.

He wore a green pinstriped suit. I'd never seen wool in such a color before. I'd assumed that shade of green was proprietary to Beech-Nut or Gerber. The cream-colored pinstripes widened at every pull of the fabric and strained against every seam. The ill-fitting double-breasted jacket was tight across his ample middle, pushing his chest up enough to give him the appearance of cleavage, visible through his thin, white polyester shirt.

I ignored the amateur actor and directed my comments to Webster. "Now that we've met, I'm Just Wondering if I'm the kind of girl you would take home to Mother?"

The big man said, "Annie, my name is Delbert Yapp. This is Mother Gertrude. She wanted to meet you right off."

The big woman added, "My son says you been writin' him. I want to know what you expect will happen now?"

I elbowed Webster. "You're killing me. How far is this gonna go?"

"You been drinking, Annie?" Vito asked, looking at me sideways.

Kate elbowed Ethan, "I think we've been away too long. What's going on with Annie and Webster?"

"Nothing," I said. "I was writing to Save Face ... I mean, Webster. A silly game is all."

Gertrude rose, "You tryin' to say you been writin' to my boy and this man too? I don't think that's a very nice game."

"No, Mother, Just wondering, I mean Annie wouldn't do that, would you?" said Delbert, his pores now drooling.

Gertrude had the girth needed to bear a son like Delbert. She also had the hair he was missing. Her arms and face bristled with dark growth. (I'm not totally unsympathetic—I understand how a woman *can* grow a mustache, just not *why* she would keep one.)

"Son, I told you not to put your picture on that evil machine! This never would've happened if you'd listened to me."

"Mother, I didn't, I promise," whimpered Delbert. "Ask Annie, she'll tell you."

"The jig's up, Webster Townsend. I figured out your payback plan."

Webster still looked confused. "Payback? For what?"

My hands flew up. "The soup! The soup!"

For some crazy reason Vito yelled, "Da plane! Da plane!"

Delbert brightened and joined in, "Tattoo, Tattoo—*Fantasy Island*. That was our favorite show, wasn't it, Mother?"

"Ooh, starring Ricardo Montalbán," Gertrude said, rolling her *r*'s and smiling like she was remembering an old flame.

Lost in thoughts of Ricardo, Gertrude seemed to have forgotten why they'd been hired.

Derailed momentarily by this off-the-wall interruption, I turned back to Webster. Denial drove my insistence. "Dodi's soup! You told me to be vigilant after I switched your soup with hers. I didn't forget."

Webster spoke like he was correcting an obstinate child. "Annie. Listen. And please don't hear what I'm *not* saying. I had nothing to do with this. Why would I write to you? I see you every week."

I studied his face, long and hard. "Are you … Is that true? … Then who …?"

Webster tilted his head toward the man in strained-pea green. "That would be Delbert, here."

I would've crawled under the table if there'd been room. I had no choice but to explain the mix-up to Delbert and his mother and ask their forgiveness. They accepted my offer to pay for their meals as a sincere act of contrition.

During dinner, both mother and son joined in the conversation, mostly recounting their favorite episodes of *Fantasy Island*. Delbert unbuttoned his jacket and relaxed. So did the hair on Gertrude's arms.

"*Fantasy Island*? Wasn't that show on in the early 80s?" Will asked.

Kate said, "Who is Ricardo Montabomb?"

Gertrude spoke as if she were the sole guardian of his reputation. "His full name is Ricardo Gonzalo Pedro Montalbán y Merino. He was Mexico's greatest star." Fanning her face with her napkin and patting her palpitating heart, Gertrude leaned in closer to Will and continued in her rolling *r* accent, "Soft Cor-r-rinthian leather."

"Yes, yes, the Chrysler Cordoba," Will said. "Montalbán was their spokesman. That was the last Chrysler I ever owned."

While they reminisced about the old TV show and its stars, I glanced over at Webster and muttered, "I think I'm going insane."

Webster chuckled. "If you're not there yet, you will be soon. Francine Porridge is headed this way."

I raised an eyebrow. "You're a riot."

"Not really. Look over there."

I heard the little girl voice before I saw her. "Hi, Webbie! Long time no see!" Sidetracked by a new face, Francine took a sharp left over to Delbert. She stuck out her hand. "Hi, my name is Francine Porridge. And yours?"

A little breathless, Delbert responded, "Delbert Yapp. This is Mother Gertrude."

Like a mother grizzly protecting her cub, Gertrude slid her chair closer to Delbert as Francine attempted to squeeze in between them.

"*Fantasy Island?* Feels more like the *Twilight Zone*," I said, barely loud enough for Webster to hear.

He whispered in a Rod Serling-esque voice, "'There is a fifth dimension, beyond that which is known to man. It is a dimension as vast as space and as timeless as infinity. It is an area which we call ...' Party of One."

The cost of my entrée of crow, followed by humble pie and acid indigestion, came to seventy-eight dollars plus tip.

CHAPTER 34

I didn't contemplate all that happened between Delbert and Webster and me until later that night. In the quiet of my home, humiliation zigzagged through my ego. Over and over I asked myself, "How did that happen? What were you thinking?" And my grand-prize-winning question only an imbecile would ask, "Just once why can't people be doing what I think they're doing?"

This latest episodic blunder reminded me of the time I believed Ned was throwing me a surprise birthday party.

The day of my thirty-fifth birthday arrived. Without saying a word, Ned left for work and the kids went off to school. No one called all day, and the mail didn't bring a single card. I was puzzled and a little upset. Then around four o'clock, Ned called to wish me a Happy Birthday and asked if I wanted to go out for dinner. He apologized for his last-minute timing.

I started to think—always my downfall. Something which had seemed a bit off before now seemed suspicious. I had one of those ah-ha moments and realized this was his poor attempt at hiding a surprise. I spent the next few hours with a big smirk on my face, primping for my first surprise party ever, wondering who would be there. I said aloud, "My family and friends left so many clues, could the solution be any easier than this?"

Apparently so. The truth was no one remembered my birthday, and Ned's invitation *was* thoughtless and last minute.

Why did my latest social blunder with Webster upset me so? The answer I found was juvenile. This (non-existent) game with Webster made me feel like the clumsy kid who finally got picked first by a captain choosing up sides. I felt special. When I found out I wasn't, I felt foolish.

My mortification intensified when I heard Webster's voice mail message the next morning. "Hi Annie, this is Save Face—I mean, Webster. Call me back."

I snarled at the phone. "Smart-aleck."

On Sunday afternoon, another call came in from him. "Hi, Annie, Web again. I didn't see you at church. Just wondering … I mean, hope everything's okay. Let me know if we're still on for Tuesday."

Tuesday? Rats. I forgot. We were scheduled to go to the Jacobsons' again to meet with more of their artists. I'd already put in hours writing profiles and product descriptions for their website. I would easily be finished by Tuesday. But did Webster need to come with me? I waited till dinnertime to call him back. I hoped to get his machine—and did.

"Annie here. I'm all set for Tuesday. I know you're busy, so I'll go by myself and email my files to you—"

He picked up. "Glad I caught you! Why don't I pick you up since your house is on the way? I want to talk about site placement and the catalog before we show Sol and Dodi. Is nine thirty okay?"

"Uh, sure."

Darn.

My ego perked up when I got a call from Gabe on Monday afternoon.

"How was the conference?" I asked. "Did you get to do any sightseeing in DC?"

"The schedule was grueling. Other than the Ronald Reagan International Trade Center, the only sights I saw were to and from the Econo Lodge in Virginia. Now I've got a week's worth of catch up. I'll be off by the weekend. Are you free for dinner?"

"Saturday's good."

"Pick you up around seven?"

"I'll be ready."

Up to this point, I hadn't mentioned Gabe to any of my friends. In the past, I'd blab every first date all over the place, only to have to call everyone the next day to tell them what an awful match the guy had been. Understandably, I was a bit hesitant. All those false starts had taught me to keep my mouth shut ... well, sometimes.

As for my kids, I admit I was stalling. Griffin would be fine. Casey was the problem.

Both my children had married in their early twenties. Casey met Sam Gallagher while she worked a booth on Boston Common during her internship at the marketing firm. The first time she brought him around, Ned and I knew. They were married eight months before Ned died, while he was still able to walk her down the aisle. He never knew we'd moved the date up to make that happen.

Griffin had married Jillian Bouchard last June. I couldn't have picked anyone better suited for him. Both couples are young, so I'm not pushing for grandchildren—just hoping.

I called Griffin first, under the guise of "can't a mother check in on her son without it being something special?" When Jillian answered, I didn't have to pretend. As Griffin's wife, the lot of communicating with him in a way that wouldn't alarm him now fell to her. For a young bride, she did quite well.

"Griffin will be pleased you're dating," Jillian said. "Tell me, how did Casey take the news?"

"I haven't called her yet."

"Well, I'm sure she'll be fine." She redirected her focus. "So, what's Gabe like?"

I gave her an edited description and mentioned he was a sports fan. I had to hold her back from asking Griffin to use his connections to get good seats for the next Patriots game.

After we hung up, I braced myself and called Casey. I told her about Gabe from the beginning—and emphasized that he'd been one of her father's friends from work.

"Nice friend," she said with a bite.

My daughter was being unreasonable, but I knew she didn't want to be. I ignored her tone.

"We've only met a few times at mixed gatherings. I'm not sure where the relationship's going, but I promise to give you regular progress reports, okay?"

"Super. Can't wait."

She forced my hand with her sarcasm. "Casey, you're too old to be acting like a brat."

"Well, seems like you can't wait to hop on the first bus leaving Dad's memory behind."

"Casey Nicole, that's enough! You know I loved your father and always will. But he's been gone for over two years."

She shot back, "I know exactly how long!"

"Casey, answer me this. If I had died, would you expect your father to spend the rest of his life alone?"

"Dad would never go chasing after women!"

"He wouldn't have to! He'd have a line of casseroles at the front door before the funeral was over. Petunia and Buttercup Ogilvy would be mud-wrestling over each other to have first crack at him!"

Lily and Violet Ogilvy, septuagenarian spinster sisters and our neighbors for years, had been nicknamed Petunia and Buttercup by Ned on the day they moved in. They loved the attention, and they loved him. The vision of them fighting over Ned broke the tension and made us both laugh.

"I'm sorry, Mom. I want you to be happy, I do."

"So would your dad."

I wasn't surprised when Casey told me she suspected something was up simply because I had cut our recent calls short. She'd recognized my MO.

Relieved when that conversation was over, I asked myself why telling my kids about Gabe, although tough, seemed easier than telling them about Jesus.

Whenever I thought about, or even rehearsed, telling my family about my new relationship with the Lord, my thoughts got jumbled and my words rang phony. I'm embarrassed to admit there were times when the truth about Jesus and all he'd done for me sounded unbelievable even to me. Doubt knew when to creep in and attack.

Lord, help me fight back!

When my boss learned of my plans to go to Orleans on Tuesday, he asked if I would take over the Hollingsworth's account, a five-star restaurant on Route 6A in Brewster. He had intended to handle the account himself but couldn't keep his Tuesday night reservation. I tried to beg off, but didn't get far. Reluctantly, I called Webster and left a message.

"If you're up for an adventure tomorrow, wear something suitable for a fancy-schmancy restaurant. I have reservations for research at Hollingsworth tomorrow at six."

As I knew he would be, Webster was at my house Tuesday at nine thirty sharp. I'd practiced what I would say in case he mentioned Save Face or Delbert. I vowed to say nothing unless he brought the subject up.

No sooner was he in the front door when I blurted, "I'm surprised you still want to do business with me, considering what a fool I made of myself."

Agh! Why can't I bite my tongue on its way out of my mouth?

"You didn't make a fool of yourself. Well, maybe a little but in an innocent way. I'm flattered you believed I was sharp enough to remember my payback threat."

"That's kind of you to say, but—"

"No buts, Annie."

Seeing I had to spend a good part of the day and evening with this guy, I figured bringing my social faux pas up again would be a colossal mistake. For a change, I'd quit while I was ahead. (Okay, *ahead* might not be the right word.)

"Hope you remembered your jacket and tie."

"You bet I did."

We met with Sol and Dodi at the Artisan House to go over the catalog and website copy. They made the final corrections and requested a few more photos. I was also able to speak with a couple of their craftsmen who worked at the gallery. All in all, the day went well.

Webster took a while to get the photos he needed because the light had to be just so. Mid-afternoon arrived before he finished. Dodi tried to feed us again. Hollingsworth was our saving grace.

On the way to the restaurant, we made a side trip to Nils Larsen's metal-sculpting shop. There spent an hour watching him hand forge magic with iron, steel, and copper.

His collection of wall sculptures, candleholders, lamps, and whimsical bird feeders kept us busy—me writing descriptions and Webster snapping pictures.

When we arrived at the restaurant, Webster put on his tie and jacket. We took a little walk around the grounds before we went in. Even in early November, the well-tended landscape added healthy color to the gray day. I caught the scent of winter bayberry. We heard the sounds of wildlife rustling in the woods nearby and the calls of local birds. Peace abounded.

Immediately, ad copy came to my mind and out my lips. "Housed in the 300-year-old Hollingsworth Dunne Estate in Brewster Township, this piece of historical architecture sits in harmony with the six acres of native trees and shrubs—a testimony to its admirable relationship with nature and history."

"Not bad," he said. "Keep going."

I continued after we entered the restaurant. "We had heard about Hollingsworth, and our expectations were high. When we stepped into the foyer, a member of their staff greeted us like family."

Webster dramatized a few lines. "The dining rooms, though formal, opened their arms."

"*Opened their arms?* You don't mind if I don't steal that line, do you?"

He feigned a pout.

The maître d' led us to a table for two, ample enough for four. We took in the room through a shimmer of soft light, alternately reflecting the gleam of sterling, the sheen of bone china, and the clarity of the crystal stemware. The fieldstone fireplaces and eighteenth-century French furniture and artwork all added to the rich, yet simple, elegance. I don't know why I was surprised that Webster knew the china pattern, the furniture period, and the artists of more than a few paintings.

Despite the romantic setting—which I would've reserved for a more intimate relationship—I decided to enjoy the company and the moment. Besides, there wasn't much chance of Gabe Reilly bringing me here on a state cop's salary.

With so much to absorb, we said nothing for a time.

I inhaled relief and exhaled stress. I caught Webster's attention and matched his previous dramatic tone as I spouted more ad copy. "Hollingsworth is an establishment best saved for special occasions—complementing celebrations as no average place could. Their very nature forbids them to rush their clientele."

He smiled. "I agree."

"Seriously, do you mind if we slow the pace? I'm on sensory overload. I'll need time if I'm to do this place justice."

"Take all the time you need, Annie."

Aromas from the fine cuisine floated through the dining rooms. I caught a hint of basil ... or maybe tarragon? The aroma of Madeira sauce wafted through but soon melded with that of tangy mango. We were hungry–but for beef or poultry or seafood? We ordered our appetizers. I chose the spinach, mushroom, and four-cheese ravioli; Webster, the Creole lobster bisque. We decided to wait on our main course.

"Initially, I balked at taking over this account. But this assignment has turned out to be a tasty one."

"I'm glad I got to go to work with you." He smiled. "No question, your clients serve better food than mine."

I laughed. "You'll get no argument from me." Our conversation centered on the skill and finesse required to create such an elegant yet relaxing atmosphere.

For his entrée, Webster chose the halibut filet with mushroom and truffle broth. I ordered the marinated grilled lamb chops. The chef's creations were as divinely inspired as those of the artisans we'd visited. We shared two desserts: warm chocolate cake with pistachio ice cream and raspberry soufflé with crème anglais. I finished with my usual black decaf, which tasted way better than the store brand I'd had that morning.

I introduced myself to the maître d' and the sommelier and asked them a few questions. At the end of the night, the chef came out of the kitchen to speak with me. He gave me some background information on himself and his staff.

"One day, I hope you and your husband will return for a meal unrelated to work."

While correcting him seemed awkward, not correcting him seemed more so. I chose to be glib. "When and if I ever find a husband, I'll be sure to do that, Chef."

Webster joked. "Can I still come with you then?"

CHAPTER 35

Before we left Hollingsworth, we browsed their specialty gift shop. I bought some pastries for my boss, and Webster purchased a book on the local history. The day had gone well, almost erasing the memories of Save Face and Just Wondering.

On our drive home, we fell into an easy conversation, which eventually led to our faith. I shared my recent struggles with fear and doubt.

"It seems like doubt crops up from nowhere. Then I feel guilty and get scared because I think that's what drew me away from church when I was younger. I don't want that to happen again. Shouldn't my faith be getting stronger?"

"Annie, having doubts doesn't mean your faith isn't growing. Years back, I used to feel ashamed whenever I doubted God or his word—I thought doubt meant my faith was weak. A pastor educated me when he said, 'Doubt is not the opposite of faith. Unbelief is.' When doubts arise, we shouldn't fear them. We should take them out and examine them closely in the light of what the Bible says."

"So you believe doubt can have a positive purpose?"

"Yes. Like fear, doubt can act as a discerning agent or a sharpening tool to distinguish between truth and error. Quite helpful in keeping us out of trouble too."

"I'm all for that!" I said.

"Another thing, in the case of a new Christian like you, the devil will try to trip you up any chance he gets. Some people make the mistake of thinking he's a harmless Halloween character, but he's real and effective."

"Why should he care about me? I can't be much of a threat, can I?"

"Oh, you'd be surprised. He wants to get you while your faith is untested and fragile, and he'll do anything to make you feel like a failure. Literally, Annie, call on Jesus the next time Satan tries to undermine your faith. He'll leave. Not that you scare him, but Jesus does."

"You're right about my thinking too much. I'm always trying to control my confusion."

"Take a deep breath and say a quick prayer. God will hear you every time." He paused for a moment. "You know, Annie, I've learned how to know God better by watching you."

"Watching *me*?"

"Yes. The way you immerse yourself in the artisans' worlds, studying their methods, personalities, and art. Your relational approach with them is a good model for those of us who seek a closer relationship with God. You've helped me."

"Really? Now I'll have to use that model myself."

Webster was patient and careful in his explanations, but he didn't condescend. I liked that. Feeling brave, I shared how angry I'd been with God when Ned died. I'd never admitted that to anyone before. I went so far as to tell him how I'd pretended God didn't exist.

Webster said he could relate because he'd reacted similarly when his wife left him after only ten months of marriage.

"After I met Nieka, for the first time in my life, I let myself get carried away with falling in love. I wanted so much to be like Philip—married and settled. He and Andrea made marriage look easy. So did my parents. When Nieka came along, I thought we could have what they had.

"When our marriage fell apart, I vowed never to be that vulnerable again. I wasn't on speaking terms with God for quite a few years—until the day I figured out that my mistake hadn't been God's fault. He didn't create me to be like Philip or to do everything like him or to have everything he had. God's plans for my life are tailored to fit me, not my brother. Realizing that has made my choices easier."

I let that sensitive moment pass before I moved to my next question. "More than anything, I want to tell my family so they'll want what I have. Any ideas?"

"What worked for you? Who said *what* to make you listen?"

"I guess, at first, Martina. But not so much what she said as what she did."

"Well, there's your answer right there, Annie. Show 'em, don't tell 'em."

That fresh revelation brought me such peace.

On Friday next, most of us were present when Vito came in late wearing a grin from ear to ear and Renata on his arm. He pulled a chair out for her and took his usual seat at the end of the table.

He didn't say much to the rest of us until after Ian delivered our drink order. Then he stood and raised his 7Up. "Please, can I have everyone's attention? We've got something to tell you."

They'd been tittering like teenyboppers since they'd arrived, so I pretty much knew what that announcement would be. I wanted to hear the words anyway.

Vito started, "Hey, you guys know how hard I prayed for my Renata to come back." He reached down and took her hand in his. She smiled up at him. "You know I never wanted a divorce." He controlled the quiver in his voice. "The thing is—"

Renata leapfrogged in, "Neither did I. That's why I never signed the papers!"

"You mean ... the divorce papers?" I asked.

Olene finished my thought. "You were never divorced?"

"Ba-da-bing!" said Vito, pumping his fist.

"Praise God!" Martina shouted.

Kate raised her hand for a high-five. "Way to go, Renata!"

"Marvelous news, marvelous," said the Professor.

Unable to hold back his tears, Vito continued. "This coming April, we'll celebrate our twentieth anniversary."

We began to clap, but Vito held his hand up. "Hold it! You only got the ba-da-bing. Now here's the ba-da-boom." He paused long enough to take a deep breath. "Twenty years to the day we took our vows, Renata is due to have our first baby!"

"A what?" Lavender acted like she hadn't heard him correctly.

I laughed. "A baby? Unbelievable! A baby!"

Will shook his head and smiled. "Well, I'll be! You take the cake, Vito!"

Vito smirked. "Renata conceived the night of the Party of One anniversary dinner."

"Vitorio!" Renata blushed.

"Well, you did," he protested. "And she sure took her sweet time telling me!"

"You should've seen his face," Renata said. "When the news sank in, Vitorio danced me around the living room while singing an Italian aria. That same night he drew plans for the nursery *and* threw his cigarettes out."

"Yup, I haven't had a single craving. Jesus, Mary, and Joseph, thank you!"

Olene hugged Renata while Webster shook Vito's hand.

After a few more toasts to the couple, Elizabeth said, "Although not as grand as yours, I have an announcement too."

Renata said, "Please tell us."

"Well, thanks to Annie's suggestion and everyone else's encouragement, I'm moving ahead with the virtual tour company. As soon as I come up with a name, I'll finish the paperwork."

"Good for you!" I said.

"Mr. Anderson has been a great help. He accompanied me to the SCORE office, where I got a start-up packet. However, I may need a little guidance in the marketing department."

I confessed, "I've already got a file started."

"Wonderful!" said Elizabeth, clasping her hands together. "We must have an official business meeting soon."

Gracie, who'd been circling the dining room within eavesdropping distance of our table, came over to hug Vito and Renata and congratulate Elizabeth.

"Maybe you'll be next, Grace," I said. "One day soon we'll be celebrating your name in lights."

Gracie sighed. "If only those lights could be on Broadway."

Will said, "You've sure got the talent!"

"Perhaps, as an option to acting," Olene said, eying Gracie's 1940's hairstyle and dress, "you might consider the field of costume design."

The Professor rapped the table with his thick hand. "My, no. Grace was meant for the stage." Then to Gracie he added, "Did I ever tell you of my acting debut at Cambridge when I was cast in the role of Othello? I pray you will experience the thrill of performing Shakespeare one day, perhaps at the new Royal Shakespeare Theatre in London. Now that is true theater! I am sure you agree that Broadway pales in comparison."

Gracie ignored his slight. "Why, Professor, I do believe you sound a little homesick. Perhaps you should plan a visit soon?"

Surveying those around the table, Will said, "New beginnings abound! This is quite the turn of events."

"There's nothing like change, marvelous change," said the Professor.

Maybe. But would change be that marvelous for us all?

Gabe was due to pick me up around seven on Saturday night—our first date sans human buffers. I lectured myself to relax, then dressed—trying not to look like I spent too much time on my appearance or so little time that I didn't care. Looking pulled together, when you're not, can be difficult. When I opened the door, I noticed Gabe had no trouble finding the right balance. Maybe choosing an outfit is easier for men because they don't think as much as women do.

On the way to the car, he asked me if I liked Italian. When I said yes, he suggested a family-style restaurant in Hyannis I'd heard of but had never been to.

We parked on Main Street and entered the small storefront establishment. A cacophony of banging pots, clattering plates, and loud chatter greeted us. The savory scents offset the noise level.

We were seated in a dark-green-leather booth with a high back—which afforded the only privacy, since the kitchen was wide open to the diners. The working kitchen was as much a stage for the cooks. The flamboyant staff flipped, stirred, and juggled with the skill of a circus act and interacted with the customers as easily as seasoned performers. Gabe and I laughed much of the night at their antics—but not at their culinary skills.

I learned more about Gabriel Martin Reilly that night. He'd married his college girlfriend at twenty-one when she was three months pregnant. They'd had a healthy baby boy. When their son was eighteen months old, his wife left to go to the corner store and never came back. She wrote a month later from Los Angeles, saying she'd filed for divorce. Gabe raised their son on his own.

"Being a single parent was tough, but I had my family nearby. Without their help, I never would've graduated from the Academy. And more importantly, I might not know the Lord. They've been faithful prayer warriors."

He pulled his wallet out to show me a picture of his son.

"He's handsome. I can see he has your features, but not your Irish skin. His mother's?"

"No, he gets that from *my* mother. She's Mexican. By some genetic rarity, I take after my father. My parents met when Dad was stationed at Lackland Air Force Base in Texas. They moved back to Boston when he got out of the Air Force."

"Do they still live there?"

"Mom does. Dad died five years ago."

"I'm sorry."

"Me too. I miss him."

I talked more about my life with Ned and our children on the Cape. Talking about issues of faith was easy with Gabe. He spoke in such a simple and practical manner and helped me understand more about God's grace and guidance.

"I want to live the way God wants me to," I said. "I haven't done such a great job on my own."

"Believe me, you're not alone. My advice to you is to pray for God's will, his *perfect* will, and don't settle for anything less. That's how I always pray."

"God's perfect will? Is there any other kind?"

"Yes. God permits us to choose his permissive will, but perfect is always best." He smiled. "Read Romans 9 when you get home."

Our evening alone was rich with easy moments and good conversation. When Gabe dropped me off, he walked me to the door, kissed me on the cheek, and hugged me like it meant something.

But what?

Will and Elizabeth walked in together the next Friday evening, looking quite pleased with themselves. Once they were seated, Elizabeth gave Will's hand a little squeeze. "Guess what everyone? Mr. Anderson and I have come up with an official name for the virtual tour business—We'll Always Have Paris!"

"The name was more your idea, Miss Elizabeth," Will said.

"As close as makes no difference, Mr. Anderson. You reminded me of that movie line at our last meeting, remember?"

"Ooh, I love that line from *Casablanca*," Gracie said. "Perfect title too!"

Before I could comment further, Vito blindsided me with a question. "Speaking of romantic movies, Annie, we haven't heard any funny date stories from you in a long time. Anything you want to tell us?"

"Me? No, nothing."

"No more funny stories?" Jeremy said. "Man, that's a bummer."

Webster said, "Perhaps Annie's stories are serious now instead of funny."

"Nothing to tell you. Sorry, guys." I gave Webster the eye.

I wasn't lying. I didn't have anything to tell them ... or anything I wanted to. For now, I still planned to keep Gabe Reilly to myself.

CHAPTER 36

In a few weeks, the welter of holiday activities would begin with Thanksgiving. Party of One-ers checked with each other to make sure no one would spend the day alone. From my experience, the four toughest holidays for singles are Thanksgiving, Christmas, New Year's Eve, and Valentine's Day. Many of us had family within traveling distance, and those who didn't were invited to join others.

Jeremy and Lavender were working at a local shelter Thanksgiving Day, then spending the evening with her parents. Will was going to a daughter's house, and Ethan was joining Kate's family at their home in Newport—even his dog Roscoe was invited. Vito and Renata would be with her brother's crew in Providence.

The Professor, Olene, Elizabeth, Martina, and her daughter would all be at Martina's. Sarge chose to work the good-money shift to give the younger people a chance to spend the holiday with family. The only one unaccounted for was Webster.

"Webster," I said, "may I assume you're spending Thanksgiving with your parents in Connecticut?"

"Not this year. They'll be in Florida visiting relatives from my mom's side."

Before I could decide whether or not to invite him to my parents' noisy affair, Martina asked him to join them. *Phew.* Since I was waiting to see if Gabe was free, inviting Webster as well might be awkward—mainly because my family would make it that way.

As for the Friday after Thanksgiving, I was going to suggest we cancel Party of One, sure that none of us would want to think about food. Then I remembered again the dinner wasn't so much about the food as about the company. I asked the group for their thoughts. In the end, we decided to keep our regular reservation.

The one charitable event I took part in yearly was the local Thanksgiving food drive sponsored largely by my employer. This was our tenth year. Five years back, I'd been put in charge of the undertaking. Since mid-September, I'd sought contributions and volunteers, created pickup and delivery schedules, and written announcements and newspaper articles.

Early on, Webster had offered to create a website for me that'd been up and running for six weeks. We tracked food items needed and posted drop-off sites and pick-up times. Many of those who needed the food might not have access to the internet, so we used the press to spread our message. We also notified churches and human services organizations. Of course, good old word-of-mouth worked best.

Cranberry Fare donated all things cranberry, including juice, sauce, and bread. Elizabeth used her fundraising skills to get gift certificates from local grocers, while Kate got her pharmaceutical company to write a check. Vito and Renata baked pies. And Lavender and Jeremy donated the remainder of the corn relish and green bean salad they'd put up from their garden.

The day for pick-ups and deliveries was the Saturday before Thanksgiving. My friends Maddie, Susannah, and Robin showed up extra early to pack the food baskets. Susannah's job was to make sure each contained the necessary staples for a healthy meal. Robin always added a card with an inspirational message. And Maddie, using what craft items she had lying around the house, made each basket look as if from an expensive boutique.

This year we would provide food for 127 families. Those on the giving side knew all too well receiving was much harder. That's why, when we delivered a basket to a family, we always left them with an invitation to be on the giving team the following year.

Positioned at the hub of all the activity, I stopped to survey the half circle of stations. Working diligently alongside my coworkers and former food basket recipients were at least twenty people I had personally invited to get involved. I was proud of them.

I thought back to the early years of this event, when I considered this particular task just part of the job. Always one to guard the lines of demarcation between my personal life and business, I took years before I asked Ned and our kids to help. Then a few more years passed before I was brave enough to invite my parents (but not before I made them sign a fake confidentiality agreement promising not to divulge anything about my teenage years).

Five years ago, I crossed another line when I asked Maddie, Susannah, and Robin to join us. This year, I made another successful leap when I enlisted the help of Party of One-ers. After painlessly overlapping home, work, and play, I wondered why I'd resisted so long.

I paused for a minute to bask in my personal growth. I felt good.

Then Gabe walked in.

Yes, I'd invited him. *Yes,* I'd given him directions. And, *yes,* I'd only done so because he said he had to work. Now here he was in the flesh, walking toward me smack in the middle of those who knew me best.

"Hi, Annie!" He came over and gave me a hug and a peck on the cheek. "One of the guys wanted to switch shifts, so I was able to come after all. Now what can I do to help?"

"Oh, good, great." I sounded as distracted as I felt. My peripheral vision caught necks stretching and ears straining. I could feel the pressure of nosey eyes. "Let's see, where do we need the most help?"

"We could use a strong man over here!" yelled Maddie, flanked by Susannah and Robin. They waved to get my attention.

Standing with Jillian, Casey whined, "Mom, there are only two of us at this station."

"Why don't you send that young man over to help your elderly parents?" Dad said in his best feeble voice.

When will I ever learn?

I prayed for a delivery team to return so I could put Gabe on a truck and get him miles away from my family and friends. God answered. Before anyone could get their paws on him, my boss recruited Gabe to reload the vans for the next trip ... with Vito and Webster.

Really, God? That's your best answer?

CHAPTER 37

The decision to invite Gabe to Thanksgiving dinner was taken out of my hands since he pulled duty that day. I wasn't sure he was ready to spend the whole day with my family anyway. My father and brothers would have grilled him; my children would have tested his sports acumen; and my mother would have fed him until he was comatose.

Billed as the "last big family Thanksgiving" at their house (which is what Mom and Dad had been threatening for about seven years now), there were four generations represented in the seventeen of us that day. Soon, the work would become too much for Mom. Until then, I decided to enjoy myself as if this day might be our last together— a concept I knew well as a widow.

Casey and Sam had picked up Griffin and Jillian on the way. I greeted the guys, then herded my daughter and daughter-in-law into a corner. If I wanted to know what happened in my children's lives, I had to go to the girls. Other than sports stats, the guys gave me *bupkis*.

"Casey, did your company get that big client you told me about?" I asked. "Are you headed for New York again?"

"Yes and yes. On top of that, Griffin and I have another television appearance scheduled on Thursday in Connecticut. I'll go on to New York right after the taping."

"How many TV appearances is this now? My children are on the fast track to fame!" I turned to Jillian. "Are you and Griffin able to turn his trip to Connecticut into a little getaway?"

"No, Griffin's only going long enough to tape the show, because we have something to do the next day."

"A school event?" I asked, knowing how busy their teaching schedules kept them.

"Uh, no, uh …"

"You don't have to tell me, Jillian. I don't want to be accused of being a nosey mother-in-law."

"I would never say that about you!" she said, "We just don't want to say anything until we're sure."

"Oh-oh …" I said, the second syllable rising.

"I know what you're thinking, and no, I'm not pregnant. My mother gets that exact same look on her face. We have an appointment with a mortgage broker. We're thinking of buying a house."

"A house?" Casey said. "Really? Where?"

"Downtown Plymouth—but we're only fact-finding now. We don't want to get our hopes up."

"That's exciting!" I said. "And I promise not to ask any more questions."

"The structure needs a lot of TLC, but my father said the repairs are manageable. And you know how I love fixing things up. Griffin can even have an office above the garage. The house could be a perfect place to raise a family."

Oops, I think the hopes are already up.

The lives of my twenty-something kids seem more complicated than Ned's and mine were at that age. I only worked full-time for a few years after we married. He was in graduate school then, so one of us with a paying job was necessary. When the kids were born, I wanted to be home. I don't know whether my kids will have that choice.

I was among the few women my age who had enjoyed being a full-time housewife and mother. More Suzie Homemaker than Gloria Steinem, I was quite content when the roles of men and women were more easily defined. I didn't want to be liberated. I wanted to be like my mother—although I never dared say that out loud. I wasn't particularly enamored with the lifestyle of braless women digging in their heels for equality. First of all, I was a mother who had nursed two babies—heck, I needed my bra.

"Turnabout's fair play, Mom," Casey said. "How're things progressing with Gabe and your Party of One group?"

In a sitting-in-the-tree-k-i-s-s-i-n-g sing-song voice, Jillian added, "Gabe's not half bad. Anything new to tell us?"

I ignored her tone. "We have a good time. Gabe and the Party of One people are all very nice."

"Your boss whooshed him out of the warehouse so fast on Saturday," Casey said, "that we didn't get a chance to talk."

"Yes, that's a real shame." I gave her my signature mother look.

I got home at quarter after seven. Full and tired, yet not sleepy, I made myself a cup of tea and snuggled in my favorite chair. I had enjoyed the day. More than that, I had this sense of anticipation ... but about what? What was I missing? What was this quirky feeling?

Oh ... wait ... there it was again. Hope.

I had the Friday after Thanksgiving off. Angst arrived right on schedule to torture me about Christmas. *You haven't bought one gift yet. Your decorations need to be up earlier than last year. Don't forget to get greeting cards. What will you wear to the office party? Shouldn't you bake cookies? Remember to ask the kids about Christmas Eve. Have you decided on a menu yet? How are you going to find time to do everything?*

I sat at my kitchen counter with my mug of coffee and basked in the sun's rays. Why did I worry? Christmas always turned out fine. I began with my shopping list. As was my habit for so many years, I started by writing Ned's name. *Whoa.* Another sucker punch from grief. When would I be free from those sore muscle memories? Since the holidays didn't come around as often as ordinary days, I might need more time to get through them.

On a fresh page, I began again. I skipped down a few lines and wrote Casey, Sam, Griffin, and Jillian. I stared at the blank lines above their names. *Are the blank lines in remembrance of Ned or in hopes of finding a replacement?*

Moving ahead, I ignored any further questions initiated by dogged ghosts. I planned when I would shop and how I would decorate. I called Mom to see what I could bring for the family party, always held the Sunday before Christmas. I did a preliminary menu for Christmas Eve, which I planned to spend at home with my kids.

On a whim, I called Maddie to see if she wanted to reinstate our gift-wrapping party. The yearly tradition had been fun when our children were little, but had been lost in the passing years. Maddie was game. She called Robin, and I checked with Susannah. We set the date. They decided my empty nest was the best location.

Of course, our party was more about catching up on each other's news than gift-wrapping. Despite our time together at the Thanksgiving food drive, we'd had no chance to talk. My married friends clung to a vicarious belief that my life as a single adult was chock full of mystery, excitement, and romance. I'd be called to account—they'd want juicy details about Gabe. A small part of me didn't want to disappoint them; a big part of me didn't want to disappoint *me*.

Of all my friends, these three had shored me up and held me tight in the hard weeks and months following Ned's death.

They would puff up like wildcats when I mentioned making changes or going on a date. If I confided in one of them, the other two would call me within the hour.

As time went by, they began to trust me to make little decisions on my own. Even now, I still feel like a preteen who has permission to cross the street if she promises to look both ways, yet going to the mall alone is out of the question. I didn't fight them.

Of course, I didn't tell them everything either.

CHAPTER 38

Very sure I wanted to stay clear of the shopping madness on Black Friday, I showed up as usual at Party of One. Awaiting me were Will, Ethan, Vito, Jeremy, Webster, and the Professor. Where were the other women?

Minutes after I sat down, I noticed Robin and her husband across the dining room. They were getting up to leave. I motioned for them to come over and introduced them all around. They left soon after, but not before I caught the look on Robin's face. I'm sure she was on her cell phone to Susannah and Maddie before her car door closed.

Though the girls knew about Party of One, whenever I mentioned any of the men to them, I bypassed those within ten years of my age to avoid their questions or matchmaking. I was amused at how excited my girlfriends would be to hear that I—a lone woman—had dined with six men in a restaurant the day after Thanksgiving. I knew the more I claimed innocence, the more intrigue they would suspect.

This is the intrigue I encountered that night: Will told his favorite golf story from September 1989 for the umpteenth time. Ethan, Vito, and Jeremy talked about Thanksgiving football plays. The Professor raved about Olene's green bean casserole and Elizabeth's sweet potato pie, while Webster and I talked business.

Funny, I couldn't think of a place I'd rather be. Except maybe with Gabe.

Gabe called Saturday. "How was Thanksgiving with the family?"

"Predictable and crazy, but fun. How about yours?"

"Unfortunately, mine was predictable too—filled with more of the same holiday idiocy and drunk driving. Maybe one year, it'll be different."

I'd heard those same sentiments from Ned year after year.

"There were no fatalities on my watch, so I'm grateful for that. Listen, my family is celebrating a delayed Thanksgiving on Sunday. Would you like to join us?"

I declined, because I'd already made plans with Casey to go Christmas shopping. She was coming around to the idea of my having a personal life, and I didn't want to do anything to hinder her progress.

Gabe followed up with an invitation to go caroling a couple of weeks before Christmas with the same gang of cops and spouses I'd met at Karen and Drew's.

"You know, Gabe, I've never been caroling before. I don't sing very well."

"Neither do I. If you don't tell, I won't."

He was so upbeat, I couldn't refuse. I wondered if this was a get-together-with-the-gang sort of thing or a real third date. Dating was so far in my past, I wasn't sure how to take his invitation.

Why do you have to over-think everything? Can't you just go and enjoy the evening?

The next week at work was hectic. Since we can't postpone deadlines during the holidays, we meet them by working overtime—three nights out of five that week. I didn't mind. I had no one waiting at home. Besides, my boss never asked us to do anything he wouldn't do himself.

Right before I left on Friday, he reminded me about our annual company Christmas party. The party was always a classy yet simple affair held in a private room at the Schooner Restaurant in Cotuit. I didn't attend the year Ned died but had gone last year. I'd struggled to feel like I belonged, even with the people I worked with every day.

"Remember, Annie, you're welcome to bring a guest."

Was I ready to bring Gabe to a work function? I was obviously hesitant, but why? I wasn't asking him to marry me or anything. This was a company party, nothing more. I thanked my boss and promised to think about a guest.

I considered ditching Party of One that night to go shopping, but I was too tired and hungry. I knew I'd be later than usual, but all I wanted was to get to our table and relax. A pleasant thought revealed itself. Like Martina, I had started to think of this group as *my* touchstone.

There was Will, always pleased to see me. Kate and Ethan and Vito and Renata renewed my faith in romance. Martina was a great encourager, and Elizabeth was so full of life. Olene and the Professor's literary discussions lifted me higher, and Lavender and Jeremy were a constant source of amazement—not always in a weird way. And Webster, well, thinking back to that first night he joined us, who would have guessed we would become friends?

I arrived at ten past seven. My spirits were buoyed even more by the sight of Gracie in a white cotton halter dress and a blonde wig. She greeted the customers ahead of me in a breathless coo as Marilyn Monroe in *The Seven Year Itch*. "Isn't the breeze from the subway delicious?"

The temperature was thirty-nine degrees outside, yet I could easily picture her standing over a subway grate with her full skirt billowing upward. The locals were used to her roles, but I heard an obvious out-of-towner say, "I didn't know Cape Cod had subways."

Will stood. "We were beginning to think you weren't coming, Annie."

Olene added, "Webster isn't here either."

Webster wasn't there? When I'd talked to him earlier in the week, he hadn't said anything about being busy on Friday. Had something come up? Like a meeting with the Jacobsons? Not that he or any Party of One-ers owed me an explanation when they couldn't attend. Still, missing a Friday night wasn't like him.

Despite the good company, I left early that night, more tired than I thought.

I didn't see Webster at church on Sunday, and he was a no-show again the next Friday. Since I'd had no reason to speak with him during the week, I assumed he would be there. Missing two Friday nights in a row, plus church on Sunday ... well, that seemed odd, if not worrisome.

I asked the others. "Have any of you guys heard from Webster?"

"I wondered about him myself," said Olene. "I have another book for him."

"I assumed you'd know, Annie," Will said, "since you've been collaborating on business, and he's been helping you around your house."

"Nope. I haven't seen or heard from him for a few weeks."

Smugness was smeared all over Vito's face. "Hey, I'm not sayin' I know for sure, but his absence might have something to do with the blonde bombshell I saw him with last week."

"A blonde?" Martina asked.

Jeremy raised a power fist. "You da man, Web!"

Not that his personal life was any of my business, but when did Mr. Social Skills have time to meet a blonde bombshell?

Lavender asked, "Vito, do you know who she was?"

Thank you, Lavender.

"No, he introduced me, but she had a foreign-sounding name, I think. I don't remember. Something like Nicky ... but not."

Blonde ... foreign-sounding ...something like Nicky. Wasn't his ex-wife's name Nieka? No, that couldn't be. I wanted to dig deeper but restrained myself.

I was relieved to see Webster's name on my caller ID early Saturday morning. "Good morning, stranger."

He didn't take the bait. "Hi, Annie. Is today a good day to come over and hang those Christmas lights?"

I hadn't strung outside lights since before Ned got sick. "The day is always a good one when I have help."

He sounded like everything was normal and didn't offer any explanations. I promised myself I wouldn't pry.

Like that's gonna happen, my conscience snickered.

Since this was the same Saturday I was scheduled to go caroling with Gabe, I got a head start by getting the lights out of my Christmas closet. Webster showed up around ten. He took great care untangling the mess of lights, hanging each string in a straight line and even balancing the colors. For his efforts, I told him to relax while I made him hot chocolate and a grilled ham and Swiss on rye.

As usual, he was compliant and appreciative … if not a bit quiet, which caused me to say, "We missed you the last two weeks. And I didn't see you at church either. I was concerned."

"No need to be."

That's all? *No need to be.* Good grief, the male species can be so frustrating. And yet I never know when to quit. "Is everything all right?"

"Fine, why?"

"Well, Vito mentioned seeing you with a woman."

"Vito should mind his own business."

"Sorry I asked."

"No, Annie, I'm sorry I snapped."

"I shouldn't have brought up the subject."

The clock was ticking, and Webster showed no signs of leaving. I waffled between wishing he'd hurry up and go and wishing he'd spill the beans about the blonde. Considering his mood and the chores he'd done for me, telling him I had a previous commitment with friends might sound insensitive and ungrateful.

At that moment, Christmas caroling in my off-key voice seemed less important than providing a friendly ear. I decided to forgo my plans to meet Gabe and the others. But before I could say another word or ask another question, Webster was out the door. Maybe I should have pushed more … or pushed less. I felt like a lousy friend.

Somehow, I managed to get to Karen and Drew's on time. I dressed warmly and wore a heavy scarf—to muffle my voice.

Karen passed out the songbooks, and we headed up her street, stopping to sing at every home that showed signs of life inside. People opened their doors and joined us. I was surprised by all those who offered us cookies and hot cider or eggnog.

Karen told me their secret. "We always send a notice around in our Christmas cards to let everyone know when to expect us."

"Our version of a fair warning," Drew said. "That way if they don't want to hear us, they can hide in their basements."

After a couple of cold hours of caroling, we went back to Karen and Drew's and warmed up by the fire. Gabe and I talked about our families and upcoming plans. We ended the night with a silly white elephant gift swap. Gabe ended up with Wild Billy, The Goat Soap for Men—I got a plastic yodeling pickle.

Despite all the holiday cheer, I couldn't shake my concern for Webster. The vision of him walking out my front door left me feeling a little sad.

But not sad enough to stop me from accepting Gabe Reilly's invitation for New Year's Eve.

CHAPTER 39

I got up early Sunday, excited about attending church—
which seemed funny because there was a time in my life when
I would've bellyached about going. I didn't *have* to go now; I
wanted to go. Church had become my second home. The more
I learned about God, the closer to him I felt. My relationship
with Jesus was—no, *is*–awesome in the biblical, not the
vernacular, sense of the word.

The pastor's sermons were powerful. He used the art of
illustration in a way that helped me remember the teaching
long after Sunday. I'd heard some ministers went on for hours.
Our pastor preached just long enough to give us something
meaty to chew on during the week.

Using my own words to talk to God was a new concept
for me, but I was getting better. Once I discovered saying the
name of Jesus felt good, I was naïve enough to tell others to
do the same. All they did was squirm and change the subject.
I guess saying his name means more when you know who
you're talking to.

Even though I didn't seek out Webster at church, he found
me. "Got time for a cup of coffee after service?"

"Sure."

On the way to a local bagel place, I made up my mind to
listen rather than talk this time. After we ordered, we grabbed
a booth in the back.

Webster took a swallow of juice and slowly set his glass
down. "The woman Vito saw me with was my ex-wife Nieka."

"Oh."

"She's single again—for the fourth or fifth time, I think. She wanted to resume where we'd left off over twenty-five years ago."

"Really?"

"Really. I never thought I'd see her again. When I answered the door and found her standing there, I was rattled, big time."

"Hmm."

"Seeing her reopened wounds I thought were healed. Ripped through scars like tissue paper. I didn't know what to do or how to feel or what to say."

I wanted to ask him *what* he did, *how* he felt, and *what* he said, but I didn't—which was quite a feat for me. Instead I said, "Oh?"

"Do you know what I realized after all these years?"

I thought, *that you still love her,* but I answered, "No."

"That I had never completely forgiven her. That shocked me as much as seeing her at the door. I thought I'd moved beyond that."

"Hmm."

"The old Nieka surfaced when I told her I wasn't interested in her proposition. That's when she asked me for money."

"Yikes."

"When humiliation and anger surfaced in me again, I needed a few weeks to spend time alone with the Lord. I was finally able to let everything go."

"Wasn't easy, huh?"

"Not so much. Annie, does my feeling vulnerable and foolish again after all these years make sense?"

"Vulnerable and foolish? Webster, you do remember who you're talking to, don't you?"

He smiled, and I knew he'd be all right.

Gabe called Monday and asked me to go Christmas shopping with him the next day. He wanted a woman's opinion, especially for the females in his family. I said yes, even though shopping was never in my inventory of skill sets. At least a weeknight would be less crowded. We agreed to meet after work.

Our stroll through the mall, admiring the decorations and listening to the holiday music, started out fine. Then Gabe stopped right in front of the women's clothing store that featured styles and colors much too bold for me. He told me this store was one of the places his mother and sisters suggested. As we entered, I doubted I could help him since I didn't know where to begin.

We walked by racks of brightly colored shawls. Everything was fringed, beaded, or appliquéd. He picked one up and asked for my opinion. I suggested we keep looking. My conservative taste fought against everything he showed me. I couldn't relate. All the clothes seemed to be designed for braver women than I.

Gabe was waiting for me to respond to one of his questions, when I heard my name.

"Annie?"

Martina stood before me, all dressed up in high-heeled boots, cropped gray woolen pants, and a pumpkin-colored fringed poncho. I took advantage of the reprieve. "Look at you—so chic! That color is great on you!"

"Thanks. I had some time before my hot dinner date, so I thought I'd run over to my favorite store."

"Your favorite store?" Gabe said.

"Oh, Martina, this is Gabe Reilly. Gabe, Martina Vargas."

Gabe extended his hand. "My pleasure. Did I hear you correctly? This is your favorite store?"

"Yes," she said. "Why do you ask?"

"Well, Annie's helping me shop for my mother and sisters. Since they're more your coloring than Annie's, maybe you can give us some advice?"

"Sure, no problem. Did they give you any suggestions?"

"My mother wants a dressy sweater and my sisters want some sort of shawl. I'm not sure what to get my nieces. Unlike me, they take after the more colorful side of our family."

I nudged Martina. "Gabe's mom is Mexican like you."

"Is that so?" Martina smiled. "Well, let's see what they have."

With her help, Gabe bought gifts for all the females in his family. Martina seemed to know what to suggest without having met them. I was impressed. We invited her to join us for coffee at the bookstore.

She looked at her watch. "Thanks, but I've gotta run. See you later, Annie. Good to meet you, Gabe."

"Your friend was very nice to help," Gabe said.

"That's because Martina *is* very nice. Running into her was a blessing. I wouldn't have done as good a job."

We walked to the bookstore. After ordering coffee from a young woman behind the café counter, we succumbed to the lure of the pastry display. We had to wait a few minutes for a table to vacate. One finally did in the corner.

"How do you know her? From work? Or church?"

"The girl at the counter?"

"No," he said, "your friend Martina."

"Martina? No, I didn't meet her at work or church—although she is a Christian—one of the most committed I know. We met at a dinner club I belong to."

"Dinner club?"

"Yes." I didn't want to give him the wrong impression about Party of One, so I changed the subject. "How's your pastry? Mine's delicious."

Soon the topic turned to Gabe's upcoming Maine hunting trip with his son. His eyes brightened when he spoke of the annual event. "This will be our fourteenth year. We don't hunt so much as hike and talk. I treasure these times before some girl snatches him up."

As I watched him talk about his only child, I became more certain that Gabe was not only a strong Christian, he was a good father and a good man—not to mention attractive, kind, and industrious. I believed he'd fit easily into my family.

In the midst of my mental pros (many) and cons (none) list, a still small voice interrupted me. *Yes, Annie, he is all that and more. But he's not the man I have for you.*

Where did that come from? Did I say that? Who said that? Was that you, God?

Gabe leaned back in his chair. He flipped his teaspoon over and over, staring at his cup.

Uh-oh, had I said something aloud? Could he tell what I was thinking? How could I explain what I'd heard?

He sat up as if he'd finished thinking and rested his arms on the table. He looked at me like he wanted to say something. Then he did. "Annie, remember when we talked about God's perfect will for our lives and how we should pray?"

"Yes …"

"Well, I believe the Lord just told me I'm not his perfect will for you. Does that confirm anything to you?"

I shook my head in disbelief. "You will not believe this, Gabe …"

CHAPTER 40

After I recounted what I'd heard in my spirit, we spent the next half hour more relaxed, enjoying the time as friends. I gave him more information about Party of One and invited him to join us.

He seemed hesitant about my invitation. "My schedule this time of year poses a problem."

"Just come when you can. And if you're worried about doing anything to embarrass yourself, don't. I pretty much have that award in the bag." When I filled him in on Save Face and Mother Gertrude, he laughed so hard he choked on his coffee.

"I'll see," he said.

Something made me say, "Martina's been a regular from the start."

"Maybe I can switch things up after the holidays."

When Gabe offered to walk me to my car, I thanked him but declined. Needing time to think, I threaded my way through the crowds toward the entrance I'd come in. Even loaded down with my purse, shopping bags, and half-filled coffee cup, there was a spring in my step. I was surprised at how light-hearted I felt. Coming to a bench at the halfway mark, I sat down to reflect.

You've basically lost your only viable candidate for romance and you're sashaying through the mall like a beauty pageant winner. What's up with that?

I marveled again at the Lord's timing. Neither Gabe nor I had been put in a position of hurting the other. He'd offered to let our date for New Year's Eve stand. I didn't know why, but I canceled. No, that wasn't quite true. I knew why. I wouldn't feel right standing with Gabe at midnight on New Year's Eve ...

Because I'd rather be standing with Webster.

What? My heart pounded; my mind raced; I tried not to hyperventilate. I managed to put my shock on hold long enough to gather my things and stand on shaky legs. I felt the urgency to get home to process this revelation. I didn't like this feeling. No, that wasn't true. I didn't like *liking* this feeling.

When did I start feeling this way about Webster?

The circumstantial evidence overtook my denial in waves. When Webster offered me the hand of peace at church, what lingered after we let go sure wasn't peace. When I took longer than usual to get ready for our times together, I mistook my primping for looking presentable. When I anticipated his visits more and more, I attributed my enjoyment to our common faith and mutual clients. And when I did things to prolong his stay, I blamed my actions on loneliness. More recently, when I worried about Webster and Neika, no matter how I rationalized, I was plain jealous.

The physical evidence convicted me too—stomach butterflies, unexplained tingling, giddiness, and non-menopausal flushness. At times when we were together, the pull seemed magnetic. I tried not to look at him, yet I found myself looking anyway. His face was always clean-shaven, his skin tone a shade of pink that made me wonder if his cheeks would feel warm—not fever-warm but just-right-warm.

I cleared my mind and throat and reviewed my surroundings to make sure I was headed toward the right exit. I stepped outside into the freezing cold and tried to remember where

I'd parked my car. Distracted by my thoughts and emotions, I slipped on an icy patch.

I flailed around to regain my balance, juggling everything in my arms, trying not to spill my coffee. Coming to a precarious stop, I braced myself against the plate glass window outside the busy mall restaurant. I peeked inside to see if I'd had an audience for my poor man's Cirque de Soleil act.

A color caught my eye. The same pumpkin-orange Martina had been wearing. I looked again. The woman was definitely Martina. I wanted to tell her what was going on with me but she wasn't alone. A man was seated across from her, partly hidden by a partition.

I wondered if this was an ordinary dinner date or a date-date. Wait, didn't she say she had a "hot dinner date"? I tilted my head for a better angle. Then I stretched my neck, trying to see over the potted plants. I was excited.

Now we'll both have someone!

I was being presumptuous, but I was too giddy to scold myself. I continued to spy on the twosome. Martina seemed quite animated, and I figured that was a good sign. If only I could see behind that irritating partition.

Oh, wait, he's moving his chair back; he's getting up; he's walking this way ...

I jerked around, my back to the window. I didn't want to be seen. I couldn't be seen. As soon as I could get my brain in gear, I ran toward the parking lot and didn't look back.

What's going on? I don't understand. How had I missed this?

I crisscrossed in and out of spaces until I found my car. I climbed in and turned the engine on to get some heat. Shivering, I took a sip of coffee, which was cold by now. I felt like I'd just stepped in a big puddle—all wet and stupid.

What was Martina doing with Webster?

CHAPTER 41

Over the next twenty-four hours, I made up my mind never to let myself be that vulnerable again. I'd rather live alone for the rest of my life than risk more hurt and humiliation. It wasn't worth the pain.

The romantic illusions I'd had were nothing more than that. I was thankful I hadn't said anything to Webster. The whole idea was nonsensical, most likely brought on by the realization that Gabe and I were not meant to be together. As far as I could see, Webster and Martina were tickled pink with each other. If that was the case, I'd be tickled too.

Well, tickled might not be the most accurate word, but begrudging didn't sound Christ-like.

The Sydney Carton line from Charles Dickens' *Tale of Two Cities* came to me: "'It's a far, far better thing I do than I have ever done. It's a far, far better rest I go to than I have ever known.'"

Such a noble act—and such a load of fiction.

No matter what happened between them, I was done. No more, finis, kaput. I was back to square one with Webster—we were friends, nothing more. That had to be enough for me.

I covered my face with my hands. "Lord, I'm drowning here. Please help me."

I couldn't forget about my company Christmas party even if I wanted to. In addition, I was the person in charge of getting the gift for our boss. When would I learn that whoever comes up with a good idea always has to execute the plan?

Early that morning, I made the trip to Sol and Dodi's to pick up the gift we'd chosen from their website. Titled "The Mentor and His Student," the sculpture portrayed a man leaning in, peering over the shoulder of an older man. My boss had said the piece reminded him of his father and him.

Sol greeted me. "All alone you've come today?"

"Yes, alone. I'm here to pick up the gift for my boss."

Dodi came in. "What? No Webster?"

"No, not today." They sure weren't making my errand easy.

Sol winked. "A fine man he is, Annie. You agree?"

"I agree."

Dodi smiled. "And Annie is a fine woman too, right, Sol?"

I wasn't sure how to react, though I knew what they hinted at was not going to happen. I smiled, half-heartedly.

Dodi chose that moment to come over and put her arms around me. She hugged me like a mother hugs a child. "Wait, dear, everything will be fine, you'll see."

I wanted so badly to believe her. Mostly, I wanted to cry.

The company party at the Schooner was more like a family gathering. Our substantial bonuses made us glad we'd splurged on the original piece of art for our boss. He loved the sculpture and couldn't stop thanking us. I was grateful I never got around to inviting Gabe or any other guest. The social interaction was less complicated and nerve-wracking. More than that, I felt like I had some of my old control back.

Keep telling yourself that, McGee, and you might believe the lie one day.

On my drive to Cranberry Fare for Party of One's Christmas celebration, I prayed I'd get through the night without thinking of Webster and Martina in any way but loving. I asked God to help me treat them as the good friends they were and to accept the inevitable.

All the regulars showed up, and everyone remembered their Secret Santa gifts. Most of the gifts were homemade or handcrafted. Jars of Vito's gravy and meatballs for Ethan. Sarge's baklava made especially for Will. Ethan's hand-carved birch tree candle holders for Martina. Lavender brought a collection of potted herbs for Olene, and Kate had made potpourri for Renata.

As Lavender's Secret Santa, I'd had my mom knit a funky hat and mittens set in gradations of purple. I hoped I'd guessed right.

Lavender squealed when she lifted them out of the gift bag. She put the hat on and held the mittens up. "Wow! Cool! The mittens have strings!"

Pleasing her was easy, which pleased me too.

Webster was last to present his gift. Since I'd yet to receive one, I knew he'd picked my name. He handed me a large flat package—a twelve-month wall calendar using Party of One photos he had taken throughout the year. Why was I surprised he'd come up with a gift I'd treasure?

Everyone scrambled around the table to look at the pictures. Each month held a collage. There were snapshots from all the progressive dinner homes and some good ones from the Sandwich Senior Center fundraiser. He had pictures of Gracie and Ian too, and even some of the short-timers like Francine, Bogs, and Tanya.

"This is a good picture of Kate and me," Ethan said. "She looks mad."

Kate laughed. "That was before I forgave you."

Lavender pointed. "That's me in the purple cape."

Sarge said. "Really? Are you sure that's not the Professor?"

I looked up at Webster. "When and how did you take all these pictures?"

"Hey, here's me toasting us, Renata," Vito leaned over and kissed her.

Elizabeth studied Olene's before-and-after pictures positioned side by side. "There's my beauty."

"Aunt Elizabeth, you promised," Olene said, still embarrassed by the attention.

"You didn't answer Annie's question," Will said. "How did we miss you taking all these pictures?"

Webster pulled out his cell phone. "Simple. I have to aim with my camera, but not so much with my phone."

Will laughed. "You're a sly one, aren't you?"

Some pictures had us holding our sides, laughing so hard. The picture of Will in his smoking jacket, walking the Bachelor's Catwalk at the auction was one.

I asked, "Will, did you ever find out who bid $500 on the day with you?"

"No, I didn't. Whoever the bidder was better claim their gift soon—before the certificate expires. Or I do."

"Mr. Anderson, my bet is on the gift certificate," said Elizabeth. "You're too busy to retire, never mind expire."

264

"Aunt Elizabeth, I'm sure you know who the call-in bidder was." Olene prodded. "Tell us."

"My lips are sealed." Elizabeth pinched her lips together.

No sooner had she said that when Ian came up to the table, holding an envelope. "Mr. Anderson, do you know anything about this?"

"Let me see, son." Will opened the envelope. "Well, I'll be ... here's your answer, Annie. Ian has the gift certificate! It reads, 'Ian Quinn is the recipient of A Day on the Town with Bachelor Will Anderson.'"

The Professor asked, "Again, Ian, how did you say you came by the certificate?"

"It came in the mail along with this old news clipping."

"A news clipping?" Will's eyes narrowed.

Ian unfolded the paper and began to read. "December 18, 1993. Today was a sad day in the life of Littleton Rubber and Plastics. A major part of its facilities—"

Will interrupted, "Oh, son, you don't have to read all that."

But Ian continued. "A major part of its facilities went up in flames along with the jobs of its 102 employees. But today is a good day in the life of mankind thanks to the actions of Littleton's Rubber and Plastics owner, William Anderson. The first thing Anderson did when he learned of the fire was to call a meeting with all his employees at the factory that same afternoon. Anderson stood on the steps in front of the rubble and announced, 'This is a setback, yes, but together we will rebuild. I am here to reassure you that none of you will go without a paycheck during the rebuilding process.' After Anderson finished speaking, he walked through the crowd, shaking hands with every employee and personally handing out Christmas bonuses."

Everyone stared at Will who looked like he wished we would move on to the next subject.

Elizabeth spoke first. "Were you able to keep your promise, Mr. Anderson?"

"Yes, I was, and I didn't lose a single employee during the rebuild. I was lucky."

"I think your employees were the lucky ones," Sarge said.

Martina jumped in. "*Blessed* is the word that comes to my mind."

Ian put the clipping back in the envelope. "Spending a day with you, sir, will be an honor. Name the date and time."

"My pleasure, son. Maybe I could take you down to meet some of the other retired execs at SCORE. Between the lot of us, you might pan a few nuggets of gold."

"I would like that very much, sir."

The anonymous bidder's spontaneous gift had a resounding effect on Will and Ian alike. Each of us had our suspicions as to the identity of the gift certificate donor. To my knowledge, nobody ever found out for certain.

We continued to go through the calendar photos. There was a hilarious one of Francine Porridge. Her features were distorted because she was leaning in too close to Webster when he took the shot. And, unbelievably, Webster had caught the expression on the face of Tanya-Lotner-Attorney-at-Law right after Sarge *served* Tanya her last supper.

The final page held a full-blown solitary photo of me. I had my elbow on the table with my cheek resting in my hand. I had a slight smile on my lips and a curious, almost dreamy, look in my eyes.

I'd never posed for his camera *or* phone. What was I thinking? Suddenly, I knew. I was wondering what it would be like to touch Webster's face.

I closed the calendar and shut down my emotions.

Near the end of the night, Webster turned to Martina. "By the way, Martina, did your girlfriend ever show up Tuesday night?"

Tuesday night? I looked at Webster, then Martina.

"Yes, she did, shortly after I ran into you. Did you get the restaurant's website fixed?"

I turned back to Webster.

"A little jiggery-pokery is all the system needed. It was up and running in no time."

They weren't on a date? The encounter was by chance? A coincidence?

I caught myself. The internal lecture went something like this: *Annie, don't go there. This news makes no difference. The whole notion of you and Webster is foolish. Remember that before you lose control again.*

CHAPTER 42

I didn't want to get up Saturday morning. Spending the day asleep was tempting—I wouldn't have to think. In the end, I got up because the phone kept ringing. The first call was from Casey, then my mother, then Maddie—all with holiday questions.

Casey said, "Have you bought anything for Sam yet? If not, I've got an idea." I took her suggestion and got through the phone call without her suspecting my mood.

My mother warned me again this year. "Save your money, Annie. Your father and I don't need a thing."

I don't know why she bothered. She'd taught me better than to ever show up empty-handed.

And Maddie asked, "Are we still on for Wednesday?"

"Yes, we are. Robin and Susannah will be here around six. We'll have fun, won't we?"

I decided not to say anything to Maddie about my recent lapse into romantic fantasy. There was no need to get her and the others all riled up for nothing.

I showered and dressed and felt refreshed. I took some time to steel myself against the barrage of wonder-ifs and if-onlys of my personal life. I managed to succeed when—enunciating every syllable to be sure I got the message loud and clear—I shouted, "You don't need anyone, Annie McGee! You're doing just fine on your own!"

When I got to church on Sunday, the parking lot was full, so I drove around back to the overflow lot. I should've remembered the children's production that morning, sure to bring additional family members. I wasn't able to sit in my usual seat but was ushered to the opposite side of the church. Since I was alone, I was expected to squeeze in wherever there was room for one. I scanned the sanctuary to locate Webster, but couldn't see much, other than those directly in my line of vision.

The pastor greeted us. Worship began with some old Christmas hymns. After the deacons made a few announcements and presented the pastor and his wife with a gift from the congregants, the children were asked to come up. They ranged in age from six to twelve, all fresh and clean in their black pants, white shirts, red ties for the boys, and red ribbons for the girls. I always loved my kids' school concerts. Casey would be wide-eyed and excited, while Griffin would be distracted and bored.

After the children's performance, the ushers came forward to receive the offering. Webster wasn't one of them. When the pastor walked to the lectern to begin his sermon, he hesitated for a few long minutes, his head bowed. The congregation was still, almost expectant.

He raised his head and spoke. "You know, this doesn't happen to me often, but when the Lord speaks I have to obey. I had my sermon all set to go, but the Holy Spirit has been giving me a different message from the moment I stepped into church this morning. I'm wise enough to know someone needs to hear it. Listen carefully and ask yourself, 'Is God speaking to me?'"

He began again. "So you're feeling pretty self-sufficient, huh? Don't think you need anyone. Doing fine on your own, you say?"

The pastor had my attention. He shifted positions. And so did I.

"Dear people, when you claim you need no one, when you claim you're doing fine on your own, there's a good chance you're hurting—perhaps a lot. Your brave shout of self-reliance comes from a deep place of fear. You're afraid you'll be hurt again, aren't you?"

I looked down at my hands sweating in my lap.

"As a form of self-protection, you've numbed your soul to cope with the pain. Let me tell you, self-protection says, 'I don't need you, Lord. I can do life on my own.' It will rob you of the richness the Lord God has in store for you."

Drawn by his message, I raised my head.

"The thing is I can't promise you won't be hurt again. That's tough news to hear, I know. However, the good news is the Lord will sustain you through heartache and joy, through grief and celebration, through life and through death.

"Today, come to the place of trusting God again. Know that he loves you and has your best interest at heart. Come humbly to the altar and pray with me now."

I don't believe God gave me much choice. Tears were streaming down my face as I made my way up front. I surrendered my life once more—this time holding nothing back.

CHAPTER 43

Wednesday evening, the gift-wrapping girls showed up, loaded down with shopping bags and wrapping supplies. I led them to the family room where there was space for the four of us and all our stuff.

Susannah studied the banquet tables. "Are these the same tables we used to use?"

"Yeah, they've been in the basement since the last time we wrapped gifts together."

"You should have waited for us," Robin said. "We would have helped you."

"That's okay. Webster brought them up for me last week."

"Webster? Is he the guy who hugged you at the Thanksgiving food drive?" asked Maddie.

"No, Webster was making deliveries. That was Gabe, an old friend of Ned's." I wasn't lying, exactly.

"So Webster is the Party of One guy? The handyman?" asked Maddie with an oh-so-innocent look.

"That's him." I tried to sound blasé.

Thankfully, Susannah changed the subject. "Your house looks nice. You put your outside lights up this year."

"Well, uh, Webster did the lights too."

"Now which one was he again the night I saw you at Cranberry Fare?" Robin asked. "Where was he sitting?"

"I don't remember." I tried to get the hounds off the scent. "Can I get you something to drink before we get started? Cider? Tea? Coffee?"

We got our gifts organized at one end of the room. As we had in the past, we set up an assembly line of sorts. Robin cut the paper to fit the packages. I wrapped. Susannah added ribbon and bows. And Maddie embellished with fresh greens, trinkets, and handmade gift cards.

Part of the fun of these wrapping parties was seeing what everyone had bought. Robin and her family had made a cookbook out of her mother's recipes and added family photos. She also got her husband a sexy piece of lingerie with the promise to wear it on New Year's Eve.

"You'll be cooking in that for sure!" I chuckled. "Better get a big apron!"

Maddie had wrapped a large box filled with doggie supplies for the puppy she and her husband had promised to get the family. She took great care wrapping a Bernina sewing machine—the prettiest package of all.

"Wow. Who's getting the fancy sewing machine?" Susannah asked.

"I am," she said with a grin, "from my husband. And I'm going to be so surprised!"

I shook my head. "So is he, I bet."

Susannah had a New England Patriots programmable electronic license plate holder for her husband. And Casey had scored a Patriots jersey for him, signed by a bunch of the players.

Holding the jersey up, Susannah said, "Annie, please make sure to thank your daughter again for me. No matter what else I buy him, this will be his favorite gift."

I held back on wrapping the gifts I had for Webster because I didn't want to get my friends going again.

Maddie said, "I'm thinking about getting my parents a gift certificate to Hollingsworth, but I'm not sure the food warrants the price."

"Knowing your parents," I said, "they'll both love the food and the atmosphere."

"When did *you* go to Hollingsworth?" Maddie asked.

"A few weeks back. They're new clients."

Susannah's eyes widened. "You went alone?"

"No, I was …we were, uh, Webster and I had dinner there on our way back from seeing our clients in Orleans."

Maddie looked at me over the top of her glasses. "*Our* clients? Does he work with you now?"

"I thought he was a handyman," Robin said, looking confused.

"No, he's a web designer and developer. And the people in Orleans were his clients first. My company is handling their marketing."

"And you needed Webster to accompany you? Oh, I see …" said Susannah.

Maddie crossed her arms. "What else do we know about this Webster?"

In some ways, keeping my feelings to myself was harder than letting them out. But I managed somehow.

I didn't get out of work that Friday until after seven. I wouldn't be in time for dinner but figured I could have coffee and dessert and wish whoever was there a Merry Christmas. Will, Olene, Elizabeth, the Professor, and Webster were present. The others were at company holiday parties. Vito and Renata had begged off. Gracie and Sarge weren't working that night, but Ian came right over to take my order.

As far as I could gather, none of us would be alone on Christmas. I wanted to double-check on Webster's plans but thought I'd ask him when he came to my house the next day. He had prearranged a final fall clean-up before the first snow.

Webster arrived early Saturday morning. I grabbed a rake and went out to help him. The air was clean and crisp and cold. No sign of snow yet. We worked to the rhythm of the sounds of frost-bitten leaves crunching beneath our feet, rake prongs grabbing at dead twigs, and metal scratching the surface of the hard, damp ground. We didn't talk much. I knew what lay beneath my silence, but what about his?

Shortly before noon, I went in to fix lunch. The tortellini vegetable soup I'd made was a good choice to combat the chill. I warmed a small loaf of multi-grain bread too. Webster's favorite dark chocolate, cinnamon chip brownies were a surprise for dessert.

After lunch, we plopped ourselves in the living room—me on my stuffed chair, Webster on the couch. My Christmas tree, centered in front of the bay window, was the loveliest one I'd had in years. Thanks to my gift-wrapping party, the gifts beneath the blue spruce looked like they belonged in Macy's New York City storefront window.

Admiring the tree, Webster noticed a cylinder-shaped, gold-flecked package with curly green ribbons at each end. He held the gift up. "Hey, my name's on this tag."

"You're not the only Webster in the world, you know. It's for my friend's son," I lied.

"You never told me you knew another Webster." He aggravated me by shaking the package a few times. "My guess is either a fire cracker or a gift certificate. Am I warm?"

"None of your business. Now put that back!"

We'd both worked hard in the fresh air and enjoyed a satisfying lunch. I should have been relaxed, but my nerves were doing jumping-jacks inside me. One minute we were talking and laughing easily, the next, stumbling over our words.

Or was it just me?

Since I'd openly admitted my feelings for Webster (well, at least to myself) and subsequently tried to abandon them (again, to myself), I felt somewhat dishonest. I hadn't said anything to Webster, so I don't know why I felt this way. As far as he knew, nothing had changed between us. The suspended moments of silence didn't help the situation.

If all those emotions weren't enough, I was tempted by the closeness of him. A long time had passed since my flesh had received any attention. I craved intimacy in ways I remembered well and missed. Did Webster sense any of this?

We were quiet—too much so. Like the calm before the storm. I waited, but I couldn't wait any longer. I'd tell him how I felt today. How? I wasn't sure. All I knew was I had to. I repositioned myself in my chair and snuck a peek at him. He was resting, his eyes closed.

Without opening them, he said, "You want to say something, don't you, Annie?"

"Uh ... how did you know?"

He sat up. "You have the itchy-fidgets. And you're too quiet."

"Well, I guess—"

"Wait. First tell me, is this going to be serious?"

"Well, maybe—"

"Can't friends spend time together without being serious?"

"Yes, we can. As long as you brought up our friendship ..."

Webster sighed. "So, you're sending me packing? Just when I was enjoying our times together."

Enjoying our times? I was pleased—excited and scared too. But, wait, what exactly did he mean? "Webster, I—"

"Annie, you don't have to say anything. Do you want me to leave?"

"Huh? Leave? No, uh … don't … I need to tell you—"

"Tell me what, Annie?"

"I'm trying, Webster, but saying what I have to say is difficult."

"Just say it."

"Well, I like you Webster, a lot, but —"

Webster got up. "Let me guess. The *but* has a name—Gabe."

"Gabe?"

"Yes, you know, Gabe Reilly, the guy you've been seeing?"

"Webster, this has nothing to do with my friendship with Gabe."

"Friendship? Annie, I know one thing. Making a date with someone for New Year's Eve constitutes more than a friendship." His tone was not pleasant.

"How did you know about that? Are you spying on me or something?" I wondered who had told him.

"I don't have to be a genius, Annie. I've seen you two together, and the word gets around."

Okay, now I was irritated. The stress got the best of me. "Webster, first of all, I believe I have the right to accept invitations from whomever I want, don't you agree? Second, it's not like anyone else has invited me."

"No, you're right. But I thought—"

"You thought what? How am I supposed to know what you think? You're not exactly transparent."

"Okay, but why didn't you tell me about Gabe?"

"Because … wait. You make my seeing Gabe sound like I cheated on you or something."

"I didn't mean to … you're right, Annie, I'm sorry. I should go."

Before I could think of something to say to stop him, he opened the front door and walked out.

Dumbfounded, I sat down and cried.

Well, that went well, Lord.

CHAPTER 44

The next morning as I dressed for church, I wondered how Webster would be when I saw him. I projected for the five miles and fifteen minutes the drive took me. What if he's still upset? What if he brings up the subject again? What if he doesn't? What will I say? I prepared responses for a number of hypothetical questions.

I walked in and found my usual seat. Halfway through the service, I realized he was not coming. Only two days before Christmas, and I was partly at fault for keeping him away. I didn't feel good.

Following the service, I headed to my parents' home to join the whole Molyneaux gang for our annual Sunday before Christmas bash. The day was full with more food and gifts than any one family needed. Again, we ended our time together with a promise to keep the occasion simple the following year. When we said those words, we meant them, but the promise never lasted the whole twelve months.

Since Casey and Griffin would be at their in-laws on Christmas Day, I planned an intimate buffet for Christmas Eve for the five of us. I loved having down time with my children and their spouses, which didn't happen often enough. We'd decided to save our gift exchanges for that night.

I was pleased with my purchases and hoped they were as popular as I thought they'd be. Even though my children are adults, I still try to give them that one standout gift like I did when they were young. Now I have Sam and Jillian to spoil too.

Thanks to Maddie's connections, I located the quilt kit Jillian wanted but couldn't afford. I got Casey and Sam the round stained-glass hanging they'd admired on the Artisan House website. Griffin was a little more difficult, but Jillian had told me about a band he loved, so I got him great concert tickets for their next Boston performance.

I hadn't decided what I'd do Christmas Day. Since neither my parents nor my kids had asked me about my plans, I figured they assumed I was spending the day with the others. I didn't say a word. Sometimes sitting home amid peace and quiet could be less lonely than being in a crowd.

I caved and phoned Webster the morning of Christmas Eve. I got no answer and left no message. With caller ID, he'd know I called.

Later that afternoon, I double-checked the packages beneath the tree and came upon my gifts for Webster. My heart sank. I wanted to give him those on Saturday, but I hadn't heard from him since he bolted out the door. So much for my plan. I put the gifts out of sight in my bedroom. The last few holiday seasons had been rough. If this one couldn't be better, then let it be over fast.

My emotions were unsteady. I had Christmas carols playing in the background when Casey and Sam and Griffin and Jillian arrived. If they'd been late, they might have found me sobbing.

"Mom, this card was tucked under the knocker on the front door," Casey said. "Don't the neighbors know by now you come in through the garage?"

"Thanks. Probably from Petunia and Buttercup, saving money on postage." I dropped the card on the hall table to free my arms for welcome hugs.

The Christmas tree was aglow A stack of kindling and logs lay in the fireplace all set to go. Lighting the fire before we opened gifts had been Ned's job. The tradition had fallen to Griffin. After he took his coat off, he went straight to the task.

I loved that all four of these young adults got along so well. Sam and Griffin were impressed enough with each other's jobs to keep talking all night. Casey would talk sports some with the guys, but she was a wife and working woman like Jillian, so they had that in common. The flow of chatter, running alongside nostalgic melodies, soothed my weary heart.

The menu consisted of appetizers and desserts. Between the Molyneaux madness of Sunday and the big dinners planned by their in-laws the next day, my kids had requested light and simple. I was pleased to oblige.

As for gifts, they were thrilled with my selections and I with theirs. I loved the grind and brew coffee machine Griffin and Jillian got me. They knew I was a freak about fresh coffee. Casey and Sam gave me a framed watercolor of the Dexter Grist Mill in Sandwich done by a local artist.

"I love his work! I know right where I'll hang this piece— on the wall in my bedroom to the left of the double windows."

Casey jumped up. "Let's go see how it looks, Mom."

"Okay, let's."

We went down the hall to my room. I held the painting up on the wall. "The colors and the scale are just right. This lovely scene will be the first thing I see every morning."

"It does look good, Mom. We're glad you're pleased."

"Who wouldn't be? You and Sam went overboard though."

"Is this gift for Webster, the Party of One guy?"

"Uh ... what?" I stared at her holding a package. "Oh, yes, I got him a little something, you know, for helping me around the house."

"What's it doing in your bedroom instead of under the tree?" She reached for the second package. "Wait, here's another one with his name ... and wrapped so beautifully. What's up, Mom? First Gabe, now Webster?"

"Nothing's up. The gifts are tokens, really." I reached for them, but she pulled them away.

"You're holding out on me, Mom. Do I have to get the others in here?"

I flumped down on the bed and shook my head. I hadn't been able to hide anything from my daughter, I swear, since she was a toddler. Her keen discernment was a curse and a blessing.

"I'm not holding out. I'm a little confused, that's all. I've known Webster for almost a year now, and I thought we were friends. Lately, I've been experiencing feelings I haven't had in a long time, feelings I didn't expect to have for him. I'm trying to work through them. Can you give me more time?"

"What about Gabe? Aren't you two still dating? Are you dating Webster too? Boy, Mom—"

"Webster and I have not been dating. Like I said, he's been helping me around the house and we've been going to church together. I think we were on the verge of talking about all this the other night, when he brought up my seeing Gabe, then—"

Casey's eyes narrowed. "Church? When did you start going to church? How did he find out about Gabe? Did you tell him?" She crossed her arms and tapped her fingers on her bicep. "What's going on?"

"First of all, Gabe and I came to a mutual, almost simultaneous, understanding that we're not meant to be together. He is a great guy though."

"Was that *understanding* because of Webster?"

"No. I don't think … maybe, oh, I don't know."

Casey asked the question I expected she would one day. "Is either Gabe or Webster anything like Dad?"

I answered as best I could. "Neither of them will ever be your dad. That's not possible. There are some similarities between Gabe and your father—like their jobs, personalities, interests, and even their builds. He's *like* your dad, but he's *not* your dad.

"As for Webster and Dad, well, that would be like comparing apples and snow globes or oranges and moon rocks. It's more of a contrast than a comparison. One isn't better than the other, but they're both so different. Webster's kind of a geek."

"Well, Mom, if knowing this helps, you can be kind of a geek yourself. I mean, you have your grocery list in a spreadsheet categorized by aisles. You spend your vacations happily organizing your cabinets, closets, and drawers. Oh, and last week you called me all excited about the community school's new course on punctuation. Uh, not all that cool, I hate to tell you."

"Gee, thanks, I think." I hugged her and felt her frustration melt away.

When Sam came in looking for us with Griffin and Jillian behind him, I gave Casey a let's-discuss-this-later glance. She didn't say a word.

On our way out of the room, I whispered, "I'll call you in a few days, I promise."

Around nine, we said goodbye in a hokey pokey of hugs. I returned to my place by the fire. Less than a minute later, I heard a knock. I shook my head and smiled. *Griffin.*

Positive I had guessed right, for he was my absentminded child, I swung the door open. "What did you forget, Grif?"

He stood there with a silly grin. "How'd you know it was me?"

"The same way I know the sun will come up each morning. Now what did you forget?"

"I forgot to thank you for the wonderful evening."

In that bittersweet moment, I noticed how much he was like his dad—an Irishman, full of blarney. I put my hands on my hips. "And ..."

He shrugged. "My lucky hat."

As I sent Griffin on his way again, I noticed the envelope on the table, marked "Annie" in a hand I didn't recognize. I walked to my desk for the letter opener. When I took out the card, a note fell out.

Sunday, December 23

Dear Annie,

First, please accept my apology for my behavior yesterday. It was inexcusable.

Second, I wanted you to know I'm taking time off to do some traveling. It may seem like an impromptu decision, but it's been in the works for a while. I'll be leaving this morning. My return date is flexible. Please let the others know at Party of One to allay any concerns. I hope you enjoy the holidays with your family and friends.

Sincerely,

Webster

I sat at my desk with the note in my hand. A minute passed before I realized Webster had been gone a day and a half. Did our muddled misunderstanding cause this sudden decision? Where did he go? What did "my return date is flexible" mean? Weeks? Months? Longer?

All I knew was I couldn't stay home alone on Christmas Day. Not this year. I called Maddie and asked if I could spend the day with her family. My asking told her I was desperate. She said yes.

I knew I'd be interrogated, but I didn't care. I was ready to talk.

CHAPTER 45

I arrived at Maddie's around noon, giving her family enough time to open gifts, eat breakfast, and scatter.

"So, what haven't you been telling me?" she said, never one to beat around a bush she could uproot with one tug.

I stalled for the right words. "Can I at least have a cup of tea?"

"Tea? I've got something better." She plopped a pint of Häagen-Dazs on the table in front of me and stuck a spoon in it. "Talk. What exactly did Webster do?"

Webster? I hadn't told anyone about him except Casey. How did she know? "I've never said anything about him."

"Are you kidding? It's not what you said, it's what you didn't say. We all know, so fast-forward to the end, then go back to the beginning. I need to know everything before I can tell you what to do."

Only Maddie. I starting laughing and didn't stop until the tears came. As promised, after our talk, Maddie told me what to do.

I was to wait.

Maybe I could have figured that out on my own, but when Maddie said *wait*, it sounded more like *hope*.

I tried to sound all nonchalant when I told the Party of One-ers that Webster had decided to do some traveling. They were as confused as I was by his abrupt decision.

Elizabeth said, "Traveling? Where's he going?"

"How long will he be gone?" Will asked.

Vito said, "When's he coming back?"

"He didn't say." I crossed my arms. "You all know as much as I do."

Lavender asked the big question. "Did you guys have a fight or something?"

"Of course not." Since I didn't qualify our misunderstanding as a fight, I didn't feel I was being dishonest.

At midnight on New Year's Eve, I wasn't standing in front of Webster. I was sitting … alone … in a movie theater … waiting, like I was told to do.

I didn't linger after New Year's Day brunch with my parents. Even though I'd had the week between Christmas and New Year's off, I had some things to do before I went back to work the next day. Part of my excuse was true. I had to do laundry.

While sorting lights and darks, I wondered how Webster had spent the past week. Was he still in the States? If so, which of the fifty? Was he in some exciting city or on a paradise island? Was he secluded or surrounded by people? Was he relaxing or working or both? He had left no clues. I could guess forever and never be warm.

Maybe he was visiting his family. If not, at least they would know where he was. I wondered if Andrea knew.

I haven't talked to her for a while. Probably should call and wish her a Happy New Year.

My excuse was pitiful, but the only one I had.

"*Shana Tova!*" I said when she answered the phone. It was one of the few Hebrew phrases I knew.

"Back at you, Annie! Nice to hear from you. And this time only months have passed instead of decades."

"I'm not interrupting a big family party or anything, am I?"

"Us? Nope. We babysat the grandchildren last night so the kids could go out. Today we're relaxing. How about you? Do anything special over the holidays?"

"Just the usual—Christmas Eve with my kids, Christmas Day at a friend's."

"Still doing Party of One? By the way, any news on that fix-up for Webster you promised? How's he doing anyway?"

That answered my question. He wasn't with them, and they didn't know he was off on some pie-eyed junket either. "First of all, I didn't promise. It was an idea that didn't work out. Second, your brother-in-law left a few days before Christmas. Said he was going to do a little traveling and wasn't sure how long he'd be gone."

"Uh, oh. That doesn't sound good. The last time he did that was when Nieka dumped him. Did anything happen?"

"Nothing I can think of." Not totally true, but I wasn't going to speculate with Andrea.

On the first Friday of the New Year, Martina mentioned Party of One's one-year anniversary coming up at the end of the month. Before we had time to decide how to celebrate,

Olene offered to host the affair at her house. We hashed out a menu for a light buffet.

Since Ian had left for Ireland the day before Christmas, Sarge suggested we time the party after his return. Nobody mentioned Webster.

On the other hand, I thought about him a lot. I went over every syllable and intonation of our last conversation, trying to see where I'd gone wrong. I didn't believe for a second he'd been planning to travel. While digging for the root cause of his leaving, I found fear and jealousy—which meant he was either running from me or us. Neither prospect brought comfort, and both made me angry.

Yes, Lord, I'll wait—but I might wait mad.

When I arrived at Olene's for the anniversary party, the transformation in her home was almost as startling as her personal makeover had been. The overgrown shrubbery had been tamed and the outside shingles repaired and painted. The front door was now a rich plum color with new brass hardware. Inside, the first-floor walls glowed in a pale shade of gold and the trim had a fresh coat of cream-colored paint. The windows were dressed with new curtain panels that allowed light to pour in.

The only thing more striking was Lavender's ensemble. She wore a floor-length lavender dress with medieval puff sleeves and a laced bodice. The skirt was appliquéd with a variety of small flying creatures, which matched the halo of purple and white flowers she wore on her head. (For someone who was always talking about finding *her center*, it amazed me that she could never get anything—including this halo—to stay put on the top of her head.)

The dress and the flower crown were semi-normal compared to the set of faerie wings she had attached to her back. Yes, faerie wings that bounced, fluttered, and shed shimmering glitter with every step.

Why, Lavender, why?

The only answer I could come up with was that she could.

A year ago, I didn't know these people at all. Once I met them, I didn't want to get too close. Now, they were an important part of my life. I knew God loved the Party of One-ers—whether they had faith in him or not. His love was unconditional. I wanted to see them like he saw them, I wanted to love them like he loved them, and I wanted to pray for them the way others had prayed for me.

As Will had on the six-month anniversary, he stood to toast me for founding Party of One. "On the occasion of our one-year anniversary, let's all raise our glasses. To you, Annie, thank you once again."

After Will's toast, Vito yelled, "Speech, speech!" and the others joined in.

I didn't plan to speak, but for some reason I wanted to. "Okay, but you might be sorry. What I want to say is more of a thank you than a speech. The message has been burning inside me for a while. Now remember, you asked, so you can't complain."

I crossed the room to the main archway and turned to face them. "First, every one of you has taught me a lesson ... or three. And I have more to learn from you yet.

"Will, you were waiting for me that first night. I was nervous and you were charming. Thank you for teaching me to enjoy and encourage the people around me."

Will tipped an imaginary hat. "The pleasure's all mine, my dear."

"Lavender, besides giving me a new appreciation for the color purple, you've inspired me to lighten up and take periodic flights of fancy."

"Ha! And what might those be, Annie?" Jeremy sounded like he didn't believe me.

Lavender poked him. "That's mega cool, Annie."

"Baby steps," I said to Jeremy. "My carbon footprint might still be a size too big for you, but I am recycling."

Next, I turned to Vito and Renata. "Vito, your faith and recovery are an inspiration. I want to be as steadfast in my prayers as you were in praying for your wife. And, Renata, while other women might've given up and moved on, you've been rewarded for holding tight to your marriage vows."

Vito patted his wife's protruding belly. "And now she has a baby prize to go with me, her booby prize!"

I faced Sarge, who stood across the room. "Sarge, you crack me up! You've taught me to be upfront and honest. I want to be as loyal to my convictions as you are to yours."

Sarge cupped her hand around her mouth and shouted, "Does that mean you'll be moving to my side of the political aisle?"

"You'll never know!" I said, admiring her persistence.

I moved on. "Professor, you've sharpened my appetite for good poetry and prose—even though there's not much chance I'll ever re-read *Beowulf*."

The Professor bowed, sweeping air with his arms. "Perhaps Tennyson, then? In his poem 'You Ask Me, Why, Tho Ill at Ease,' there is a line—"

Vito interrupted. "That guy's got more lines than my cousin Carmine the gigolo."

When the laughter died down, I continued. "Olene, you had the courage to trust others to help you grow. I was thrilled to be part of your re-discovery."

Olene blushed. Elizabeth reached over and squeezed her hand.

"Kate and Ethan, we had fun watching you get to this place. I admit we weren't always patient bystanders, but the wait paid off!"

"Sure did," Ethan said before he kissed Kate's cheek.

"Ian, you blessed me the first time I entered Cranberry Fare as a party of one. Your servant's heart is the best recipe for success. We suspect your stint at the restaurant is coming to an end. One day soon, we'll be reading about you in *Inc.* magazine."

"If that be the case, I'll have Mr. Anderson to thank." Ian raised his glass to Will.

I turned to Elizabeth. "Miss Elizabeth, you've made me realize growing up without growing old is possible. I want to maintain the spirit of a twenty-five-year-old with the same grace you have."

She fluffed her hair with one hand and made googly eyes like a flirty teen.

"Gracie, you are a joy and a professional—hostess *and* actress. When you reach the stage in New York, we'll all be able to say, 'we knew her when.'"

In character, Gracie misquoted Norma Desmond from *Sunset Boulevard* released in 1950. "And I'm so ready for my close-up, Mr. DeMille."

Lavender tilted her head. "Gracie, do you think the energy in New York is positive?"

Like the brass ring on a carousel, Sarge grabbed the chance to tease Lavender again. "Lavender is torn. She'd love to visit, but she's afraid the chi can't flow and the feng can't shui in the Big Apple."

I held my hand up. "Now you promised not to interrupt, so let me finish! Martina, you're one of my heroes. Your lifestyle and faith never contradicted the other. That authenticity was an invaluable witness to me."

I raised my glass to toast them. "To you all! Thank you for a wonderful year."

Vito yelled. "Hey! What about Webster?"

Martina said, "Yes, Annie, what do you have to say about Webster?"

He'd been gone a month. Vito's big mouth didn't surprise me, but why was Martina chiming in? "Uh, well ..."

"Yes, what about me?"

Webster's voice had come from behind me.

I flinched. "Where did you come from? How did you ...?"

"I didn't mean to scare you, Annie." He stood there grinning.

I didn't grin back. "I'm sure that's exactly what you meant to do."

"So, Annie, what were you going to say about me?"

"You've been gone so long. I'll need time to come up with something nice."

He winced. "Ouch."

I spent the rest of the evening avoiding Webster and keeping my eye on him at the same time. Did I have a right to be irritated with him for showing up without any explanation as to where he'd been or why he'd gone? I don't know, maybe not, but my feelings didn't change. His appearance that night was awkward and disconcerting.

I stayed around to help Olene and Martina clean up. When I saw Webster huddled in conversation with Will and Elizabeth—about his oh-so-mysterious travels?—I slipped out the back door.

CHAPTER 46

Webster called early the next morning. When I saw his name on my phone, I toyed with the idea of not answering— for about a nanosecond.

"Hi, Annie. Any chance I could stop by this morning?"

"I guess so," I said, kicking myself for sounding so carefree.

"Would ten o'clock be okay?"

"Ten thirty would be better," I said, playing as hard to get as I dared.

By the time Webster arrived, I looked the best I could on a Saturday morning without raising suspicions.

He was the first to speak when I opened the door. "You skipped out last night before we had a chance to talk."

"*I* skipped out. You're kidding, right?"

"Yeah, pretty dumb opener coming from me." He dropped his head. "I'm sorry, Annie."

I sighed. "Come on in. Why don't we agree to begin again?"

"I'd be a bigger fool than I already am to abnegate the generosity of your offer."

Of course, you would. I ushered him into the living room and released my inner Emily Post. "How about some hot chocolate?"

"Sounds great."

"Let me take your coat." While hanging his coat in the front hall closet, I caught sight of his unopened Christmas gifts on the shelf. I got them down and put them on the table in the foyer. When I returned to the living room with the mugs of cocoa, Webster had put coasters out on the coffee table in front of the couch.

I set the mugs down. "So, tell me, Mr. Townsend, where have your exciting travels taken you these past thirty-three days?"

Darn. That sounded like I'd been counting.

"Exciting? The word *thoughtful* might be more indicative of my travels. I spent over ten days house-sitting at my parents' place in Connecticut and the rest of the time in DC, sightseeing and taking photos."

I pushed. "Then why the big mystery?"

"No mystery. Just needed some time to think."

Before I could ask about what, he reached behind him and pulled out a gift-wrapped package. "Belated Christmas gift," he said, reacting to the confused look on my face.

"How did you get that past me?"

He smiled. "I'll never tell."

I held my finger up. "One minute." I retrieved the larger of the two packages from the foyer. "Might be a bit dusty," I cracked wise. "You go first."

I knew by the chuckle he tried to stifle that he'd heard my comment but chose to ignore it. Instead, he tore the wrapping, then used his penknife to cut the tape on the cardboard box. He tugged until the item came out.

"A copper bird feeder! Wow. This looks like Nils Larsen's work ... Hey, this is the squirrel-proof feeder I wanted! Thanks so much, Annie."

Personally, I thought a bird feeder was kind of a boring gift, but Webster acted like Ralphie in *A Christmas Story* opening his "'official Red Ryder, carbine-action, two-hundred-shot, range-model air rifle with a compass in the stock and this thing that tells time.'"

He hugged me.

The scent of him—spice and pine and all things fresh—took my breath.

Webster handed me the gift he'd smuggled in. It was a limited edition of Jane Austen's *Pride and Prejudice.* He remembered. I was pleased.

Before I could thank him, he pulled a small box wrapped in red metallic paper with a tiny gold bow out of his shirt pocket. "Your turn again."

Without a word, I opened the box. Inside was the cloisonné brooch I had admired the day of our visit to the jeweler's studio. "After all this time you remembered?"

"I cheated. I bought the pin that day."

I found his spontaneous act even more touching than his choice of gifts. "Well, you deserve a proper hug for your thoughtfulness." I stood. He followed suit. I had to stretch to reach my arms around him.

I didn't plan to, but I may have hung on a few seconds longer than I would have hugging anyone else. Webster responded by not letting go. Without warning, our embrace became electric, shocking dormant senses back to life. The charge made moving apart nearly impossible. With all the restraint I could muster, I backed away. At least I *think* I was the one who backed away.

I needed a moment to find my voice. "Let's sit. We need to talk."

"Yes, we do."

I took a deep breath and focused on his eyes. "At church the Sunday before Christmas, Pastor had a message that spoke directly to me. I've tried so hard to act like I don't need anyone. I was afraid if I cared about someone, I might get hurt again. I wasn't trusting God."

"Was that the Sunday he changed his sermon up at the last minute?"

"You were there? The church was so full I didn't see you."

He shook his head. "You're mistaken, though. I'm certain that sermon was meant for me."

"Please, let me finish before I lose my courage." I cleared my throat. "I've been struggling with feelings I haven't had for a very long time. As we just experienced in our hug." I felt my face redden. "The struggle's not only physical. Do you know what I'm trying to say?"

He studied my face and settled on my eyes. "I hope so, Annie. The truth is I've been fighting my heart since the first day I met you."

"Truly?"

"Truly."

I felt the heat of a full-out blush. "Why didn't you say anything?"

"I don't know. First, I couldn't believe what was happening. Then we became friends. I didn't want to ruin that. When I saw you with Gabe, I felt like a fool. Mostly, I was afraid."

"Webster, for the record, Gabe and I were never serious."

"I know that now." He responded to my head-tilt query. "Email prayer chains are highly underrated as a source of gossip."

"So it seems. Are you still afraid?"

"A little," he said.

"Me too."

I didn't know if I shook from nerves or joy. He placed my hand upon his face. His cheek was warm, just-right-warm. How did he know to do that? He pressed his lips against my palm, then leaned in. His eyes held mine and drew me closer. I felt the warmth of his breath and smelled a hint of chocolate. I paused to be sure. I moved forward to accept his kiss—his lips, a perfect fit.

We backed away and stared at one another. I knew. There were no words, just wonder. We held hands for a long while, experiencing the joy of our mutual revelation. We didn't speak.

All we did was smile—a silly thing for people our age to do—but we couldn't help ourselves.

"Annie, I don't want to move, but I think we'd better. We may be tempted to do something we would certainly enjoy, but later regret."

In that moment of weakness, I couldn't imagine regretting doing anything with Webster. Even though I knew he was right, I didn't want him to go. "How about a walk then?"

"Good idea." He breathed in and out slowly. "It's twenty-six degrees outside. That should do it."

We bundled up and headed out. A light snow fell. In our heightened state of unawareness beyond anything but us, the world was a white blur. We held hands and walked, confessing little secrets and revealing big dreams.

Back at the house, in the foyer, Webster kissed me again. "I should go," he said, like he was tripping a safety valve.

"I know. One more thing before you do." I handed him the second gift.

He laughed when he recognized the cylinder-shaped package he'd shaken the last time he was at my house. Inside, he discovered a hand-decorated scroll with an invitation to be my date on New Year's Eve at Hollingsworth.

Dropping his head, he said, "What a jealous dope I was." He wrapped his arms around me and held me tight. "Can we go any time or do we have to wait until next New Year's Eve?"

"Maybe the next holiday. What's coming up?"

"Groundhog Day," he said, "in five days."

"Works for me!"

He chuckled as he walked out the door. Waving from his open car window, he took his time driving up the street.

The phone rang fifteen minutes later. I knew it was him.

"I'm checking to make sure what happened was real," he said.

"Still is."

"On my way home, I realized I forgot to tell you something."

"Oh?"

I thought he was smiling when he whispered, "I love you, Annie McGee."

I knew I was. "I love you too, Webster Townsend."

Awed by the wonder of God's ways, I couldn't stop thanking him. First, for superseding my own best-laid plans. Second, for giving me Webster. And third, for reassuring me that I still had time left before my libido expired.

So this is what God's perfect will feels like?

After everyone arrived at the next Party of One, I asked for the floor. "Last week at the anniversary party, I neglected to thank one person. If you don't mind, I'd like a do-over." I faced Webster, back in his seat where he belonged. "Web, you're quick to listen, slow to speak, and kind to others. Those are the qualities I admired about you," I paused for effect then dropped the bomb, "even before I fell in love with you."

I waited for the impact to hit the group. Instead, their remarks knocked me sideways.

"About time!"

"Finally!"

"At last!"

Lavender rummaged in her backpack and pulled out a rumpled sheet of paper. "According to my calculations, Professor, you won the pool!"

Like Ethan and Kate had been, we were the last ones to know.

The following morning, Webster and I walked hand-in-hand into the bagel shop in town. Francine Porridge's shrill laugh and little girl voice stopped us short. I surmised she had a live one. We placed an order to go. Unfortunately, we had to walk by her booth to get to the exit.

I tried not to stare but couldn't help myself when I heard, "Yuh, I like my big breakfasts, all right. I like my pancakes, my waffles, my bacon, my sausage ... yuh, I like my big breakfasts."

There was my ex-coworker's brother-in-law (my former blind date) sitting across from Francine, doing a cocky Detroit lean, his head tilted, and his arm up over the back of the booth. He seemed quite pleased with himself and Francine.

"I adore breakfasts!" said Francine in a baby girl squeal.

Smiling, my joy spilled over for Francine and ... what was his name?

CHAPTER 47

On a sunny day in early spring, Webster and I went for a walk along the canal, now a favorite site of ours. Watching the sun glisten over the water, we talked.

"When I'm with you, Annie, I feel like I'm standing on solid ground for the first time in my life."

"Solid ground, huh? For me the feeling's more like floating on Cloud Nine."

He reached for my hands. "Maybe we can do both?"

"A marriage of great minds, you mean?"

He smiled. "Would you like to make that marriage legal?"

I hesitated before I spoke. "If you're asking what I think you're asking—the answer is yes!"

When he pulled a small box from his pocket, I was astonished he'd managed to surprise me again. I gasped when he revealed its contents—the blue sapphire ring I'd tried on at the artisan jewelers. He placed the ring on my finger. We kissed … and kissed again.

"How did you know to get this one?" I asked, staring at my left hand.

"Well, you showed a polite interest in the display case of diamonds but turned giddy when you saw the sapphires."

"I did?"

"You did."

"This ring is such a unique piece, I can't believe it was still there after all these months."

He leaned in and whispered in my ear, "It wasn't. I've had the ring in my office, filed under *h*."

Once again, as so few could do, Webster left me speechless … almost. All I could say was, "Under *h*?"

"*H* for Hope."

There's that word again.

I'd spent years convinced I'd done everything right. Webster had spent years searching for significance. I was sure I could find the way. Webster wasn't sure he wanted to try. Together we found Hope and Love.

That was the real power of Party of One.

We headed back to the car through the stream of cyclists and walkers who'd gathered on this perfect day. Webster wended through the crowd, holding my hand, pulling me along behind him. Bringing up the rear gave me a good view of his jeans— those light blue, flared, stretch-denim Wranglers.

I smiled. When did those outdated jeans become endearing to me? The back left pocket, worn along the trace of his wallet, was a shade lighter. If given time, that wallet would wear through that pocket just as time with Webster had worn through to my heart.

I loved what those jeans represented—Webster's reliability, humility, and ability to disregard the hubris of fashion. They reminded me people are deeper than their first impressions. To discover how deep, I needed to dig through my petty prejudices.

Gee, who knew those Wranglers had so much to say?

And would they keep talking once I drop them off at Goodwill?

EPILOGUE

After his three-week visit home in Ireland, Ian returned with vigor and determination to begin his business. He cut his hours at the restaurant. Privately, he admitted, "The only reason why I'm not quitting altogether is so I can remain under Mr. Anderson's tutelage."

In mid-February, Gracie moved to New York City as a live-in nanny for a drama instructor and her husband. Through the instructor's theater connections, Gracie got a small part in a way-off-Broadway play a few months after she arrived. Her performance earned her rave reviews in some industry rags and blogs. She emailed every one of them to us.

Ethan and Kate, now formally engaged, cut back their Party of One attendance to once a month. We expected the change, especially after Will sold Ethan his old house in Sandwich. The young couple was hard at work restoring the sixty-year-old colonial, hoping to complete the work before their wedding.

Sarge became a full-fledged member of Party of One in early March. When Webster expressed surprise she'd given up her poker night and the lucrative night shift to join us, she shot back, "I gave up nothing. My poker night was changed to Wednesdays, and you guys don't tip that well anyway."

Olene, maintaining her style and self-confidence, became the group's top recruiter. When we asked her where she found all these people, she said, "You can tell a lot about a person by the books they read."

Her first recruit was a twenty-something, budding mystery writer who jotted down notes during our mealtime conversations. (What could be so mysterious?) Then there were the identical twins—women in their sixties who still dressed alike. One read romance novels; the other, true crime. A middle-aged widower who liked westerns arrived early and stayed late every week. He hadn't missed a Friday since Olene's invitation.

Martina, still a prep cook at Cranberry Fare, was delighted when her son (visiting from Houston) and her daughter (down from Boston) surprised her by joining Party of One on the night of her fiftieth birthday.

Though Gabe had told me he would stop by after the holidays, a few months came and went with no sign of him. When the group decided to host another progressive dinner, I gave him a nudge. He agreed to come.

When he asked me what he should bring, I told him something Mexican—but, unlike Save Face/Delbert, not his mother. He hung up laughing ... but showed up. Martina smiled and Gabe came back ... again and again.

On April 1, Lavender received her massage therapy certificate. She rented garage space from a couple who owned an inn on Route 6A in Sandwich. Even though most of her clients were friends and coworkers—many of whom couldn't afford to pay—she insisted she was living her dream. I believe she was. She kept a part-time position as a research assistant while waiting for her paying clientele to grow. And, thankfully, the innkeepers bartered massages for a portion of the rent.

Jeremy's promotion at work meant relocating to Seattle in early spring. He and Lavender kept in touch but neither seemed devastated by his cross-country move.

Vito and Renata attended until their son was born on April 12, the same day as their twentieth anniversary. It was not a coincidence but a Caesarian, due to Renata's age. They named him Vitorio Jr., but called him Torey.

In the seven months after their reconciliation, Vito had lost thirty-five pounds. "Renata cuts my portions in half," he said, "and calls it the 'live free and longer diet.' Hey, as long as I can live longer with my wife and my son, I'm a full man."

Professor Whitley's class schedule continued to accommodate the Party of One time slot. When Elizabeth's virtual tour company, We'll Always Have Paris, *toured* England at a local retirement center, she invited him to recite a few lines from *Othello*. He dressed for the part and performed with as much panache as he would have at the Royal Shakespeare Theatre in London. He got a standing ovation—from those who were able to stand.

On nights when more showed up than the section could handle, the couples would move to a separate table. After all, the purpose of the Party of One remained the same—to give singles a chance to share a meal with others.

As for Webster and me, once our relationship evolved from friendship to romance, we changed things up some. Instead of lounging around my house alone, we spent more time outside, exercising our bodies and self-control. The quiet breakfasts and lunches at my kitchen counter turned into less intimate meals in public places. We wanted to grow as a couple before we married. To do that, we needed to honor God ... and behave.

I called Gracie in early June to tell her about the first Party of One wedding.

"The Fourth of July? They're getting married on the Fourth of July? Don't you think staking your claim to someone else on Independence Day is rather odd?"

"Ironic maybe, Gracie, but not sacrilegious."

"Tying the knot on Independence Day is sort of like breaking up on Valentine's Day or dying on your birthday. Well, maybe not quite the same, but I'm just sayin'."

"What are you talking about? They'll have fireworks every year to help them celebrate. This is your save-the-date call. Do you think you'll be able to come?"

"I wouldn't miss their wedding for a leading role on Broadway."

"Why don't I believe that, Gracie?"

"Oh, you know what I mean."

Mr. Will Anderson and Miss Elizabeth Hanssen were married on July 4. The wedding took place at an old church in the center of town.

There was a buzz among the guests when Will walked in. His back was straight and his head held high as he strode out in his tartan kilt with full regalia. He was the very picture of a silver-haired Scottish laird awaiting his queen.

I'm sure Miss Elizabeth met his expectations, looking regal in an antique lace ivory sheath with three-quarter sleeves and a ruched satin band at the waist. A delicate visor veil, accented with baby's breath and lavender, framed her face. She carried a simple bouquet of ivory roses.

The minister spoke loud enough for us to hear—mainly because he had to speak loud enough for the bride and groom to hear. The ceremony was simple and traditional, well-suited for Will and Elizabeth.

The crowd cheered after the minister said, "I now pronounce you husband and wife. You may kiss your bride."

Their lips touched but didn't linger. Not used to public displays of affection, they seemed a little embarrassed when the whole thing was over.

Later, in the receiving line at the reception, I whispered to Elizabeth, "Leave it to your husband to find a way to wear plaid on his wedding day."

Elizabeth whispered back, "You do know the whole Scottish theme was my idea, don't you? I didn't want to leave anything—or any plaid—to chance."

There were definite clues Elizabeth had had a hand in the theme. The tartan of Will's wool kilt was the same pattern as Olene's and Kate's taffeta bridesmaids' shawls and the ribbons on their bouquets and Ethan's boutonnière.

Gracie asked, "Where are you kids going to live now?"

"We found a single story, two-bedroom condo in South Sandwich," Elizabeth said, "with a separate library to serve as our Paris office. It has a double-car garage too."

Will added, "I figured at eighty-four, I'm finally ready for one of those fifty-five and older communities."

Martina joined us. "Will, I'm sure you'll be one of the youngest ones there."

"I don't know about that," Will said, gazing at his wife. "But with Miss Elizabeth on my arm, I'm sure to be the envy of every man in the place."

Elizabeth said, "Correction, Mr. Anderson—it's Mrs. Anderson now."

I couldn't have been more pleased the way things turned out for this sweet couple—a poignant reminder that life isn't over unless we refuse to keep living.

As for when Webster and I would marry, we fell somewhere in between Ethan and Kate, who wanted to wait until everything was perfect, and Will and Elizabeth, who realized time was a commodity they couldn't afford to waste.

Webster thought September might be good. My wedding planner, Ms. Libido, and I thought August sounded better.

August it was!

ABOUT THE AUTHOR

After years of writing and editing for business and ministry, Clarice G. James now enjoys writing smart, fun, relatable contemporary fiction. Readers are likely to find a thread of romance, a sprinkling of humor, and/or an element of mystery throughout each story.

When she's not writing or reading, Clarice enjoys organizing author and writing events and working on home decorating projects.

Party of One was one of five finalists in the 2011 Jerry Jenkins Operation First Novel contest. Her debut novel, *Double Header* (Mountainview Books LLC, 2015) was one of three winners in the 2014 Operation First Novel contest. *Manhattan Grace,* her third manuscript, is on deck.

Clarice grew up on Cape Cod. Married for over twenty years, she was widowed in 1998. Eight years later, she was blessed to remarry. She and her husband, David, live in Southern New Hampshire. Together they have five children and ten grandchildren. She has been a follower of Jesus Christ since 1980.

HOW TO ORDER:

To purchase a copy of *Party of One*, ask at your local bookstore or order online through one of the following sites:

Amazon www.amazon.com
Amazon Kindle

If you enjoy *Party of One,* please post a review on one or more of the following sites:

Amazon www.amazon.com
Barnes & Noble www.barnesandnoble.com
Goodreads www.goodreads.com

You can reach Clarice at cjames@claricejames.com or find her on Facebook at https://www.facebook.com/clarice.g.james. She'd love to hear from you.

DISCUSSION QUESTIONS

(May include spoilers!)

1. Have you (or a close friend or family member) ever lost a spouse? If so, what similarities did you find in Annie McGee's life?

2. Who is your favorite person at the Party of One table? Which character did you most identify with? Which one would you most likely have as a friend?

3. Did you learn anything about communicating with those processing grief? How would you reach out to them?

4. Can you relate to Annie's reluctance to interact with her tablemates outside of this event? Why or why not?

5. Annie and Gabe's relationship was not meant to be. Have you ever experienced something similar? How did you handle it?

6. What did you think of Martina's faith and her style of evangelizing? Have you ever tried to convince another person to believe what you believe? How did you fare?

7. What would make you open to hearing more about a person's faith?

8. Casey had some issues with her mother moving on with her life romantically. How much influence should parents and adult children have on each others' lives?

9. How long do you believe a widowed or divorced person should wait before they consider dating?

10. Are you an extrovert or an introvert? Are social situations difficult for you? Or are you the life of every party?

11. Have you ever been lonely in a crowd? Do you know why? How do you overcome loneliness?

12. If you were single, would you consider joining a Party of One fellowship? (Read more about the Party of One on the next page.)

THE PARTY OF ONE:

A FELLOWSHIP FOR THOSE TIRED OF DINING ALONE

And let us consider how to stir up one another to love and good works, not neglecting to meet together, as is the habit of some, but encouraging one another, and all the more as you see the Day drawing near. ~ Heb 10:24-25 (ESV)

The Party of One, A Fellowship for Those Tired of Dining Alone, was founded in 2013. Its purpose is simple: to fellowship with single adults at a communal table.

During the eight years she was widowed, Clarice G. James developed a heart to reach out to singles and others who had slipped through the cracks between active couples and busy families. Party of One extends an open invitation to all who are "tired of dining alone." Its members include men and women of all ages, some single by choice, single by circumstances or "spiritually" single. It also includes those who are called to encourage them.

Beliefs

- People need to belong; we believe some of you belong with us.

- It's healthy to laugh out loud.

- Whining and complaining do not attract friends.

- We know we can't please everyone, but we do our best to please as many as possible.

- We can learn new things if we listen and remain teachable.

- We are called to reach out to the lonely.

- We are the only ones responsible for making our life interesting. The rest of the world is not going to do it for us.

- We will always make room for one more!

If you're interested in starting a Party of One Fellowship in your area, email Clarice G. James at cjames@claricejames. com or call her at 603-578-1860.

Fellowship is a place of grace, where mistakes aren't rubbed in but rubbed out. Fellowship happens when mercy wins over justice.

~ Rick Warren, *The Purpose Driven Life: What on Earth Am I Here for?*

REFERENCES & RESOURCES

(BY GENRE, IN ORDER OF APPEARANCE)

Books and Poems

Ch 20: *Beowulf,* Author unknown, 700-1000 AD

Ch 29: *Children of Húrin*, J. R. R. Tolkien, Harper Collins, 2007

Internet References

Ch 11: "Fingers of God," Wikipedia, hosted by Wikimedia Foundation

Ch 14: "Geek vs. Nerd," Wikipedia, hosted by Wikimedia Foundation

Movies

Ch 1: *Dirty Dancing,* director Emile Ardolino, produced by Linda Gottlieb, 1987, Lake Lure, NC and Mountain Lake, VA

Ch 1: *Picnic,* director Joshua Logan, produced by Columbia Pictures Corporation, 1955, Culver City, CA

Ch 2: *Gone With the Wind*, director Victor Fleming, produced by David O. Selznick and Selznick International Pictures in association with MGM, 1939, Los Angeles, CA

Ch 15: *On Golden Pond*, director Mark Rydell, produced by IPC Films and Incorporated Television Company (ITC), 1981, Lake Winnipausakee, NH

Ch 19 & 31: *Casablanca,* director Michael Curtiz, produced by Warner Bros., 1942, Burbank, CA

Ch 20: *Miss Congeniality,* director Donald Petrie, produced by Castle Rock Entertainment, 2000, Beverly Hills, CA

Ch 32: *You've Got Mail*, director Nora Ephron, produced by Warner Bros., 1998, New York City, NY

Ch 38: *The Seven Year Itch*, director Billy Wilder, produced by Charles K. Feldman Group and 20th Century-Fox, 1955, Beverly Hills, CA

Ch 46: *A Christmas Story,* director/writer Bob Clark, produced by MGM, 1983, Los Angeles, CA

Epilogue: *Sunset Boulevard*, director Billy Wilder, produced by Paramount Pictures, 1950, Los Angeles, CA

Television Shows

Ch 1: *Jeopardy*, a game show created by Merv Griffin, 1964 to present

Ch 33: *Fantasy Island*, a series created by Gene Levitt, 1977 to 1984

Ch 33:*Twilight Zone*, a series created by Rod Serling, 1959 to 1964; 1985 to 1989; 2002 to 2003

Plays

Ch 12: *Othello*, William Shakespeare, 1603

Ch 18: *The Dining Room*, A.R. Gurney, 1982

Songs

Ch 9: "It's a Small World," lyrics & music by Richard Sherman and Robert Sherman, published by Lyrics © Walt Disney Music Publishing Company, 1962

Ch 31: "Marrakesh Express," music and lyrics by Graham Nash, produced by David Crosby, Graham Nash, and Stephen Stills, 1969

Ch 31: "As Time Goes By," music and lyrics by Herman Hupfeld, 1931

Made in the USA
Middletown, DE
07 November 2019